The Time S

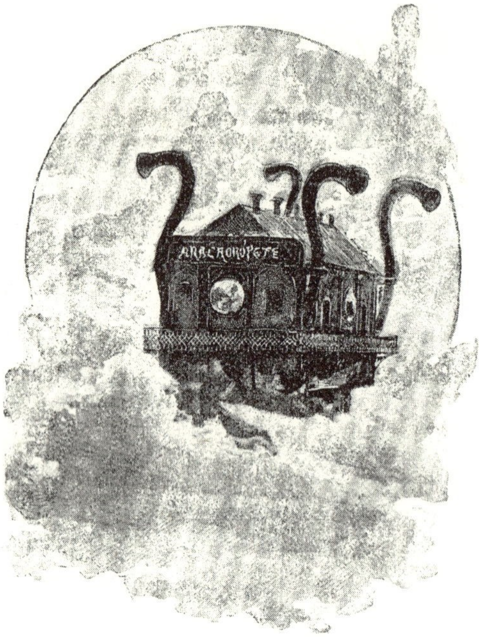
ANACRONÓPETE

The Time Ship

A Chrononautical Journey
ENRIQUE GASPAR

Edited, translated, and introduced by
Yolanda Molina-Gavilán and Andrea Bell

*With illustrations by Francesc Soler
from the original 1887 edition*

WESLEYAN UNIVERSITY PRESS
MIDDLETOWN, CONNECTICUT

Wesleyan University Press
Middletown CT 06459
www.wesleyan.edu/wespress
© 2012 Yolanda Molina-Gavilán and Andrea Bell
All rights reserved
Manufactured in the United States of America
Designed by Dean Bornstein
Typeset in Adobe Caslon Pro by The Perpetua Press

Wesleyan University Press is a member of the Green Press Initiative. The paper used in this book meets their minimum requirement for recycled paper.

Wesleyan University Press gratefully acknowledges the support of the Program for Cultural Cooperation between Spain's Ministry of Culture and United States Universities.

Illustrations in the introduction were provided by the Biblioteca Nacional in Madrid, which kindly gave permission for them to be reprinted here.

Library of Congress Cataloging-in-Publication Data
Gaspar, Enrique, 1842–1902
[Anacronópete. English]
The time ship: a chrononautical journey / Enrique Gaspar; edited, translated, and introduced by Yolanda Molina-Gavilán and Andrea Bell.
 p. cm.
"With illustrations by Francesc Soler from the original 1887 edition."
Includes bibliographical references.
ISBN 978-0-8195-7238-7 (cloth: alk. paper) — ISBN 978-0-8195-7293-6 (pbk.: alk. paper) — ISBN 978-0-8195-7239-4 (ebook) I. Molina-Gavilán, Yolanda. II. Bell, Andrea, 1960– III. Title. PQ6613.A87A6313 2012
863'.5—dc23
2011041423

5 4 3 2 1

Dedication

To Olga, Ana, and Antonio
—Yolanda Molina-Gavilán

*To my parents, Clyde and Joyce Bell,
whose love makes time and space look small*
—Andrea Bell

Publication of this book was made possible by a grant from Figure Foundation.

Contents

Acknowledgments   ix

Introduction: *The Time Ship*'s Place
in the History of Science Fiction   xi

Chapter 1: In Which It Is Proved That FORWARD
Is Not the Byword of Progress   1

Chapter 2: A Lecture within Everyone's Reach   8

Chapter 3: Theory of Time: How It Is Made,
How It Is Unmade   14

Chapter 4: Which Deals with Family Affairs   23

Chapter 5: Cupid and Mars   35

Chapter 6: The Vehicle as School of Morality   43

Chapter 7: Away!   50

Chapter 8: Retroactive Effects   56

Chapter 9: The Gradual Reduction and
Ultimate Elimination of the Army   65

Chapter 10: In Which a Seemingly Insignificant
Yet Greatly Important Incident Takes Place   77

Chapter 11: A Bit of Tiresome, Though Necessary, Erudition   85

Chapter 12: Forty-eight Hours in the Celestial Empire   93

Chapter 13: Nineteenth-century Europe Meets
Third-century China   102

Chapter 14: An Unexpected Guest   110

Contents

Chapter 15: The Resurrection of the Dead
    before Judgment Day   117

Chapter 16: Where All Is Explained and All Is Entangled   127

Chapter 17: Bread and Circuses   137

Chapter 18: Sic Transit Gloria Mundi   152

Chapter 19: Shipwrecked in the Sky   161

Chapter 20: The Best One; Not Because It's Better
    but Because It's Last   169

Notes   179

Bibliography   191

Acknowledgments

Yolanda Molina-Gavilán: This project wouldn't have been possible without the support of many people, but the greatest gratitude must be directed to Art Evans, the veritable soul of this Early Classics of Science Fiction series; to Suzanna Tamminen, director and editor-in-chief of Wesleyan University Press, who first welcomed our project; to our editor Parker Smathers, who patiently answered all our technical questions about the manuscript; and to Rosemary Williams, copyeditor extraordinaire.

Andy Sawyer, the British Library's Science Fiction Librarian, gave Enrique Gaspar's time machine some unexpected publicity when, in 2011, he included *El anacronópete* in a special exhibit on science fiction. That exposure, along with articles in *El País* (Madrid) and the London *Times*, brought us in contact with Gaspar's great-granddaughter Christine Buchanan, who has given us a richer appreciation of the author as a committed playwright and devoted family man. They and others have made working on *The Time Ship* especially rewarding.

Yet, if I am to start at the beginning, I should reserve a special thank-you to my sister Ana, who first put a copy of *El anacronópete* in my hands, making it possible for me to begin dreaming about translating it. My siblings Olga, Ana, and Antonio are always a frame of reference and a source of loving encouragement. Another special thank-you is owed to Dean Betty Stewart at Eckerd College who generously approved a subvention to Wesleyan University Press to help defray publication costs. I also thank Eckerd College for awarding me a professional development grant to conduct archival research at the Biblioteca Nacional in Madrid, where I was assisted by very expert and knowledgeable staff. Allan Meyers, as my collegial chair, was instrumental in defraying some research costs, and as a colleague also offered invaluable advice, particularly in regard to the subtitle of our translation. I am grateful as well to my colleague Thomas J. Di Salvo for his continued and engaged support in all my research endeavors. I extend particular thanks to the students in my "Applied Spanish: Translation" course in fall 2008, who so enthusiastically took on the task of critiquing one of our chapters. And, of course, I could not have found the peace of mind to complete this work without Massimo.

⌛

Andrea Bell: A project like this is much more enjoyable with the help of others, and I have many people to thank for making my work on this book not just possible but immensely gratifying as well. In 2007, Hamline University dean Fernando Delgado awarded me a CLA Grant to conduct research in Spain. I am indebted to Angel Carralero of the *Asociación Española de Fantasía, Ciencia Ficción y Terror* for helping me arrange meetings with Agustín Jaureguízar in Madrid and Miquel Barceló in Barcelona. Señores Jaureguízar and Barceló generously supplied us with hard-to-find information about Gaspar's novel and other early works of Spanish science fiction. Whenever I was particularly stumped by a translation puzzler, my Hamline University colleagues María Jesús Leal and Walter Blue would graciously and expertly set me on the right track. Deepest thanks to Huiying Yin, Zhijun Li, Ken Lan, Scott Relyea, and Thomas Radice for carefully checking the Chinese terms, romanizations, and dynastic histories; any errors that remain are the fault of the translators. I appreciated chatting about this project with Kim Koeppen, Mark Berkson, David Davies, Jermaine Singleton, departmental colleagues, and others within and outside the Hamline University community who shared my enthusiasm for Gaspar's novel and may now, I hope, find pleasure in reading it.

Yolanda and I were fortunate to read excerpts of this translation at two meetings of the American Literary Translators Association; members welcomed us warmly and were a great resource as we worked.

I'll close with love to my entire family, a special thank-you hug for Chris, and a scritch for Lagsi.

Introduction

Nineteenth-century Spanish literature is not usually associated with fantasy or science fiction. The realist and naturalist schools of writing represented by larger-than-life authors such as Benito Pérez Galdós, Pío Baroja, Leopoldo Alas (Clarín), Vicente Blasco Ibáñez, and Emilia Pardo Bazán had the undivided attention of most critics and readers alike. Yet that latter part of the century was also shared by Enrique Gaspar, a prolific playwright who for almost fifty years remained deeply involved with the Spanish theater while engaged in a parallel career as a Spanish diplomat abroad. Besides writing for the stage, Gaspar produced a handful of novels that dealt with the social impact of the science and technology of his day. One of these was *El anacronópete*, translated here as *The Time Ship: A Chrononautical Journey*, a novel he published in 1887 and that now has the best claim of being the first work of Western fiction to describe a time machine, anticipating as it does H. G. Wells's celebrated time travel novel by eight years.[1]

The novel derives its title from the name given the time machine by its inventor. The "anacronópete"—from the Greek "ana," going backwards, "cronos," time, and "petes," he who flies—is a huge mechanical contraption powered by electricity and designed to be navigable through both time and space.[2] The story features four protagonists, two men and two women. Don Sindulfo García and Benjamín are Spanish gentlemen together endowed with the intellectual and financial resources necessary to indulge the passion for scientific discovery characteristic of European gentlemen of leisure in that era. Clara is Don Sindulfo's niece, pure, innocent, and in love with a secondary character named Luis, the captain of the Spanish hussars. Juana, or Juanita, as she is also affectionately called, who completes

Introduction

the main quartet, is Clara's maid, a saucy country lass who functions as both gadfly and comic foil.

Don Sindulfo is Clara's uncle and guardian, but he wants to force her to become his wife, and this unsavory wish motivates him to use his time ship to transport the two of them back to a day when he could act on his desires with impunity. Benjamín, Sindulfo's bookish protégé, is obsessed with the belief that, by traveling backwards in time, he can learn the secret of immortality, thought to be in the possession of the Chinese. Don Sindulfo, Benjamín, Clara, and Juana, along with a dozen French prostitutes and a squadron of Spanish hussars, take off, most of them unwillingly, in search of more permissive times, the key to eternal life, and, in a particularly Spanish Catholic twist on the Enlightenment spirit, scientific knowledge that will lead to the better appreciation of God's majesty. Along the way they witness a decisive nineteenth-century Spanish battle, rescue a third-century Chinese empress, survive the catastrophic eruption of Mount Vesuvius, and behold the parting of the Red Sea. Finally, they journey all the way back to the origin of the universe itself before their surprising return to the present.

The Time Ship's Place in the History of Science Fiction

The Time Ship belongs to the tradition of the imaginary voyage story, a narrative form popular among those who wrote "science fiction before the genre," as Brian Stableford calls the works he examines in his history of science fiction's origins. There are examples in ancient Greek literature of imaginary voyages to distant or made-up lands.[3] Since the license to critique society from some invented distance is one of the imaginary voyage genre's main virtues, it follows that many of the works are social satires, utopias, and morality tales. Some early examples from Spain include *Viage [sic] de un filósofo a Selenópolis* [1804; A Philosopher's Voyage to Selenopolis, author unknown], Joaquín Castillo y Mayone's *Viaje somniaéreo a la Luna, o Zulema y Lambert* [1832; A Somniaerial Trip to the Moon, or Zulema and Lambert], and Tirso Aguimana de Veca's *Una temporada en el*

Introduction

más bello de los planetas [1870–71; A Season on the Most Beautiful of Planets].

Physical settings for these narratives included cities, islands, and the cosmos, and the fantastic voyages were typically achieved by such conveniences as a dream, an enchanted object, a supernatural guide, suspended animation, mesmerism, or some other non-technological means. With the modern revival of the form (the sixteenth century onward), the startling notion of traveling through *time* was introduced. According to Paul Alkon, describing events that hadn't yet happened went against Aristotelian aesthetics and was the business of seers and prophets. "The impossibility of writing stories about the future," says Alkon, "was so widely taken for granted until the eighteenth century that only two earlier works of this kind are known."[4] These are Francis Cheynell's pamphlet *Aulicus, His Dream of the Kings sudden Comming to London* (1644) and Jacques Guttin's *Epigone, histoire du siècle futur* [1659; Epigone, History of the Future Century]. Literary historians believe that the first narrative to propose travel not to some vague future period but to specific dates was Samuel Madden's satire *Memories of the Twentieth Century* (1733), in which an angel appears in the year 1728 bearing letters that describe important British and European events that will take place in the eighteenth through twentieth centuries.

With the 1881 publication of Edward Page Mitchell's "The Clock That Went Backwards" came the notion of linking time travel to a mechanical device. But it wasn't until 1887 that a machine specifically engineered to permit controlled displacement in time—Gaspar's vessel, the *Anachronopetus*—made its literary debut. It was followed the next year by Wells's unfinished serial, "The Chronic Argonauts," whose publication Wells suspended after three installments in the April through June 1888 issues of the *Science Schools Journal* and which he re-created and published as *The Time Machine* in 1895.

One may easily wonder what inspired Enrique Gaspar to compose *The Time Ship*. Two obvious influences on his thinking at the time were the French astronomer Camille Flammarion and the author Jules Verne. Gaspar had, in fact, come to know Flammarion in Saint

Introduction

Nazaire, Brittany, and apparently offered to adapt his novel *Lumen* for the stage, with music by Offenbach, because Flammarion had told our author, in a friendly letter dated 18 October 1875 and addressed to "Mon cher Monsieur Gaspardo," that he hasn't yet had time to think about *Lumen* being staged or about master Offenbach either.[5] Flammarion's writings on science were, of course, widely read throughout Europe; many of his works were translated into Spanish between 1874 and 1884 and were hugely popular in Spain. Gaspar's narrative gives a clear tip of the hat to him when, in Chapter 9, Don Sindulfo describes a battle in reverse, just as Flammarion's cosmic voyager Lumen had done when witnessing the Battle of Waterloo from a star.

Jules Verne's fiction was even more of a sensation than Flammarion's; according to Nil Santiáñez-Tió, Verne was the second most translated and read French author in Spain, after Zola. Verne's tremendous success with the staging of *Around the World in 80 Days*—more than 400 performances in its first run—did not escape Gaspar's notice, and his own work had all the makings of a zarzuela (a comic operetta) that could have rivaled Verne's box-office sensations. Writes Jean-Michel Margot:

> *Around the World in 80 Days* brought something new and extravagant to the Paris stage: it featured new landscapes, exotic people, live elephants and serpents, natural cataclysms and strange transportational vehicles for the audience to enjoy without leaving the comfort of their theater seats. . . . nothing was neglected, including ballets and music written especially for it, sumptuous sets and clever machinery.[6]

The Time Ship was similarly grandiose: had it been staged, its lavish sets would have transported audiences to Paris, Morocco, China, and Pompeii. Viewers would have been treated to the 1878 Paris Universal Exposition, a sprawling military battle, bloodthirsty Moors, imperial China, Roman gladiators, a flood of literally biblical proportions, the origins of the universe, and an audience-pleasing tale of young love overcoming all obstacles. All that plus a marvelous and intricately

Introduction

described time machine complete with futuristic laundry, galley, and observation deck.

By the 1870s, when popular science writing was becoming fashionable in Europe, Gaspar had embarked upon his diplomatic career. His lengthy overseas postings put him at a competitive disadvantage in the Spanish theater world and contributed to the financial and critical failure of some of his recent stage efforts. Gaspar, though far from wealthy, kept up a rather costly and indulgent lifestyle while living in China and in all likelihood penned *The Time Ship* in the hope that it would sell well. As a man with a finger on the pulse of European entertainment tastes (as best as could be done while based in the Far East), Gaspar took note of the public's growing enthusiasm for science themes in general and the scientific romance in particular, and this might be one explanation for populating his novel with a time machine, scientific theories, and technological marvels.

Scientific disquisitions outweigh narrative progression in the opening chapters of *The Time Ship*; they give the novel a rather slow start and characterize Don Sindulfo as a pedant. He and Benjamin use the language of science and technology to make a lengthy, rational, and authoritative-sounding case for the feasibility of time travel. Perhaps in the hope of emulating Flammarion, Gaspar saddled his otherwise breezy, fast-paced adventure with long pages of erudition about Chinese customs, and he shoehorns an extended monolog on graphology, lifted almost verbatim from Carrasco's *Mitología universal* [1864; Universal Mythology], into the middle of a treasure hunt in ancient Rome. This may have seemed necessary to Gaspar as a means of establishing the verisimilitude and scientific plausibility crucial to the plot, his characters, and the central conceit of the time machine. It might also, as Arthur B. Evans says was the case with Albert Robida's works, "serve certain implicit pedagogical ends, if not for the instruction of science, at least for the acclimatization of humankind to science" and, we would add, for the acclimatization of Europe to the very notion of Spanish scientists.[7] National pride is a frequent motif in the novel and may have served to challenge the general perception, held at home and abroad, that Spaniards had contributed

Introduction

little or nothing to the European scientific revolution and that, indeed, science in Spain was "slow, backwards, anachronistic and derivative."[8] In the opening chapter, tramcar passengers are amazed to learn that the time machine's inventor is a Spaniard and compare him with the only other famous Spaniard they can think of, the legendary nineteenth-century bullfighter, Frascuelo. One of the French tramcar passengers has a fit of nationalist pique at France having been bested by Spain. Linking scientific achievement with Iberia might also have been Gaspar's response to Jules Verne's disdainful comment, in *From the Earth to the Moon*, that "as to Spain, . . . science is not very favorably regarded in that country. It is still a backward state," for while Gaspar himself might criticize Spain, he was patriotic and disliked it when others found fault with his homeland.[9] In an interesting confusion of fact and fiction, *The Time Ship*'s narrator dismisses the inventions and discoveries of Robert Fulton, George Stephenson, Samuel Morse, and Jules Verne, saying that their steamships, locomotives, telegraphs, and fantastic journeys were but child's play compared to Don Sindulfo's Anachronopetus. The narrator even accuses Verne of being unoriginal: "As for the Nautilus," he says, "long before Verne our compatriot Monturiol [a Spanish engineer] had already conducted a highly successful [submarine] test with the *Ictíneo*."

By the 1870s, Verne had produced at least one Spanish imitator, Antonio de San Martín, whose 1871 novel *Un viaje al planeta Júpiter* [A Voyage to the Planet Jupiter] borrowed heavily from Verne and anticipated Gaspar's orientalism in the character of Troung-vinkhy, a Chinese scientist who engages in interplanetary travel by hot air balloon. "As happens in so many nineteenth-century science fiction novels," writes Díez, "the Chinese scientist enlightens his young travel companions, and by extension the reader, through relentless astronomic explanations: in this way, literary imagination combines with presumed scientific accuracy and truth in an effort to suspend the reader's disbelief."[10]

In his essay on *Una temporada en el más bello de los planetas*, Brian Dendle counts among that text's weaknesses "the didactic and scien-

Introduction

tific elements . . . [that] are presented in banal fashion in the form of discussions of scholars which take place almost parenthetically inside, but barely connected with, the novelistic intrigue."[11] Gaspar's narrative shares that defect, but to a much lesser degree. Though the scientific digressions in *The Time Ship* are unevenly lumped into a few specific chapters, much of the time they contribute to establishing plausibility and the Brechtian estrangement Evans says is typical of the transition from the primarily didactic to the plot-furthering roles of science and technology in science fiction's development. Gaspar's novel is significant, then, not only for the invention of a time machine but because of the extent to which scientific and technological didacticism is subordinated to the plot.

If money worries and the ability to spot a trend were factors in Gaspar's writing a scientific romance, what inspired him to dream up a time machine? Could it have been that the sting of his recent theater failures hurt all the more because the critics accused him of being out of touch and ignorant of contemporary life in Spain? Gaspar knew there was some truth to that; in many of his letters to friends he mourns that his work is suffering because of his isolation. From faraway China, writing a social satire in which one can fly about freely through time and space in pursuit of direct observation and experience might have been, on some level, a satisfying exercise in wish fulfillment.

A Few Points of Comparison between *The Time Ship* and *The Time Machine*

On some levels, comparing *The Time Ship* with Wells's *The Time Machine* is an interesting enterprise, given that the two authors must have been thinking more or less along the same lines, but we must keep in mind that Wells in all probability never read or even heard about Gaspar's time machine narrative, so there is no real question of influence. Moreover, we consider Gaspar's and Wells's works to be vastly different in content, tone, purpose, and reception. There can be no disputing that each author held fast to his conviction that art

Introduction

could—indeed, should—be used to educate, challenge, inspire, and ultimately improve society; however, Gaspar's time-machine novel is more light-hearted and entertaining than Wells's, the social criticism more satirical, the moral lessons less somber and urgent. Nor is there any question that Wells's novel struck a chord with artistic and intellectual communities in a way Gaspar's certainly did not. For a number of aesthetic, economic, political, and social reasons, *The Time Machine* has never been out of print, has been adapted numerous times to the stage and screen, is the subject of countless academic studies and has made the name H. G. Wells synonymous with the time machine trope. In contrast, Gaspar's earlier introduction of the time machine was first conceived as a comic opera—never staged—and later published as a novel—ignored by the critics and consigned to the grave. Nevertheless, *The Time Machine* is so well known that we suspect readers will enjoy considering some ways in which the two novels overlap and diverge. We shall leave it to Wells scholars to more thoroughly compare the two texts.

The greatest similarity, of course, is that both Gaspar and Wells introduce machines designed to transport passengers through time. Physically, the vehicles are quite different, as is the quality of the ride. Wells's time machine is a one-seater, small enough to fit in a corner of the inventor's home laboratory, though presumably large enough to accommodate a second person, given that the Time Traveler, having grown fond of Weena, a character he meets in the future, had hoped to bring her back with him. Its designer anticipated little need to eat, sleep, move about, attend to personal hygiene, or be protected from the elements while en route. Time travel itself is harrowing and dangerous. The dazzling succession of light and dark is "excessively painful to the eye" and the machine travels at such a vertiginous speed that the protagonist's ears are filled with noise and the landscape becomes a dizzying blur. The Traveler feels confused, terrified, and verging on madness. "The fact is that . . . the absolute strangeness of everything, the sickly jarring and swaying of the machine, above all, the feeling of prolonged falling, had absolutely upset my nerve."

Introduction

When he tries to stop the vehicle, he brakes too abruptly and is "flung headlong through the air."[12]

Not so on Gaspar's elaborately described Anachronopetus. Modeled after a large sailing vessel and described as resembling Noah's Ark, it has room enough to carry well over thirty passengers plus scientific equipment and provisions for months of travel. One can stroll the interior corridors, descend to the hold, visit the observation room, and use wondrous tools to cook meals and wash clothes.[13] Powered by electricity, the time machine moves at different speeds, travels so smoothly that its passengers scarcely realize they are underway, and can hover gently over northern Morocco while the Battle of Tetouan rages below.

Another interesting difference between the two authors' visions is that, in Wells's case, time travel is achieved with only minimal movement through space; the Traveler notes that he has departed from and returned to the same physical place, his laboratory, though at opposite corners of the room. Gaspar's machine, on the other hand, can be programmed for destinations in both time and space.

We also note that neither author is above giving science a helping hand now and then by having his characters discover or invent some substance with convenient (and conveniently unexplained) attributes: Wells's lunar explorers in *The First Men in the Moon* (1901) have their Cavorite (the fictional Dr. Cavor's gravity shielding material) and Don Sindulfo has his García fluid. The latter allows Gaspar both to acknowledge and overcome the paradox of time-traveling oneself out of existence, for the magnificent García fluid chronologically "fixes" people and objects and prevents them from fatally regressing as they travel backwards in time. At least one critic of the day remarked sternly on what he perceived as Wells's shrinking from temporal paradoxes in *The Time Machine*; in an 1895 issue of *Pall Mall Magazine*, the writer Israel Zangwill commented, "Wells . . . was not oblivious to the possibility of paradox in time travel, but his failure to use it seems to indicate that he simply did not know how to respond to such puzzles."[14]

Introduction

Because the modern reader is so familiar with the concept of time travel, it can be hard to imagine a time when this idea was breathtakingly new. Both Gaspar and Wells have their inventors publicize their temporal experiments, although in neither case is doing so essential to the plot. It is interesting to see how the scientists' claims are received by their fictional audiences. In *The Time Machine*, the dinner guests are skeptical both at the beginning of the novel, when they hear the Traveler expound his theories and describe his plans, and toward the end when he recounts his adventures. Even the physical evidence—the scale-model trial machine in the second chapter and the flowers the Traveler finds in his pocket after he returns—does not persuade some of his friends. Gaspar's Don Sindulfo has a much easier time of it. The public that flocks to hear his theories and witness his departure in the second and third chapters of the novel is primed for spectacle and cheers his every claim. The audience at the Universal Exposition may not understand the sage's scientific explanations, but they embrace them nonetheless. Endorsement by the French government and the august Scientific Congress lends the inventor unassailable credibility. Don Sindulfo deftly contends with the lone questioner in his Paris audience and is hailed a genius. His planned journey is considered neither foolhardy nor impossible but as an opportunity to correct the *Iliad*, hire Molière, protect the wine industry from the perils of vine disease, and restore French morality.

Not always the logical and dispassionate scholar, H. G. Wells's Time Traveler could be irrational and impulsive; he doubts himself and his theories and sounds a cautionary note at the end of the sixth chapter when he says, "Very simple was my explanation, and plausible enough—as most wrong theories are!"[15] As Hammond observes, "he takes foolish risks [and] feels the normal human emotions of anger, fear, petulance and dread."[16] Don Sindulfo, in turn, is petty, vengeful, cowardly at times, and selfish; he is a flawed and discredited character, which undercuts his authority as a model of reason and science. Although his fellow time travelers never challenge Sindulfo's knowledge of science and engineering, they seriously doubt his sanity. Gaspar portrays Don Sindulfo, and to a lesser extent Benjamín and

Introduction

the entire scientific community they represent, less than sympathetically, to great comic effect, but also to argue, reformist that he was, that Spain's illusions of progressive leadership are built upon shaky foundations.

Moving beyond these textual features to the question of reception and influence, while there can be no disputing the importance of Wells's novel in the development of science fiction, no such claim can be made for *The Time Ship*, even if we limit our examination to the genre's history in the Spanish-speaking world. An exhaustive search has uncovered no published reviews of the novel besides the comparatively recent ones listed in our Bibliography; Gaspar's narrative did not attract much critical attention when it first appeared, nor did it spawn a wave of imitators. In the introduction to his anthology of early Spanish science fiction, Julián Díez claims that Gaspar's novel received mention in specialized U.S. publications, though he does not identify them by name and we have yet to unearth them.[17] But it would be wrong to state that *The Time Ship* played no role in the development of science fiction in Spain. It was fully in keeping with the aesthetic of the times, reflecting modernist sensibilities, a newfound belief in the perfectibility of individuals and society, and both optimism and misgivings about the consequences of science and technology.

Díez's history of early Spanish science fiction shows a clustering of new scientific fiction written by Spanish authors soon after Wells became known in that country. When José Martínez Ruiz (Azorín) wrote a piece of scientific fiction with a distinctly anarchic bent, his epigraph was a quote from Wells: "We are at the beginning of the beginning."[18] As was the case in other countries, several of the more established Spanish writers of the day such as Miguel de Unamuno and Ángel Ganivet dabbled in the artistic and ideological potential inherent in this new mode of scientific fiction. Leopoldo Alas (Clarín) authored "Cuento futuro" [1886; Future Story], an apocalyptic tale rooted in Old Testament myths that describes a decadent culture similar to that of the humanoid Eloi in Wells's *The Time Machine*. Straddling the turn of the century, the journalist Nilo María Fabra would show

Introduction

the greatest dedication yet by a Spanish writer to the emerging genre. In keeping with a positivist sensibility that sought to regenerate both art and society, Fabra published a handful of stories that put science and technology at the service of a utopian vision of the future.

In those days, of course, science fiction was not yet named or really recognized. However, the modernist manifesto, coupled with Spanish angst triggered by unrest at home and in the former colonies, inspired a number of Spanish authors—the prestigious and the unknown alike—to compose what genre historians now identify as precursors to science fiction. Enrique Gaspar was among them. There is nothing to suggest *The Time Ship* or any of his scientific-themed plays gave particular direction or inspiration to a Spanish sf movement at the time. Recognition came late to this novel, as it did to its author. But Gaspar and *The Time Ship* were part of the larger process that gave rise to science fiction in Spain toward the end of the nineteenth century and now, at last, the novel—republished several times, translated, and acknowledged as a landmark science-fictional work—is getting its due. Gaspar's narrative has been the subject of a handful of recent critical studies and will, we expect, inspire more. *The Time Ship* truly has traveled through time and space, and its influence on future science fiction may yet be felt.

The Time Ship's Author, Enrique Gaspar

Enrique Lucio Eugenio Gaspar y Rimbau (1842–1902) was born in Madrid to two theater actors, Juan Gaspar and Rafaela Rimbau. The influence of his parents and the theatrical milieu in which he was raised instilled in Gaspar a lifelong love of the stage. According to Leo Kirschenbaum's authoritative biography of the author, "Enrique's earliest impressions were of listening rapturously to his mother and father as they recited verses from the classical and contemporary drama, and of making strenuous efforts to memorize the pleasant sounds of words whose meanings he could not comprehend."[19]

After the death of his father when the boy was six, his mother married a famous architect, Sebastián Monleón, and took her three

Introduction

children to the city of Valencia, on the Mediterranean coast, where she continued her acting career. The young Gaspar studied humanities and philosophy before getting a position at a commercial bank run by the Marqués de San Juan. He took this position to help his family financially; his true calling, however, was the pen, and writing was an occupation he would never abandon. By age seven he had composed a quatrain; at thirteen he wrote the libretto for a zarzuela entitled *Consecuencias del amor* [The Consequences of Love] and at fourteen years of age he became the co-editor of *La Ilustración Valenciana*, a weekly illustrated magazine. He also had his first public triumph with a one-act play called *Un miope sin quevedos* [A Short-Sighted Man without Pince-Nez] that was performed at the Princesa theater in Valencia. He had wanted to write a play in which his mother could act, and when *Un miope* was warmly received by the Valencian audience, Enrique decided to immerse himself wholly in the theater and in writing.

As soon as Gaspar could afford to move back to Madrid he did so and, with the help of the actor-impresario Emilio Mario, pursued a playwriting career in the capital city, where he famously said he "joined the rolls as a beggar; as a Spanish writer, that is."[20] Once there and partly in response to chronic financial need, he became a rapid and prolific writer, able to turn out one-act plays in just a few hours when necessary. The difficulty he had earning a living as a playwright is understandable, since opera was at its peak of popularity then and monopolized theater audiences. In 1863, the same year Gaspar moved to Madrid, Verdi himself directed his opera *La forza del destino* [The Force of Destiny] at the Spanish Royal Theater. Also, the current fashion of translating plays from the French did not encourage Spain's writers to produce original scripts, thus leaving the theater scene somewhat bare.

During this formative period, Gaspar was a regular at coffee houses and at the Ateneo club in Madrid, becoming friends with fellow novelists and playwrights such as Pedro Antonio de Alarcón and Adelardo López de Ayala. He also traveled back and forth to Valencia to keep in touch with the literary scene there. Gaspar had a sparkling

Introduction

Portrait of Gaspar in his youth.

personality and cut a fine figure. In 1902, the year of Gaspar's death, Fernández Bremón remembered him for the benefit of his future biographers thusly:

> He was not very tall, yet his figure was well proportioned. When he was young he caught people's eye because of his graceful and regular features, his slender blond moustache and his long goatee, which would have given him an effeminate look had it not been for the serious virility of his face. He dressed with care and had a slight Valencian accent. (154)

As to his character, Bremón reports that Gaspar was considered somewhat immodest by his fellow writers because he would answer back at the critics after negative reviews, but explains this as the natural response of an innovator confronted with the status quo (154). Cabello de la Piedra, in his article "La escena española en el siglo XX: Enrique Gaspar" written only months before the playwright's death, confirms Gaspar's passionate, energetic nature and compares him to a

Introduction

Gaspar as Spanish Consul in Marseille, at his desk.

doctor whose preferred curing methods are amputations, cold showers, cauterizing irons, and other drastic measures. Yet the picture he paints is not that of a vain man, since "Enrique Gaspar keeps neither first drafts of his works nor anything that praises him" (n.p.).

When he was twenty-three years old, Enrique Gaspar married Enriqueta Batllés y Bertán de Lis, with whom he had been in love for years. Given that she was a Valencian beauty whose father was Dean of the University of Valencia and whose mother was an aristocrat, it is no surprise that her parents did not really approve of their son-in-law's socially inferior background. The failure of some of his plays and the birth of his two children made Gaspar realize the necessity of a regular income, so in 1869, at age twenty-seven, he joined the Spanish diplomatic corps as vice-consul. Undoubtedly, his personal connections (such as Adelardo López de Ayala, who was then Foreign Affairs Minister) and his liberal ideology (the 1868 liberal revolution had just ousted Queen Isabella II) helped him obtain a government post.

Gaspar's diplomatic career was burdensome and long. After 1870,

Introduction

when he left for his first foreign posting, to Sète, in southern France, "[he] was destined never to return to Spain save for occasional brief leaves, for he did not attain sufficient financial security to warrant his abandoning the consular service."[21] Being exiled, as he considered it, from the land he loved was emotionally and professionally taxing; his passion for the social drama necessitated intimate and sustained contact with both Spanish society and the theater world but his consular work prevented it. Over the next twenty-seven years Gaspar's diplomatic career would require of him extended postings to France, Greece, and China. He wrote his friends bitter lamentations about the cultural poverty and isolation he experienced in some of the towns he lived in, and from his correspondence we get a picture of a dedicated man of letters with a passion for both musical theater and serious social drama, who, although feeling trapped into earning a living at another profession, nevertheless retained his sense of humor. Becoming a consul in China had taken some doing, for example, since King Alfonso XII's restoration to the Spanish throne in 1875 had suddenly placed Gaspar on the wrong side of the political fence. He had to resort to his many connections to secure this post, and referred to this fact with his usual wit, saying "There are so many people interested in my case, that they are considered a political faction called the 'Gasparinos.'"[22] In the end, his salary was increased and he was posted to Macao, "so that I could study theater," as he wryly commented.[23] Yet he wound up being disappointed, for contrary to the romantic China of his imagination, he found Macao to be foul smelling and not very refined. Gaspar remained at his consular post in China from 1878 to 1884 and during this time suffered a crisis as a playwright. Several of his plays were rejected by the Vico y Calvo theater company in Madrid, in spite of praise from critics and fellow playwrights like Cañete, Tamayo, Nuñez de Arce, and Echegaray. His plays were not deemed popular enough to make a profit and he took to writing newspaper articles as a source of additional income; his work for the *Diario de Manila* brought in 250 pesetas every month, a healthy supplement to his consular salary of about 417 pesetas a month.[24] It is from this period that we derive the image Kirschenbaum paints of a

Introduction

hardworking Gaspar who "kept watch night after night, a cigarette in hand, the ashtray overflowing with stub ends" as he labored to make ends meet (327).

In the latter stages of his diplomatic career, Gaspar's oft-made request for a transfer to the Ministry offices in Madrid was finally approved. A recent string of successful stagings in Barcelona and Madrid, such as those of La lengua [1882; The Tongue], and *Las personas decentes* [1891; Decent People] brought him back to life in theater circles. Gaspar's talent and lifelong campaign to bring realism to the Spanish stage were at last being recognized: "For the first time, the critics agreed in praising him; they acclaimed the triumph of realism and hailed Enrique Gaspar as its master."[25] Along with his transfer to Madrid, Gaspar was promoted to the rank of Consul of the First Class and his salary was again increased. This domestic post lasted a mere three months, however, and at the end of it he was forced to continue his career abroad. In 1886, Gaspar was sent to the French-Pyrenees town of Oloron Sainte-Marie, where he stayed for four years and where his daughter Enriqueta was wed.[26] His inability to oversee personally the direction and performances of his plays worked against him and the stagings were not always successful. He also failed to realize his dream of securing a seat on the Spanish Real Academia de la Lengua [Royal Language Academy], because he did not reside in Spain.

At fifty-four, at the peak of his professional career and while he was posted to Marseilles, his dear wife died, very suddenly, of influenza. Gaspar was devastated. Full of sorrow and frustration, alone and in deteriorating health—he suffered from chronic bronchitis, asthma, emphysema, and heart trouble—his one solace was the theater. According to Kirschenbaum, Gaspar saw almost every play that came to town, sometimes over and over again. "One of the series of Marseilles sketches drawn by Sem, the noted French caricaturist, shows the hall of the Grand Théâtre completely empty save for the actors on the stage and their audience of one, Enrique Gaspar, sitting in the middle of the auditorium intent on the performance, a solitary figure amid the rows of vacant seats."[27]

Introduction

Caricature of Gaspar by Ramón Cilla in the Spanish weekly *Madrid Cómico*, 7 November 1896.

In 1900 Gaspar's failing health forced him to retire early and he was granted a pension by the Spanish government. Weary and discouraged by the eternal fickleness of theater audiences and critics, and looking old beyond his sixty years, he went back to Oloron to live with his daughter and son-in-law, Rafael Lavigne. Don Enrique, according to a family friend, although confined to a wheelchair and on oxygen because a stroke had left him partially paralyzed and unable to write, never complained; on the contrary, he remained outwardly cheerful and endeavored to put people at ease. On 7 September 1902, Enrique Gaspar died after a severe asthma attack. His friends and admirers in Valencia lobbied in vain to have a monument erected in his honor, and although he was eulogized in the press at the time[28] and has been the subject of a few critical studies since, his contributions to the theater have been largely eclipsed by those of more celebrated Spanish playwrights.

Introduction

His Literary Output

Enrique Gaspar's literary career spanned about fifty of his sixty years. Even as we offer the English-speaking public a translation of one of his novels, and one that matters to the history of science fiction, we cannot ignore the fact that Gaspar's place in Spanish literature was earned not for his science-fictional efforts but for his social dramas, a genre he pioneered in Spain at great personal cost. Gaspar wrote prolifically throughout his life, mostly for the stage. His production alternates between light, inconsequential comedies whose main purpose is to provoke laughter and his more engaged social dramas, which are more representative of his theater as a whole. His plays may be grouped into three categories, according to theme: those of amorous intrigue, where love is a device used exclusively to move the plot along; those of social criticism, always aiming to educate; and lastly, his plays of scientific ideas. *The Time Ship* belongs to both the first and third categories.[29]

Gaspar was an insatiable reader, appreciative of Spanish Golden Age writers like Calderón de la Barca and of French playwrights like Louis-Simon Auger. Richard Brinsley Sheridan and William Shakespeare were his favorite English authors and among his contemporary Spanish playwrights he admired Adelardo López de Ayala and, especially, Manuel Tamayo y Baus. His foremost biographer, Daniel Poyán Díaz, also offers clues to the source of Gaspar's inner drive to renovate the theater: Spanish Krausism[30] and its passion for liberalism and progress, which meant the reform of old-fashioned traditions, equality for women, a certain dose of anticlericalism, and the belief that duty should drive the individual, an ethical system also found in Ibsen's theater (139).[31] Thus, as a playwright and in keeping with this philosophy, Gaspar focused the content of his more engaged plays on controversial social and political issues of the day such as class struggle, political corruption, middle-class hypocrisy, and feminism. These subjects were approached in a direct way but always through the use of humor, for a placating effect. Gaspar eschewed the high-

Introduction

flown poetic metaphors that were the romantic fashion of the day and drew instead on some original idea to drive the plot. In his 1874 play *El estómago* [The Stomach], for example, all the characters end up being controlled by their digestive organs. And in 1882, his play *La lengua* tackled the subject of female education through the cliché of women's malicious tongues. Furthermore, his innovations were very much concerned with form as well as content. Thus, he asked the actors to drop the use of exaggerated gestures in favor of more realistic ones, championed the cause of switching from verse to prose—which went against the norm of the times—and wrote dialog that was caustic and concise. This new, more realistic type of social drama did not always make him a hit with critics and the public, although some of his plays did achieve instant success, such as *Las circunstancias* [1867; The Circumstances], *La levita* [1868; The Frock Coat], *Lola* [1885], *Las personas decentes* [1891], and *Huelga de hijos* [1893; A Sons' Strike].

In short, Gaspar's "serious" plays echo life's real problems of the day and share a desire to educate the spectators. Their setting is urban and, like the audience, most of the characters belong to the bourgeoisie, although at times they come from the lower classes and introduce class conflicts. The problems these plays tackle may be described as negative or pessimistic, although their resolution invariably condemns the petits vices or defects that provoked them.[32] His plays were praised by influential critics like Emilia Pardo Bazán, Josep Yxart, and Julio Cejador y Frauca,[33] but disregarded and even despised by others. By and large, his light, comedic pieces did well, while his more serious naturalistic work and his attempts to reform the national theater were routinely misunderstood and criticized. As Wadda C. Ríos-Font reports, "Gaspar's innovations were . . . evaluated by audience and critics according to the criteria applied to melodramatic theater, and his plays were judged deficient rather than revolutionary" (240).

According to Kirschenbaum and others, between 1860 and 1902 Gaspar published some forty-two plays and zarzuelas, over twenty poems, numerous essays and newspaper articles, two travel narratives, and six short novels, several of which were adaptations.[34] Even

Introduction

though most of his literary works are not well known today, Gaspar was a pioneer and an innovator of the late nineteenth-century Spanish stage, as critics Leo Kirschenbaum, Daniel Poyán Díaz, and Juan Antonio Hormigón now recognize.[35] His social plays were ahead of his time, paving the way for the works of later, better-known authors like Joaquín Dicenta and Benito Pérez Galdós; the latter, only one year younger than Gaspar, is considered the founding father of Spanish modern drama.[36]

The Time Ship: Structure, Critical Reception, and Analysis

The Time Ship had a previous incarnation as a three-act, thirteen-scene zarzuela, and when Gaspar adapted the work as a novel he followed many of the structural conventions of the original musical form. The narrative is divided into two parts (or acts) whose scenes correspond to the different places and times where the time machine stops. The "cast" fits the typical arrangement of zarzuela paired voices: two main singers (Don Sindulfo and Clara), a comical duet (Benjamín and Juana), another duet to complete the two love triangles (Luis and Pendencia) and a chorus of male and female voices (the Spanish hussars and the French ladies). The subject matter is basically the same in both texts and entire paragraphs are almost identical. The zarzuela was never performed; however, the undated manuscript, donated by the author's granddaughter Doña Inés Gaspar, may be found at the Biblioteca Nacional in Madrid.[37]

Nil Santiáñez-Tió and Augusto Uribe, the two Spanish science fiction critics who have helped give *The Time Ship* new life, stress the importance of its timing vis-à-vis Wells's *The Time Machine*, yet stop short of offering a full critical analysis of the novel in its own right.[38] *The Time Ship* has been regarded as simply derivative of the science-ridden adventure tales for which Jules Verne was becoming famous. Yet Gaspar's work is more than a simple divertissement à la Jules Verne. It has a specific Spanish tone and its underlying themes, steeped in wit and irony, imply social, political, literary, and even religious and philosophical criticism.

Cast list of *El anacronópete* on the second page of the zarzuela manuscript.

According to María de los Ángeles Ayala, Gaspar's ethical preoccupations emerge both in his plays and in narrative works like *The Time Ship*. She lists the role of women, the substitution of the liberal arts by experimental science, the selfish interests behind apparently

Introduction

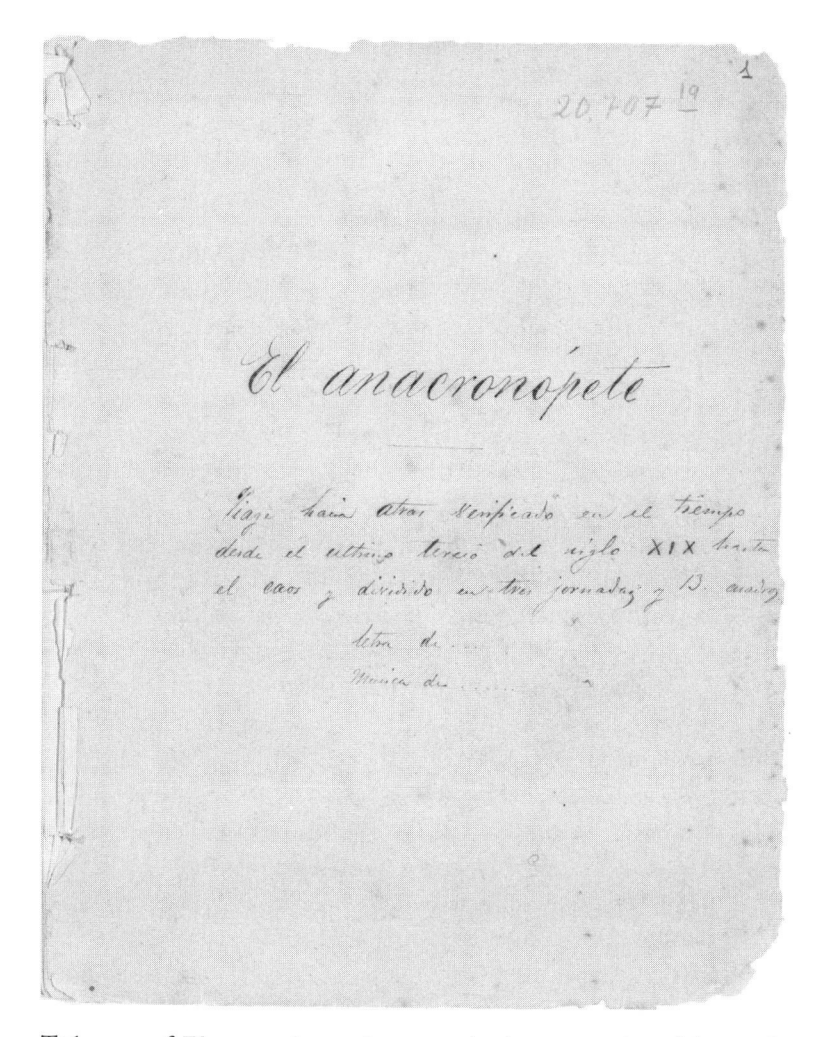

Title page of *El anacronópete* as it appears in the manuscript of the comic operetta.

altruistic behavior, and the social role of the man of science among the subjects that Gaspar's body of work interrogates (409).[39] To those concerns we may add a healthy questioning of Spain's sense of its own past and the role of religion in society.

Introduction

The specific Spanish essence and point of view we mention, plus the role of science in the novel, must all be understood through the prism of humor. Santiáñez-Tió underappreciates the role comedy plays in *The Time Ship*, considering the "quite funny jokes" to be on a par with all the "annoying digressions" it contains or at least to have no ulterior importance, whereas comicality is in fact key to understanding the novel's serious commentary.[40] Daniel Poyán Díaz, a critic who has written two volumes on Gaspar's literature, emphasizes that although Gaspar used scientific ideas in his writing mostly for comical effect, they were also tools that served a higher purpose, that of denouncing both the ridiculous uses of science and the flawed motivations behind the technological advances of his day. Poyán believes that, in *The Time Ship*, Gaspar purposefully imitates Jules Verne's imaginary voyages in order to amuse, just as he pokes fun at the use of electroshock as therapy in *La sordera política*, ridicules hypnotism techniques in *La cura prodigiosa*, laughs at the idea that animals may have a language in *Pasiones políticas*, and derides the theory of the transmigration of souls in *La metempsicosis*.[41] Ayala notes that Gaspar mocks the preoccupation with the advancement of science on several other occasions, as in his tale "La artillería postal" [The Postal Artillery], included in *Majaderías* (409).

Santiáñez-Tió recognizes that Gaspar "seems to be aware that scientific discoveries have real consequences for the development of society"[42] and makes explicit in the novel that Don Sindulfo believes his technological wonder will produce beneficial results (that is, French morality will improve through the redemption of the prostitutes who are entrusted to him). Yet, Don Sindulfo is a flawed character, a kind of "mad scientist" whose intrinsic motivation is not the progress of humanity but personal gain. His egotistical wishes regarding his young niece Clara are ridiculed throughout the course of the novel, most sharply by Clara's maid, Juana, with her running commentary on her master's foolishness. Here we see an example of Gaspar's preoccupation with the advancement of the social mores in Spain during his time and his preferred method of dealing with it: humor.[43]

Don Sindulfo, being an older, respectable bourgeois male, embod-

Introduction

ies the traditional authority figure. He is in charge of the expedition at first but is quickly superseded by his junior companion, Benjamín, who offers a contrast to the scientist. The reader soon understands that the more sympathetic Benjamín must be a character closer to Gaspar's own heart and represents a younger, more progressive yet down-to-earth generation. He is poor (Gaspar's finances were a constant concern throughout his life) and he is a linguist (the author spoke several languages); therefore it follows that the younger scientist is more open to understanding and possibly accepting the outside world. Also, Benjamín is passionate about his subject of study, archeology, just as Gaspar was about writing plays. The contrast between practical-minded, courageous but somewhat naïve Benjamín and his more hidebound and fanatical friend Don Sindulfo will be made clear toward the end of the novel when the head of the expedition suffers a fit of suicidal rapture. Could Don Sindulfo be a reference to the famous Enlightenment-affirming comment of Goya's drawing, "The sleep of reason brings forth monsters"? If so, the novel's "hurried ending" is not incongruous, as Uribe claims; rather, in keeping with Gaspar's philosophical and literary outlook, the ending can be read both as a commentary on Spain's scientific backwardness and loss of international influence and as a call to his countrymen to abandon any vain illusions of grandeur they may have been harboring with regard to their country's place in the world.

 A preoccupation with Spain, from its history to its standing in the world of the 1880s, is a constant thread throughout the novel. Undoubtedly, Gaspar witnessed a particularly turbulent period in Spain as the century drew to an end.[44] It could be argued that when he chose to steer Don Sindulfo's time machine backwards, Gaspar was looking to remind himself and others of better, more stable times in the past. In this light, it is not surprising that the travelers' first view of history is the not-so-distant 1860 Battle of Tetouan, in which the Spanish forces were victorious and managed to hold on to their territorial possessions in Morocco. Significantly, the choice of destination is made by the socially conservative Don Sindulfo, who wants to hover over and witness the battle he describes as epic, memorable,

Introduction

and honorable for the Spanish army. The episode is presented in a humorous, undignified manner though, with the soldiers moving backwards in time while the travelers' ears are filled with Juana's waggish commentary. Furthermore, the battle does have dire consequences for our characters, since they end up carrying two dozen fugitives from the enemy camp aboard their vessel. The second stop and only other episode from Spanish history the travelers visit is in 1492, right before the fall of Granada, where Benjamín acts as a sort of oracle to Queen Isabella. Again, witnessing this key event, which generally represents the unification of Spain as a nation, could be regarded as a nostalgic look at Spain's past glories. Yet it is shown merely as a casual stopover by a practical Benjamín in need of provisions and the episode ends up having no consequences for the travelers. It could be concluded, then, that Gaspar does not glorify Spanish victories in battle, nor does he seek to alter history's course or assign disproportionate weight to Spain's role in global history. Seen in this light, the novel's ending and the narrator's parting words underscore Gaspar's ironic view of any patriotic illusions of grandeur.

Another aspect of the fabulous adventure told in *The Time Ship* is its religious dimension and here again we see Gaspar's use of irony at work. In the first chapter the narrator explains Don Sindulfo's decision to go back in time by clearly linking it to the scientist's philosophical principle, which may be summarized as follows: understanding what God has already created will bring us closer to divinity, and avoiding the future will keep us from nihilism and the danger of questioning or denying God's existence. Santiáñez-Tió takes at face value Don Sindulfo's wish to travel to primeval Earth in order to get closer to God, and concludes that there is a definite link between science and theology in the novel ("Introducción," 18). Yet, the fact that Don Sindulfo's moral character and temperament are discredited early on, and that his reckless actions lead toward destruction, points to a different understanding of Gaspar's intentions in this regard. Also, the narrator's voice in the paragraph preceding Don Sindulfo's declaration of religious intentions is clearly ironic: finding out whether a fossil belonged to a human or to Sancho Panza's donkey, a fictional character

Introduction

if ever there was one, is given as an example of what great service to humanity the travelers may provide. This and other ironic twists add to the impression that Gaspar is commenting on the state of science in Spain, encumbered by religious intrusion. We couldn't agree more with Ayala's assertion that Gaspar's ample use of irony and mordant humor does not obscure deep thought or social criticism.

Notes on *The Time Ship*'s Publication History and Our Translation

The first edition of *The Time Ship*, prepared by Daniel Cortezo and illustrated by Francesc Gómez Soler was published by Biblioteca Arte y Letras, a Barcelona publishing house that became part of a modernist, progressive, and European-leaning cultural wave.

Enrique Gaspar was matched in his passion for innovation and visual splendor by Soler, the celebrated Catalan painter and set designer. Set design was just coming into its own during the late Romantic period as a field that showcased both artistic creativity and technical prowess, and Soler has been recognized by historians as the foremost Catalan stage decorator of his time, a genius of popular set design who created "instructive spectacle" for the theater-going public over the course of a long and illustrious career that included creating sets for major productions in Catalonia, Cuba, Venezuela, and New York and serving as the principal scenographer for Barcelona's magnificent opera house, the Gran Liceu.[45]

Francesc Gómez Soler i Rovirosa (1836–1900) was born into an affluent family in Catalonia, Spain. He studied drawing and painting locally under Marian Carreras and Llorenç Ferris, and his artistic sensibilities were initially influenced by the liberal values that swept through western Europe in the wake of the French Revolution. Soler spent many years traveling in Europe and trained under leading scenographic artists such as Charles Antoine Cambon, Thierry Ricquier, Henri Philastre, and Félix Cagé, which turned him away from the Italianate style then favored in Barcelona and made him an adherent of French naturalism. It also brought him firsthand knowledge of new technologies and popular innovations in set ornamentation

Introduction

that he later incorporated into his many creations for the Catalonian theater, as well as for popular festivals, parades, political ceremonies, and other grand civic events for which set designers were hired and charged with making the world, as it were, a stage.

When designing for the Spanish stage, Soler "placed faith in magnificence and greatness";[46] the productions he mounted, whether for Wagnerian opera or children's entertainments, were wonders of fantasy, ingenuity, and excess. According to one account, "His stagings were the first to make the public cry out in awe, almost in unison" ["Sus montajes fueron los primeros que hacían exclamar al público, casi a coro: Oh!"].[47] He experimented with placing short curtains downstage near the proscenium arch in order to reinforce spatial perspective and plasticity, and stretched painted curtains across the top of the stage to depict ceilings or sky.[48] One innovation the Catalan artist had noted during his travels and later helped introduce into Spanish theater was the visual and conceptual division of the work into segments, a style for which a stage adaptation of Enrique Gaspar's fantastical light opera would have been perfectly suited, whether along the structural axis of geographical setting or number of scenes. Aiming to bring greater depth to the theater space, one of Soler's specialties was illumination: he was fascinated by the possibilities for three-dimensionality afforded first by gas and later by electric stage lights, and is credited with the idea of plunging the audience into darkness during the performance, a novel experience at the time that enhanced the feeling of intimacy and heightened theatrical illusion but was seen as an eccentricity that disconcerted both audience and critics at first.

As both Gaspar and Soler were committed to artistic renewal and change, it is only fitting that the publisher Daniel Cortezo would ask Soler to illustrate some of the texts Cortezo was overseeing during his editorship of Biblioteca Arte y Letras. Two of the press's 1887 offerings, in fact, were illustrated by Soler: a translation of Salvatore Farina's *Oro Nascosto* as *Oro escondido* [Hidden Gold] and Gaspar's *The Time Ship*. In both cases, the drawings reveal the hand of a scrupulous artist with a penchant for detail and verisimilitude who uses light

Introduction

and shadow to enhance the sense of depth. While the artwork in *Oro escondido* is domestic, sedate, and decidedly representational, *The Time Ship*'s drawings—even some of the more incidental ones—imply emotion and action; they capture well the novel's humor as well as its dramatic tension, and, like Soler's stage designs, evoke an aura of the fantastical even while remaining grounded in realism. The influence that Far Eastern art, particularly Japanese print, had on modernism and art nouveau in the late 1800s and early 1900s is evident in the cover illustration, which suggests wonder and exoticism through the portrait of an Asian woman (presumably the Empress Sun-che) gazing at the Time Ship, trapped within what appears to be its own private universe. Creative and prolific as a leading set designer who held sway in Barcelona through the last decades of the nineteenth century, Soler's aesthetic can be fully appreciated in the illustrations he created for the *The Time Ship*, drawings so insuperable they have been reproduced in each subsequent edition of the novel, including this one.

Between 1881 and 1890, Biblioteca Arte y Letras published high-quality works chosen with an eye for novelty or modern value and beautifully illustrated by the best engravers and artists of the time. The 1887 edition of *The Time Ship* included two additional narratives entitled *Viaje a China* [Trip to China] and *Metempsicosis* [Metempsychosis] and its cover was simply entitled: *E. Gaspar, Novelas*.

Sadly, *The Time Ship* had to wait over a hundred years, until 1999 to be exact, for a second edition, this time in electronic diskette form. This electronic edition was the result of efforts made by the *Asociación Española de Fantasía, Ciencia-Ficción y Terror*, a well-established Spanish science fiction club, to recover hard to find turn-of-the-century Spanish science fiction novels. A few years earlier, Nil Santiáñez-Tió had resuscitated Gaspar's novel by including several fragments of *The Time Ship* in his 1995 anthology of early Spanish science fiction, *De la luna a Mecanópolis: Antología de la ciencia ficción española (1832–1993)* [From the Moon to Mechanopolis: An Anthology of Spanish Science Fiction (1832–1993)]. Santiáñez-Tió's and the Association's attempts to recover Spanish proto–science fiction

Introduction

specimens certainly paid off, since the following year *Círculo de Lectores*, a Spanish general-interest book club, came out with a special print edition of Gaspar's novel. This 2000 reprinting of the original Biblioteca Arte y Letras text was reserved for members of the club and hence was of limited circulation. Yet, this renewed attention clearly helped the novel to become better known among Spanish science fiction circles, and in 2005 Gaspar's novel was again republished, this time by Minotauro, one of Spain's leading sf publishing houses. Theirs is a hardcover book, beautifully illustrated with the original drawings by Soler from the first edition and prefaced by a brief note from the editor highlighting the fact that *The Time Ship* is the earliest-known time machine story. Finally, as befits any science fiction text, *The Time Ship* has been scanned by Google and a digital copy is readily available online, the book having entered the public domain.

Our translation is based on the 1887 text edited by Daniel Cortezo, although, as far as we can tell, the subsequent editions do not deviate from the original. This has been, as all translations are, an exciting and demanding endeavor.

The title was our first challenge, along with the neologism Gaspar used for his travelers, *anacronóbatas*. Though wishing to emulate Gaspar's playful spirit by coining a similar neologism for the English title, we eventually found "The Anachronopetus" too cumbersome and opted instead to keep the flavor of the original Spanish by adding "A Chrononautical Journey" as a subtitle to *The Time Ship*. Likewise, within the narrative we rendered *anacronóbatas* as the more straightforward "time travelers" and "voyagers." Other puzzles were closer to that word's equivalent in Spanish: *rompecabezas*—literally, "head-breakers." Often these were puns or mispronunciations, like in Chapter 9 when Juana made us scratch our heads over her rendering of the Spanish *personas* as *presonas*, in reference to the French streetwalkers confined on board. Since the mistake Juana made is both a common vulgarism and a veiled reference to the word *preso*, meaning prisoner, we first tried "impresoned" and then "presoners," preferring in the end "*captive*-ating ladies" even though it didn't lend itself to mispronunciation. Gaspar challenged our wits in many other instances, such

Introduction

as in Chapter 18 when, again thanks to Juana, we had to translate a Spanish phrase disguised as Latin into an English phrase disguised as Latin. We can only hope that some of these "head-breakers" will have found their way into English in a competent and even felicitous way.

One of *The Time Ship*'s secondary characters, an aide-de-camp named Pendencia, is from Zaragoza and his regional speech mannerisms are transcribed by Gaspar into Spanish spellings like "quince camaradaz máz" and "no cea uzté bárbaro" for "quince camaradas más" and "no sea usted bárbaro" (meaning, respectively, "fifteen more comrades" and "don't be a brute"). This way of substituting an /s/ sound (transcribed with an "s") for an /θ/ sound (transcribed with a "c" or "z") is a dialectal characteristic known as *ceceo*. To a Spanish reader at the time this way of marking Pendencia's speech would have suggested that he hailed from the southern Spanish region of Andalucía, was of a working-class background, and had received little in the way of formal education. Pendencia also mispronounces certain words and at times expresses himself in a roundabout way, perhaps in an attempt to compensate for his educational shortcomings. In any case, the impression his speech causes is comical. Many literary translators we consulted recommended caution when dealing with accents; what we have tried to convey, as Gaspar did—that is, both through Pendencia's words and the way they are written—is a personality rather than an accent. Pendencia may be a common man cast in the role of comic, but he is clever and honorable, speaks directly as well as figuratively, and can imitate formal registers, even though he often gives himself away in the process. His spelling ("My hart a waytz," Chapter 5) probably vexed his teachers no end but his epistolary style makes Juana swoon.

A good portion of the novel's action is set in third-century China, so we shall close our Introduction with a few words about the romanization method we used. At the time Gaspar was living in Macao, the phonetic representation of Chinese in the Roman alphabet was just being systematized by the British diplomat and sinologist, Thomas Francis Wade (1818–95). He introduced his system in 1859 and Gaspar, being part of the consular service, became familiar with

Introduction

it. When Gaspar included Chinese words in his novel he usually, but not always, used what we now call the Wade-Giles method and that is the style we use in our translation, for although modern readers will be more familiar with pinyin, we feel the archaic transcription style better preserves the sense of exoticism and estrangement Gaspar's original readers would have felt. In some cases, Gaspar's transcriptions were inconsistent and some of his information about China was flawed. Whenever possible, we have added notes to clarify his meaning.

We first became acquainted with this early Spanish time travel story in 2000. Five years later, brief but very complimentary articles in the cultural sections of Spanish newspapers about the new and beautifully illustrated 2005 Minotauro edition further encouraged our idea of making this historically important, delightfully humorous work available to English-speaking readers. As Santiáñez-Tió reminds us, a history of science fiction that remains ignorant of key early sf Spanish texts will be incomplete and, let us add, erroneous. Brian Dendle's research, for example, offers proof that the interstellar trip described in Aguimana de Veca's *Una temporada en el más bello de los planetas* was actually written almost twenty years before Verne's *De la Terre à la Lune* [1865; From the Earth to the Moon], but was not published until 1870–71, when Jules Verne's commercial success made it less risky for Spanish publishers to print similar works. Happily, *The Time Ship*, now in English and preserving Soler's superb illustrations, can take its place in the increasingly accurate and inclusive account of science fiction's history, thanks to Wesleyan University Press and its internationally minded *Early Classics of Science Fiction* series.

The Time Ship

CHAPTER 1

In Which It Is Proved That FORWARD Is Not the Byword of Progress

Paris—focus of excitement, center of movement, nucleus of bustle—looked different that day. This was no orderly procession of locals and foreigners making their way to the Exposition at the Champ de Mars, either to satisfy base curiosity or to make a technical study of the advances of science and industry. Nor did those faces reflect the happy pleasure with which the inhabitants of ancient Lutecia, mangling English words and dressed to the nines, hasten each year to watch the grand prize stakes in the equestrian events, with each person capable of paying the price of the handicap and together of liquidating the floating debt of some foreign State.

Granted, although it was a time of universal competitions, for this was the year 1878, it was not an age for races, as no more than ten days in the month of July had transpired. Furthermore, there was no to-ing and fro-ing; that is, none of the usual occurrence where people who are out for amusement cross paths with those who are working or idle. All were headed in the same direction, a look of wonderment on their faces. The shops were closed; trains from the four cardinal points spilled forth passengers who, storming omnibuses and horse-drawn carriages, had but one cry: "To the Trocadero!"

The little steam boats on the Seine, the ribbon rail, the American tramway, that is, every mode of locomotion that exists in the modern Babylon, redoubled its efforts toward that attractive object of common desire. Although the heat suffocated like in the dog-days of summer, two human rivers overflowed the sidewalks since, not counting privately owned vehicles, Paris, with her fourteen thousand carriages for hire, could only transport two hundred and eighty thousand people at a time, allowing for ten two-person trips per carriage. Since the number of inhabitants had risen to two million by virtue of the day's entertainment, which everyone wished to attend, the result was that one million, seven hundred and twenty thousand individuals had to travel on foot.

The Champ de Mars and the Trocadero, the theater for that singular presentation, had been overrun since daybreak by the impatient crowd that, lacking the fee for the lecture that would take place in the palace's banquet hall at ten o'clock in the morning, was content to witness the second part, on the Exposition grounds, for the price of admission. Those without access to those grounds stormed the bridges and avenues. The most indolent or least fortunate were reduced to spreading out through the upper reaches of Montmartre, the bell towers of churches, the hills of the Bois, and the promontories of the Parks. Tile roofs, obelisks, columns, commemorative arches, observatories, artesian wells, domes, lightning rods—anything offering some height had been taken over by force, and stores ran out of umbrellas, parasols, straw hats, fans, and refreshing drinks with which to combat the sun.

What was happening in Paris? Let us be fair. Those people, who admire themselves by placing their mediocrities on pedestals so that the world will take them for geniuses and who enjoy mocking themselves during their endless leisure time, were, on this occasion, stirred up for ample reason. Science had just taken a step that was going to radically change humanity's way of life. A name—hitherto obscure and Spanish to boot—was coming to erase with its brilliant intellect the memory of the leading experts of the learned world. For indeed, what had Fulton done? Applied to maritime locomotion Watt's or Papin's experiments so that ships sailed with greater speed, more easily overcoming the waves' resistance with their impulse force. But leaving a port on Monday to reach another on Tuesday in which previously, with the wind in your sails, it would have been impossible to drop anchor before Saturday, cannot be called saving time but, at most, losing less of it. Stephenson, inventor of the locomotive, made it devour space along two metal nerves; but to cover greater distances in fewer minutes was always to go in search of tomorrow via the pathway of today. I say the same of Morse: transmitting a thought over wire by means of an electric agent does not alter the fact that, though the current may be able to circle the globe four times in one second, the idea, in each revolution around the equinoctial line, takes one two-hundred-and-fortieth of a minute to return to its point of origin. That is to say, the result is fatally hindmost when it comes to time. Furthermore, the inability to dispense with the conductors renders graphic the definition of the electric telegraph that one individual gave as, "A very long dog that barks in Moscow when its tail is pulled in Madrid."

The so-called marvelous hypotheses of the famous Jules Verne were but child's play compared to the grandness of the real invention by the modest Zaragozan, resident of the Royal Seat of Spain. Journeying to the center of the earth is but a matter of opening a hole through which to confirm descent, imitating the residents of Ergastiri who, many centuries before the Christian Age, had already penetrated the chasms of Laurium in order to mine argentiferous lead.[1] The trip was shorter, but the road the same. Voyaging through the air by the ingenious theory of the bellows offers no other advantage than reducing navigation to the will of the aeronaut by omitting the ropes that Jourdan used to move the Montgolfier balloons and scout the enemy's position in the Battle of Fleurus.[2] To go to the pole and await the thaw is a matter of pure patience: servile though wise imitation of those people who, in order to shop at a store, wait until the store is having a clearance sale. As for the Nautilus, long before Verne, our compatriot Monturiol had already conducted a highly successful test with the Ictíneo.[3] To tell us about what dwells at the bottom of the seas, we need only assemble a congress of divers. And above all (forgive me if I repeat myself), to depart alluvial terrain on Monday in order to arrive in the Eocene on Tuesday, the Permian on Wednesday, and the Sea of Fire by week's end; to travel by air from France to Senegal in twenty hours or to reach the end of an underwater trip later or earlier, but always afterwards, encompasses an idea of posteriority that renders science's mission monotonous, invariably running after tomorrow as if it already knew yesterday.

The world is mankind's house, and its inhabitants as they multiply add stories to the structure, with the goal of living more comfortably, but they are not careful to study the foundations to make sure that the building will withstand the crushing weight being added to it. When, a half-hour later, we see so disfigured the pattern we witnessed thirty minutes before, can we have such blind faith in the tales history tells us of the primitive times upon which we base our future conduct? If, through a series of deductions, Boucher de Perthes believed he had proven the existence of fossilized man, is it not possible that the femur he assumed to be human belonged to some relation—on the zoological scale—of Sancho Panza's mount? The past is absolutely unknown to us. When studying it, the retrospective sciences proceed almost by induction, and so long as we are unaware of yesterday it is pointless for us to ramble on about tomorrow. Before turning to nihilism through hypotheses about the future,

FORWARD is Not the Byword of Progress

let us learn to believe in God by drawing near to the marvelous origins of his vast architectural work.

Such were the philosophical principles of Don Sindulfo García, Doctor of Exact, Physical, and Natural Sciences. His application of them was the spectacle to which those people, craving excitement, hastened *en masse*, with the anxiousness and doubt that are naturally awakened by that which one cannot fathom, in spite of living in Paris, the self-anointed brain of the world.

"But see here, Captain, sir," inquired of a Pavian hussar a gentleman who, along with nineteen other individuals, was heading by omnibus to the setting of the event. "You, as a Spaniard, must know about the Time Traveler's device."

"Begging your pardon," replied the hussar. "I know how to fight my country's enemies; to be civil with the men and gallant with the ladies; I know discipline, tactics, and strategy; but when it comes to flying through the air, at school I only learned how to be tossed about in a blanket when my tobacco pouch wasn't full enough to supply my schoolmates."

"Nonetheless," the questioner insisted, "It seems to me that you, as a countryman of the machine's learned inventor, must have more exact notions of it than a foreigner would."

"I'm honored to call myself a Spaniard and, moreover, I am Señor García's nephew, but I am no more informed about the subject than the next man."

News of the kinship between the captain and the scientific colossus redoubled the curiosity of the travelers, who began trying to find in him traces of his uncle, just as in the desert plains of Marathon or among the vineyards of the Catalonian countryside we search for Miltiades' steps or Attila's steed's helmet. The women asked if Don Sindulfo was married; the men, if he had won any medals; and everyone, if he was related to Frascuelo.[4]

"But, in short, what is he trying to do?" asked one.

"What we French are tired of doing," exclaimed a hotheaded patriot. "Traveling through the air."

"Yes, but with a set direction and at a dizzying speed," a French national guardsman prudently contended, noting that the hussar was handling his saber, his only intention in fact being to settle it more readily at his side.

"I do not deny," put in a fourth, "that it is a great and marvelous thing to be able to plow the atmospheric currents at will; but sooner or later this would have come about. What human intelligence does not conceive is that, with this vehicle, one can go backwards in time, leaving Paris *today* after eating in Véfour and arriving *yesterday* at the monastery in Yuste and drinking chocolate with Emperor Charles V."

"That's impossible," everyone shouted.

"For we the ignorant," continued he who held the floor. "Not so for the science that endorsed the invention during its last congress. In any case, soon our doubts will be resolved. Today, Señor García departs for chaos in his Time Ship, whence he proposes to return within a month, bringing back proof of his fabulous expedition."

"I'll wager the inventor is a Bonaparte loyalist who wants to re-seat the traitor of Sedan on the throne of France," thundered the patriot.

"Or bring back the Terror with Robespierre," said a supporter of the Legitimist cause, clenching his fists.

"Let's not be hasty," argued a sensible one. "If the Time Ship leads to the undoing of what's been done, it strikes me that we should congratulate ourselves because this will allow us to repair our mistakes."

"You're right," exclaimed a henpecked man who was plastered against a wall of the coach. "As soon as the line is open to the public, I shall buy a ticket for the night before my wedding."

Everyone was still enjoying this witticism when the omnibus (not without great risk of flattening the packed crowd) stopped at the head of the bridge and the passengers, disembarking, fought their way to their destinations as best they could.

What we have just heard seems like fiction, and yet nothing could be more real. Doctor Don Sindulfo García was preparing to conduct a practical experiment to resolve the most arduous problem the annals of science have recorded to this day: traveling backwards in time.

FORWARD is Not the Byword of Progress

What analysis of the problem had been done? To what class of bodies belonged what, up until today, had been an abstract idea? How could it be dismantled? What agents did one use for that? What monstrous system was it that threatened to arrive at the truth by going backwards, in a century that seeks its ideals in tomorrow and accepts "forward" as the formula for progress?

The following chapter will tell us.

CHAPTER 2

A Lecture within Everyone's Reach

THE show was divided into two parts. First, the Spanish sage would bid farewell to his colleagues, the authorities, and his Paris audience in a lecture at the Trocadero Palace, during which he meant to make those less versed in the sciences understand the main principles of his invention by replacing technicalities with common demonstrations. The second part would entail elevating the monstrous device from the Champ de Mars up into the atmospheric zone where the trip would take place. In order to witness this latter event, people need only pay the entrance fee to the Exposition fairgrounds, climb to high ground, or spread out in some flat, open space. And this, as we have seen, is just what the masses had done from the break of day, testing the prudence and fists of the police, who eventually succeeded

A Lecture within Everyone's Reach

in preventing a takeover of the Palace of Industry. Among the many who claimed the right to hear the doctor's words, relatively few were chosen. The main hall, though spacious, was not large enough to contain so many people. None of the spectators was following the anti-fat[5] treatment, and yet one could say that they had all lost weight, since every seat held at least one-and-a-half people. The entrances were clogged and the aisles jam-packed with the type of crowd that patiently awaits the opportunity to advance one step, knowing all the while that it will never reach its goal.

The Presidents of the Republic, the co-legislative bodies, and the Cabinet were all present, as were the diplomatic corps and delegations from Institutes and Academies. Members of those learned bodies intermingled with military officers parading their bemedaled and beribboned uniforms and also with the modest priest bearing only the Cross of Golgotha over his black or purple cassock. A few dinner jackets—not many, since in France it's a rare bird who doesn't own a uniform—acknowledged civilian status as though in shame among the oceans of silk, waterfalls of Spanish lace, mountains of diamonds, and clouds of hair. Some of the women's coiffures were as black as tempests, others were as blonde as stratus clouds wounded by the setting sun, and almost none were of that color that announces snow in the winter of life, since to be a woman and to be old is now becoming incompatible with the land of Violet and Pinaud.[6]

Finally the time came. A wave of curiosity rippled across the place. The doors were thrown open by two janitors and the scientific committee entered, with the hero, that modesty so becoming of talent showing on his face, walking to the right of its president. Everything about him was commonplace. His first name, rather than that of a sage, seemed to belong to the old man in a comic opera. His last name was not linked by means of any particle to those patronymic lists which, like that of Paredes or Córdoba, provide leafiness to family trees and stop cold the disrespect that allows Malibrán, an illustrious offspring of the Garcías, to be as infamous in the world of the arts as Bernaola is in the one of crime.[7] He carried his fifty years not with the haughty pride of the titan who brings his own stepladder to climb up to heaven, but with the resignation of the porter carrying a trunk. Smallish, his long hair smooth and perfectly combed, his suit well brushed and seeming to hang off his thin frame, he had one of those faces that seemed to have been made in accordance with the name it would have to bear. In brief, he was worthy of the name Don Sindulfo García and merited the nickname his maidservant had bestowed on him: Pichichi. Such was the outward appearance chosen by Wisdom to astound the world, proving once again that under a bad cape hides a good drinker.

The delegation sat beneath the massive pipe organ; the president rang a silver bell, the session was opened, and the Time Ship's inventor proceeded to the rostrum amid a torrent of applause that was brought to an end not by his reedy voice but by the movement of his lips, which made the crowd realize he had uttered "Gentlemen," the sacramental opening of any speech.

Silence restored, the hero expressed himself thusly: "I will be brief, because the more hours I spend, the more I widen the gulf that separates me from the yesterday I am proceeding towards. I will speak plainly: since my theories have been endorsed by the learned world, all that remains is to make myself understood by everyone else. Nevertheless, I will answer any objections that may be put to me. My purpose, as everyone knows, is to go back in time, not so as to put a stop to the constant forward motion of life, but to unmake its work and bring us closer to God as we travel toward the origins of the planet we inhabit. But in order to explain how time may be undone, we must first learn of what it is composed.

Let us proceed in order. God made the heavens and the Earth, the former dark and the latter in chaotic form. He then said: 'Let there be light,' and there was light. And so we have the sun floating in the celestial vault and the orb suspended in space by solar attraction. Everyone knows, since Galileo demonstrated the principle of the Earth's rotation, that the world moves; but what science has not yet explained is why the Earth performs its rotary movement from west to east and not the other way round. This is what I will expound as the basis of my time traveling system."

A Lecture within Everyone's Reach

A whisper of satisfaction came from the audience and the sage continued his speech:

"In the beginning, the Earth was immersed in chaos; it was a huge ball of fire that, like any incandescent body, exhaled those vapors we know by the name of radiation. Fixed on its axis, as any other recently created work would be, it had yet to begin the rotating motion the Creator had assigned to it. Its heat was infinitely more intense on the east because the sun kept bathing it with its rays on that side. Those of you who have seen bituminous substances melt in a pot will have observed the enormous quantity of vapor they release. Imagine, then, how much the fusion of a spheroid whose volume is 1,097 million cubic myriameters would discharge. Even the layman can grasp that evaporation such as that could not happen without each emission being accompanied by a bang and a repercussion. Well, given that when a cannon is fired the recoil makes the cannon jump back, each radiation discharge should generate dislocations in the globe. And since the discharges were becoming more and more frequent and intense on the eastern side of the planet due to the larger amount of heat the sun was giving off, the recurring backwards movements caused by the constant jolts resulted in the spheroid rotating on its own axis from west to east. This was cleverly foreseen by Providence for the periodic succession of day and night and will be as enduring as its Omnipotent Lordship wishes the central fire of its motor to be."

A lengthy cheer welcomed such a novel, daring, and unexpected theory. The doctor, without moistening his lips—a detail noticed by the audience, so used to seeing their speakers use water for that purpose throughout their perorations—picked up the thread thusly:

"Every phenomenon obeys a cause, and yet two-and-a-half centuries have passed since the inventor of the thermometer and the geometric compass, that wise man of Pisa who taught us how to count seconds and measure the beating of arteries by the isochronous movement of the pendulum—since Galileo, in short, told us that the Earth was moving. Not until today has the reason for such a simple fact been revealed to us. But, is this enough? Absolutely not. If every phenomenon obeys a cause, it is also necessary that it reach an end, produce a result, fulfill a purpose.

'The Earth is moving,' cries a man, and immediately Science wonders: 'Why does it move?' 'Because of heat release,' answers Observation, and yet immediately afterwards Philosophy cries halt, shoulders its guns, and exclaims, 'And what does it move for?'

Let us answer Philosophy. The Earth is moving in order to make time. Our planet which, as we have seen, was no more than an incandescent mass, eventually solidified its crust, saw colossal mountains rise up from its surface, filled its bosom with seas, clothed its barrenness with an amazing flora, and populated itself with the richest fauna. How did this miracle occur? Very simply: through the action of time, the succession of days or epochs over whose work presided the wisdom and will of the Supreme Maker, who allows the revolutions to continue for the benefit of man's perfectibility and admiration of his omnipotence. The globe's transformations, then, are the work of time. But who is that creator? Where are his materials? What is his laboratory? The creator is radiation, its materials are found in the gaseous zone, its laboratory, space. TIME IS THE ATMOSPHERE. All the wonders that nature, science, art, and industry lay before us today for our admiration, that we believe to be the genuine expression of progress and that fill us with pride, come entirely from that region where until today man has been able to find nothing except air, rain, lightning, thunder, and half a dozen other meteorological accidents. Restrain your impatience, for I shall prove what was just said with a practical demonstration. I like conviction to reach the soul through the sense of sight."

A wave that threatened to become an explosion convulsed the crowd. The president rang his bell and the lecturer, having turned his back for a moment, faced the audience again, holding in his hand a top hat whose cylinder was encased in one of those enormous gauzes a man uses to announce he is in mourning to everyone who had not asked him because they could not care less.

The gauze, having been prepared for this purpose beforehand, was wrapped around the hat five or six times and attached to it at one end only. Don Sindulfo began to unwrap it, to the hilarity of the crowd who used that occasion, as all other circumstances in life, to abandon itself to its frivolous and unruly nature.

The sage, deaf to the world, carried on with his task. He let the crepe that was stitched to the crown on one side flutter away and, displaying the hat's silky felt and pointing to its now-uncovered cylinder, said:

"Behold the Earth in its incandescent state, just as God saw fit to launch it into infinite space. As you can see, it is fixed, immobile; and yet, suddenly, radiation as represented by this gauze produces a discharge; this, in turn, causes a dislocation of the globe and the sphere begins to gyrate on its own axis, setting off time, which is nothing but constant motion."

And as he said this he stretched the gauze out with his right hand, simulating a rising column of smoke, while with his left hand he turned the hat around almost imperceptibly.

"Behold time," he continued, indicating the crepe.

"Do you want to know how it turns into minerals, plants, and living beings through an uninterrupted succession of seconds? How we get from seaweed to the greenhouse, from kaolin to diamonds, from caverns to architecture, and from trilobites, with their three lobules, to men's foreheads and infinitesimal calculus? Follow time with me to its own atmospheric laboratory."

Every face showed astonishment. The doctor flashed a small smile of triumph, a herald of his convictions, and clearing his throat continued as we shall now see.

CHAPTER 3

Theory of Time: How It Is Made, How It Is Unmade

"Anyone who has watched a pot of soup boiling on a stove will perforce have seen the phenomenon of transformation, made manifest by the steam as it escapes up the chimney. The first thing the steam does is cool off and turn into drops of water that halt the boiling process if they fall into the pot's depths; or else it becomes soot, if condensation occurs far enough away from the fire to permit solidification. That is to say, if the pot were to continue boiling during an uninterrupted stretch of years, a film or crust—the by-product of the vapor's emissions—would eventually form on the surface of the soup, similar to what forms on the hearth, and it would petrify over time. Let us apply this principle to our case.

Theory of Time

This hat is the Earth; its gauze, steam. The steam rises and condenses, but the earth rotates and envelops the steam just as a sash winds 'round the dandy's waist or a turban, the head of a Muslim. And thus you can see how, by means of this rotating, the first layer of crepe covers the silk of the hat in the same way the sphere's first solid film covered the igneous mass of the planet. The gauze appears full of folds and clefts. What do they represent? The hills and plains, the work of time. Where was this time produced? In the atmosphere. Does that mean that the Himalayas and Príncipe Pío mountain, the valleys of Josafat and Andorra fell to us from the clouds? Without a doubt. How? Thusly: the fearsome hurricanes that reigned back then swept the fused substances of the Earth's surface toward a given point; when clumped together, they formed points. Just as when we blow on a bowl of semolina soup and the surface forms little bumps. Moreover, the continuous electrical discharges opened trenches or depressions in the globe's crust, creating channels through which flowed the incandescent mass that became today's mineral veins. Finally came the torrential rains that, cooling and solidifying the orb, caused the formation of primitive land, that is, the first solid stratum (counting from the bottom up) of this eighty-kilometer crust that serves as our pedestal.

'Hold on there,' someone will object. 'I see in these atmospheric revolutions nothing but agents modifying the globe's properties, not the idea of time. The world doubtless is the product of time; nevertheless, reason does not admit that the minerals, flora, and fauna it contains are the product of lightning, hurricanes, or rain.'

'What is time?' I will ask in reply. Time is movement; in inaction there is neither before nor after. What has left its mark upon the Earth? Radiation, caloric release; in the end, steam, the aftermath of these discharges. Of what agents was this steam composed? Of all those that today make up our planet, and the proof is that, if the Earth had not moved, the gases, disappearing into space, would have left us world-less as they carried off through evaporation all of the Earth's substances. Therefore the atmosphere, endlessly receiving the planet's exhalations and returning them transformed, is the laboratory where cosmic metamorphoses take place, where movement occurs and where, as a result, time is produced.

What! You see nothing in rain but the drop of water, in lightning only the spark, in a hurricane, the gust of wind? Lift up your spirits and praise the Creator who in those fluids sends us the never-ending tomorrow, as almost seven thousand years ago he sent you the today you live in and the marvels you admire. The clouds hurled down the Hagia Sophia in Constantinople and Pope Sixtus V's obelisk in the Eternal City, bringing us in their drops the red porphyry of Egypt with its embedded white crystals. Down from their laboratory came the waters of Luxor and Pompey's column. The vermilion with which David and Bathsheba's son ordered Jehovah's temple painted: what else created it but the cinnabar that was showered upon Almadén in La Mancha? Lime and carbon set loose from the nimbus's depths gave you the houses you inhabit, by furnishing you with the chalk pits and limestone whence you extract mortar and carve corbels. In the same downpour that contained marl for bricks came kaolin which, together with feldspar, vitrified to provide you with bowls to eat from and porcelain with which to decorate your sitting rooms. The trains that cross Mount Cenis and St. Gothard, and the steamers, like the Vega, that now plow their way across the Bering Strait—where would they be without the atmospheric action that made coal by decomposing vegetation from the carbon era? Will you deny that each drop contained the seed of an engine or a schooner and each storm that of an entire train or fleet? But it did not only rain modes of locomotion: from the howls of the gaseous zone the fireplace, public illumination, and womanly caresses were shaken loose. For hydrogen, once extracted from coal, created gasworks, while its residue, having metamorphosed into coke, gathered the family together around the love of the hearth or cemented peace between husband and wife when, as crystallized carbon, it was presented in the form of a diamond. The compass and the electric telegraph had lightning as inspiration. What would become of humanity without the mercury that signals variations in temperature and serves in the extraction of gold and silver? But there is still more. In the constituent elements of the atmospheric phenomena God permits shells, turtles, birds, reptiles, and second-phase mammals to come to Earth as embryos. Then, in the tertiary era, He allows air, purified by the absorption of carbonic acid by carboniferous flora, to blow so compatibly for the organic family that the microscopic life forms fallen to Earth in raindrops develop, crossbreed, and enlarge, turning into mastodons, hippopotami, horses, bulls, buffalos, stags, dromedaries, tigers, and lions. Finally, quaternary land gives us the mammoth, the urus, the cervidae, and the megathere. At last Providence, to crown its work, takes a bit of the clay fashioned for this purpose during six days or epochs and, shaping it into a figure, imparts unto it its divine breath, calls it man and proclaims it, by virtue of its intelligence, the king of creation. Gentlemen, the concentric wrappings of the gauze symbolize the geological ages of nature. These ages should be considered the world's mathematics. Are they not the product of atmospheric evolutions? They are. Do we not count the age of the globe by them? We do. So, if each layer of film is a series of centuries, then each drop, each spark, each gust must be a fraction of a second. Ergo, the hours hover about in space. Let us contend, then, that time is the atmosphere."

Enthusiasm, hitherto repressed in the auditorium due to wonder, erupted at the first opportune pause and a storm of clapping and shouts of acclaim resounded through the lecture hall, spreading out into the corridors where people applauded in the spirit of imitation. One of the attendees, rising up from his seat to the great puzzlement of the audience, who thought he was leaving the room, faced the sage and said:

"Will you allow me to express a doubt?"

"As many as may occur to you," replied Don Sindulfo.

"If the speaker considers time to be like a thick sash, mustn't one assume that, given the depression of all spherical bodies at their poles, the Earth's poles remain bare of wrappings just like the crown of the hat and the ring or circle for the head were left gauzeless in the demonstration?"

"Without a doubt; and that merely confirms my thesis. Given that the atmosphere is time and that time is formed by events, if no one has yet traveled to the poles, then at the poles nothing has happened; and having no need of the crepe or wrapping where there is no vital spark, this atmospheric economy has been nature-the-tailor's thrift."

Hearty laughter greeted the scholar's witty rebuttal and, unperturbed, he took up his lecture once more.

"Nothing simpler, ladies and gentlemen, than to unmake a body when the elements of which it is comprised are known to us. If I know that this symbol of mourning on my hat is made of concentric layers of gauze rolled around the cylinder, then by winding them in the opposite direction from that taken during their binding I will assuredly end up uncovering the hat's crown; this, when applied to the cosmos, means that by dint of unwinding geological zones, one will come upon chaos. Now then: how does this unmaking take place? In order to explain satisfactorily I must refer to my apparatus. The *Anachronopetus*, or Time Ship, which is a kind of Noah's Ark, owes its name to three Greek words: *ana*, which means 'backwards,' *cronos*, 'time,' and *petus*, 'one who flies,' thereby justifying its mission of flying backwards in time. For in effect, thanks to the Time Ship, one may have breakfast at seven in nineteenth-century Paris, partake of lunch at noon in Russia with Peter the Great, dine at five in Madrid with Cervantes—if he has the means to that day—and, overnighting en route, disembark at dawn with Columbus on the beaches of virgin America. Its motor is electricity, a current that science, though it had tried and come close, had not been able to make travel without conductors until now—and a current that I have managed to subdue by conquering its speed. That is to say, with my machine I can just as easily circle the globe twice in one second (average speed), as I can make it go at a snail's pace, ascend, descend, and come to a dead stop. Excepting its impulse agent, all else are mechanical processes whose explication would awaken no interest, especially in a public that knows by heart the works of Jules Verne: works of entertainment which, if they cannot be compared with the solemn scientific nature of my theories, nonetheless contain hypotheses based on physical and natural studies that relieve me from giving vexing explanations about the regulator, compensators, thermometers, barometers, chronometers,

Theory of Time

high-powered lenses, potassium receptacles, Reiset and Regnaut's device for producing breathable oxygen, and sundry other elementary details. I rise to the center of the atmosphere, which is the body that we are trying to unmake and that I shall continue to call time. Because time—in order to become wrapped up in the Earth—marches in the opposite direction to the planet's rotation, the Time Ship, so as to unwrap time, must travel contrariwise to it and in step with the spheroid: that is, from west to east. The globe takes twenty-four hours for each revolution on its axis; my machine navigates at a speed 175,200 times faster, with the result that in the time it takes the Earth to produce one day in the future, I can undo 480 years of the past.

Now, the first thing that leaps to mind is that, at whatever height and speed of locomotion this is checked, the Time Ship need only describe one orbit around the earth like that which satellites describe around the planets; and that is indeed how it would be, were the atmosphere to remain immutable. But since I unmake the atmosphere, with each orbit I undo its work by one day and there, wherever I stop, is yesterday.

Let us see how this phenomenon is proven. It is commonly said that in order to preserve sardines from Nantes and peppers from Calahorra one must extract *the air* from the tins. Wrong. What is extracted is *the atmosphere* and, as a result, *time*, because air is nothing but a composite of nitrogen and oxygen, whereas the atmosphere, in addition to consisting of eighty parts of the former and twenty of the latter, carries within it a bit of water vapor and a small dose of carbonic acid, all elements that never separate when filling a vacuum. But let us move away from science and approach common reason. Let us imagine that the world is a tin of sweet red peppers from which we have not extracted the atmosphere. What happens when it is sealed without this precaution? Time begins to exert its influence and produce its effects. First of all, molecules stick to the can's walls, molecules that, when amassed and solidified, would petrify over the years and in whose essence we would find the mineral seeds of primitive rocks. Next, we observe that the substance gets covered with a kind of verdigris that is none other than primal vegetation. And finally the animated little life forms in the water vapor, having reproduced and developed, tunnel their way through the mixture, enriching it with the manifold variants of the animal kingdom.

Can you still doubt that the atmosphere is time? Then let us turn the original supposition around. Let us assume that we have extracted the air and that we open the tin one hundred years after sealing it. What do we see? The peppers in a perfect state of preservation, no time having touched them; thus, if the atmospheric action should have destroyed or altered them, and the lack of this action has kept them completely whole instead, there is no question that what we are eating one century later is the vegetable life of a century before and that, therefore, we have gone back one hundred years. Clearer still. We have not extracted the air from the tin and we open it at the moment when decomposition begins; if we take a spoon and with it start to remove the layers of mold that encase the peppers, their reddish color, not yet changed, eventually will be uncovered as a result of displacing the harmful atmosphere. Well, this is the theory of time. The world, still too young for the central fire to have disappeared, is nonetheless covered with these films of mold that the Time Ship will unwrap with the help of four great spoons or fixed pneumatic devices at its angular edges; with which not only shall I unmake the trifling twenty leagues of gases that surround the globe in concentric layers, but once I dislodge them I shall navigate in the void, preventing my vehicle from burning up in the atmosphere's friction. Because, returning to similes: the atmosphere is nothing but the agglomeration of imperceptible atoms, just as a beach is nothing but the gathering of millions of grains of sand. Or if you want it made more graspable still: the atmosphere is a vast public square full of people on a day of revolution. If a foolhardy and unarmed man were to try to run with a dispatch from one end of the plaza to the other against the tide of public opinion, the result would be a push here, a shove there, resistance from all quarters; he would no doubt perish in the waves of that mutinous horde, just as the Time Ship would disappear, burned to a crisp by friction and motion. But, what does a prudent governor, representing science in this case, do? He gives a horse to the one charged with carrying the dispatch (the electricity applied to the Time Ship), surrounds him with a cavalry squadron (the four pneumatic devices), and commands them, lances at the ready, to exit via one of the adjacent streets. The phenomenon at work is known to all. The atoms scatter before the lancers; the molecules at the rear try to fill the gap caused by the atoms' displacement or dispersal; but, as the cavalry advances more quickly than the rearguard mutineers and those in front flee beyond reach of the pikes, the groups disappear and the dispatch, free of all resistance force, happily reaches the end unhindered, galloping across the void that the squadron's lances are opening up for it.

The delirious audience was about to explode in enthusiastic shouts; but it stopped upon seeing that the interrupter was getting to his feet again and, facing the lecturer, cried:

"With all due respect, I should like to voice a doubt."

"I'm listening," said the sage.

"If by this process, which is beyond refutation, one travels backwards in time, will it not be that, as the time traveler sheds years, he becomes younger?"

"Unquestionably."

Here the gentle sex's response took the form of a joyous cry.

"So the traveler will end up non-existent by virtue of shrinking?"

"That is what would happen if science had not foreseen all."

"And how, sir, do you neutralize those effects?"

"Quite simply: by making myself immutable thanks to a current of my own invention. Do I not travel towards the past? Well, just as sardines can be kept fresh for the future, I can protect myself against the yesterday that is my tomorrow. It is the process of preserved foods applied with opposite effect to animal life. And now that this is settled, permit me to bring my lecture to a close, as the hours are passing and this evening I must have an audience with Philip II to find out if the pastry maker from Madrigal was or was not the Portuguese king whose disappearance will soon cease to be one of history's enigmas."[8]

A torrent of hurrahs flooded the lecture hall. Men threw their tricornes into the air; women covered the speaker's podium with flowers; and the organ, on which was being played a march composed for the solemn occasion, could scarcely be heard above the frenzied shouts of the overflow crowd.

At last our illustrious citizen, surrounded by the scientific assembly and followed by the throng, managed to reach the door; and offering a "Three cheers!" to the *past* as a new rallying cry for civilization, he climbed over the balustrade, descended Trocadero hill and headed off toward the Time Ship, which rested its huge bulk in majesty on the esplanade of the Champ de Mars palace.

CHAPTER 4

Which Deals with Family Affairs

G REAT effects are not always the result of great causes. We need only cite the Peloponnesian Wars, which History always attributes to an eminently political cause but which owe their origins to the kidnapping of three of Aspasia's young lady pupils by some jovial young men from Megara. What's more, Pericles, who malicious tongues say may have been involved with the lady teacher himself, must not have approved of the stunt. And it seems to me that the poor man must indeed have liked Aspasia because, when she was accused of impiety and he took charge of her defense, all he could do was cover his face with his cloak and cry on the Pnyx hill like a child, which certainly earned the good disciple of Anaxagoras her absolution.

The Time Ship

All erudition aside and contrary to appearances, Don Sindulfo's invention did not result from his love of science either, but from a family—or should I say, a purely personal—interest.

A few words about his life.

When he was still very young, our hero found himself alone in the world, a doctor of science and the owner of an immense fortune whose returns he annually invested almost entirely in gadgets of the best foreign manufacture to enhance his study of Physics and Mineralogy. Being as prodigal in his studies as he was miserly in everything else, he reached the age of forty without gaining even a rudimentary knowledge of love. All of his affections crystallized in his friendship with Benjamín, another know-it-all, ten years his junior but almost as oblivious as Don Sindulfo to all earthly things. In truth, he had no time for anything but learning Sanskrit, Hebrew, Chinese, and some two dozen other difficult languages, having a matchless aptitude for them. Although they did not live in the same house, one could say they lived together, since Benjamín hardly ever left García's place, where he could count on his daily chickpea soup at two and his stew at eight. For this reason Benjamín, who was poor, was able to solve the problem of saving without having, and Don Sindulfo found a grateful stomach that would tolerate his impertinent remarks.

Early one morning, Zaragoza's newspapers and the Peninsular ones announced the sale of the museum belonging to a well-known Madrid archeologist who had passed away a few weeks earlier. And since Benjamín, who never let the grass grow under his feet when it came to antiques, had expressed a wish to acquire a few trinkets, his friend decided to help him out by moving them both to the seat of the royal Spanish court and placing his purse and his knowledge at the antiquarian's service.

No sooner said than done. They arrived in Madrid and rented a modest room in Las Peninsulares,[9] and on the day of the sale they went to the collector's study. Benjamín would have bought everything if he had had the money, but his poverty of means restrained him, and he even needed Don Sindulfo's prodding to buy a few items. Truth be told, you would have to be a saint not to lose your shirt over that pile

Family Affairs

of wonders. There, inside a leather case and in a fossilized state, was the eye Hannibal lost during the siege of Saguntum; next to it stood the tip of the ox Apis's horn; a bit farther on lay a moldy rifle which, since it had been found loaded with hempseeds, was supposed to have belonged to Ambrosio and until then had been considered only a legend.[10] But, since the prices were not within the means of every purse, Benjamín had to limit his aspirations and focus on acquiring a relatively important medallion. Time had corroded part of the inscription, but what one could still make out, which was

SERV C   POMP   PR
JO   HONOR

left no doubt as to its provenance, which the catalog claimed was a commemorative tribute made by Gaius Servilius, prefect of Pompeii, in honor of Jupiter.

They were just about to leave the museum when the rapt aficionado's attention was caught by the ridiculously low price on a rather unusual mummy. Indeed, the sarcophagus was not of Egyptian shape, nor was the embalming procedure the one which, according to Herodotus, was practiced in Thebes and Memphis, whereby the chest is opened with a sharp Ethiopian stone to extract the ventricle and refill the abdomen with myrrh, cassia, and palm wine. Nor had the mummification been accomplished as Colonel Bagnole notes, with the resin the Arabs call *katran* that is extracted by fire from a very common bush found on the shores of the Red Sea, in Syria, and in Arabia Felix. The mummy's cardboard-like state seemed natural since, lacking any incision mark whatsoever and not being wrapped in the traditional strips of cloth or sporting any hollow spots, one could not say it had ever been bound at all. The catalog modestly said: "Mummy of unknown origin," and this absence of ancestry or history made it worthless in the eyes of those who ordinarily are only proud of often apocryphal family trees.

Benjamín, with his observant spirit, set his five senses to the study of the tiniest details. Spotting a bracelet or metal ring boasting a Chinese inscription that was fitted to the right heel, and which common people had taken to be an ornament, he could not contain a cry of surprise.

"What's the matter?" asked Don Sindulfo.

"I have just made an extraordinary discovery."

"What?"

"Listen to what this inscription says: *I am the wife of Emperor Hsien-ti, buried alive for having claimed to possess the secret of immortality.*"

"Hsien-ti!" cried Don Sindulfo, now sharing his friend's enthusiasm. "The last descendant of the Han dynasty?"

"Dethroned in the third century of the Christian era by Tsao Pi, founder of the Wei dynasty."

"Meaning . . ."

"Meaning that these people, the cradle of world civilization, possessed, if not the secret of immortality, at least that of the fabled longevity of biblical times."

Don Sindulfo, awaiting no further explanations, took out his wallet and drew a bill of exchange on his banker, entrusting the Peninsulares inn with the transportation of his newly acquired objects. Among these was another last-minute find, a petrified bone that had cost them its weight in gold, since it was nothing less, according to the catalog, than a man's fossilized shinbone, discovered around Chartres in some fields dating back to the Tertiary Period.

The two inseparable friends thought of nothing else but their preparations for the trip back to Zaragoza, where they could throw themselves fully into their scientific research. And yet, a meddling garbanzo bean crossed their path and altered the majestic monotony of their existence. When they went one afternoon to settle their account and bid farewell to the banker, a brawny Zaragozan widower who had made his fortune during the first civil war[11] by supplying the loyalist army, they engaged in the usual chatter, beginning:

"And how are they treating you at the inn?"

"Poorly. It's French food, so you never know what you're putting in your mouth. We're leaving Madrid without having once tried a good old Castilian-style stew." And continuing on:

"Now then, today will be the day you satisfy your whim, since I've just gotten hold of some butter-tender garbanzo beans from Fuente-Saúco."

"But that would be too much trouble."

"No it wouldn't."

"Yes, it would."

"'Twouldn't." "'Twould."

As a result, they stayed to eat at the banker's. And the banker had a daughter, and the daughter was a mute who, despite lacking the power of speech, left no thought unexpressed and made herself perfectly understood by using her hands and feet. I do not know which of those two communicative devices she employed more often during dinner, but the long and the short of it is that by the time dessert was served, forty-year-old Don Sindulfo, seated on her right, was as in love with the child as a young cadet. The aforementioned daughter certainly merited it, since every line of her body reached its maximum curve and each of her attributes would incite anyone to become Espartero, not only to pursue them, as in Bilbao, but to embrace them, as in Vergara.[12]

The trip was postponed, the visits, repeated. Wishing not to entrust the gadgets' safety to mercenary hands served Don Sindulfo as grounds for the suitability of the marriage during his talks with Benjamín. The latter's agreement heartened the sage; the question was duly popped and the banker, who always happened to have Saúco garbanzo beans on hand every time a marriageable man came along, said yes with the delight of a sick man hearing his tumor is benign. As for the young lady, we need not record whether she took the news well, since it is common knowledge that, when it comes to marriage, even mute women rejoice.

The large dowry was settled, the wedding presents arranged. And since one of the conditions was that they take up residence in Madrid, the sages returned to Zaragoza to properly pack up their laboratory. A month later, husband, wife, and friend set up house on Tres Peces Street in the City of the Royal Crown.

Mamerta, for such was Mrs. García's given name, turned out to be of excellent disposition, and the fact that she liked to be around Benjamín more than her husband was hardly surprising, if we consider that the former, being a polyglot, was teaching her sign language in several different tongues while Don Sindulfo could not manage to make himself understood in his own. Women go crazy for a good chat. She also had a passion for men in uniform. But Don Sindulfo, knowing this to be a young woman's weakness, would at times wear his own uniform from the national cavalry, the one he wore during the biennial,[13] and that would keep her happy. Her only defect was that she could not be crossed. She would instantly have a fit of hysterics that would turn into a series of blows rained down upon the nape of her husband's neck; and the man, bent on saving it, thought it prudent to let her do as she pleased from then on so as not to excite her nervous system. Another feature of hers worth noting was that she would faint the minute she saw a threaded needle, and this kept her from attending to the housework, in spite of her good intentions. As a result, she spent her days putting her hair up in her dressing room, signing with Benjamín, or playing on the guitar a tune that no one had taught her and no one could recognize, but one she would invariably play in the same rhythm, at identical pitch, and to similar effect: breaking the eardrums of those who heard it.

Six peaceful and joyous months like this slipped by for the trio, after which came summer and with it, the annual sea-bathing cure the banker took in Biarritz to slim down, without ever succeeding. His daughter, who treated herself to the same cure in order to fill out, with no better results, often accompanied him. Given that Mamerta, in spite of her marriage, was not getting any fatter, it was decided that she would go along with her father that year as usual to soak in the waters of the empress's favorite beach.[14] They arrived and dove in, but such was their bad luck that the banker suffered a dizzy spell while performing a clever maneuver and drowned. His daughter signaled for help, the lifeboat darted in to the rescue, the young lady was slow to avoid it, and after its prow struck her on the back of the head two bodies were taken ashore instead of one. As the father had been the first victim and Mamerta had made a will in favor of her husband,

Don Sindulfo found himself the owner of a considerable fortune which, when added to his assets, allowed him to emulate Croesus' fame.

"Welcome, misfortune, if thou comest alone," says the proverb. And no saying was ever more relevant, since it was from that moment on that our sage's tribulations began, though one might consider them tribulations willingly borne, given the benefits they bestowed upon science.

Also dying around that time was one of Don Sindulfo's sisters, as rich as him, long-time widow, and mother of a tender, fifteen-year-old rosebud named Clara. Upon departing this earthly plane, that is to say, Pinto, the land where she lived, she designated her brother the girl's tutor after bequeathing him the proper legacy, with no other condition than that he not separate the orphan from Juanita, a lass four years older than Clara, for as long as she lived. Clara had been brought up with Juanita and loved her madly despite her lowly status, for Juanita was only one of her maids.

Our sage's mourning for his wife, his solitude-inducing hobbies, and the circumstances that inclined him toward isolation led him to change residences, and the two inseparables took their retorts and crucibles, their rain gauges and compasses, their fossils and stones, and set out to bury themselves in Pinto among Clara's childlike simplicity and Juanita's innocent remarks. Juanita, a country lass and her parents' daughter, would tell any number of home truths to one and all in that fresh, saucy manner Madrileños use when they abandon themselves to their instincts. The Maritornes[15] did not take a fancy to the two sages and she started by assigning a nickname to each of them. She called Don Sindulfo Uncle Pichichi, and the languages professor, the "gasbag."

But, oh, human frailty! That same man, who had reached the age of forty without experiencing any of the attractions of the daughters of Eve, needed no more than six months of fraternization to then be unable to resist their magnetic pull. Not knowing that his case with the mute had been a marriage of convenience fobbed off on the first bidder, he came to imagine that his own face was genuine currency with which to acquire undamaged goods at a low price, and he was always shoving it in front of his niece who, innocent and loving, saw nothing in it but an uncle's face.

One day a few months later, Don Sindulfo—stimulated by what our hero judged to be the triumph of his charms and supported by Benjamín, who was always ready to flatter his protector's weaknesses—declared his impudent thoughts to his ward. This earned him a flat refusal, but one that was watered by Clara's bitter tears, since she was hesitant to explain the reason for her rejection.

"Good Lord, man, come over here!" said Juanita, approaching her master after finding out what had happened. "Do me the favor of looking at the lines on your face in this mirror. Do you think my mistress should like marrying a pair of bellows?"

"Insolent woman!" cried Don Sindulfo, blinded by fury. "Don't make me throw you out into the street."

"Me? Not you or anyone else. I'm here because it was the testtater's will and the law is on my side. I'm a court-ordered maid."

"But, on what basis do you deprive me of all hope?" asked the tutor humbly, seeing if sweetness would profit him more.

"Well, Meester,[16] the thing is, the Missy and I care more for soldiers than for scientists."

"What?"

"What I mean is, she's head over heels for her cousin Don Luis, the Captain of Hussars, and I love his orderly, Pendencia. They'll be arriving at the Madrid garrison in three days time and if you make any trouble you'll find your learned self in a pickle."

That revelation, confirmed by his niece, was the coup de grace for Don Sindulfo, whose passion, fanned by jealousy, reached its boiling point. The captain, more in love with his cousin than ever, arrived in the capital the following week and within two hours made a personal appearance in Pinto. But the front door of the house was locked and bolted in his face by Don Sindulfo, with the order that he not show himself there again under pain of disinheritance. Luis's first impulse was to seek protection in the law against the tutor's heartless arbitrariness, but Clara was not old enough for the judge to overrule paternal dissent and, even if she were, she would not have gone against her mother's dying request, which forced her not to marry anyone of whom Don Sindulfo disapproved.

Suffering and waiting were required, then. When one loves and is loved, one endures everything with patience. But from then on the house became a hell, since letters came and went with the help of the orderly and the Maritornes, and the sage was consumed with fruitless surveillance and pointless weight loss.

"Oh!" the wretched man would cry in despair, "Why did the law become so lax? Happy were the times when a tutor had the right to impose his will on his pupil. I wish I could transport myself back to that age, mistakenly called dark, when respect and obedience to one's superiors formed the basis of society! How I wish I could go back centuries!"

"Would to God!" Benjamín chimed in to complete the duet. "That way we could land in China during the Hsien-ti Empire and solve that enigma the mummy started, to which end I have uselessly read all that historiographers have written about the followers of Confucius and Mencius."

That single prevailing idea came to achieve monomaniacal proportions in both their minds. The polyglot dreamed in Chinese and his colleague spent his days extracting air from the containers with the pneumatic machine, to be analyzed and separated into its elements. But all was in vain until Providence—wishing, as it does in most discoveries, to appear disguised as happenstance—came unexpectedly to their aid.

One afternoon when the new Don Bartolo,[17] driven by his jealousy, tiptoed into the kitchen intent on catching the pigeons that often escaped the hawk by sheltering near the stove, he found Juanita spelling out a letter from Pendencia, one she hurried to hide in a place she knew Don Sindulfo would not look.

"What are you doing?" he asked her.

"Learning," she said without missing a beat.

"You'd do better to keep yourself entertained by cleaning the chimney, which has a foot of soot and an army of cobwebs."

Family Affairs

"You'll find that plus the whole of creation in there. That's the work of time. And very likely no one has swept it out since the day you were born."

Don Sindulfo, who was holding a knife, was wielding it with the undoubted intention of committing murder; but, he stopped himself in time and began scraping the hood of the stove with it as if to soothe his fury.

"So amuse yourself," he added, "by removing the layers of grit and you'll see how you make the burners shine."

"Oh, please, don't make me laugh! If that were possible, you'd already have made yourself as good as new by scraping the extra layers of years off with a knife."

Don Sindulfo feigned getting tough, when a sudden idea crossed his mind and left him standing on one foot like a crane, looking for all the world like Cain when he heard the Lord ask him, "Where is Abel thy brother?" That common housemaid, who lacked the least scientific understanding, had just set him off toward reaching the solution he had been chasing with such zeal.

From that moment on he got down to work. Physics, Mathematics, Geology, Dynamics, Mechanics, Sublime Calculus, Meteorology, the whole of human knowledge, spurred on by his love and flogged by his jealousy, finally offered up to him their most secret mysteries and, reducing his invention to one single formula, he established the axiom that going back in time was nothing other than unsooting time.

A few years, all of his capital, and a great deal of his niece's besides, were invested into building the Time Ship. Meanwhile, the young lovers waited patiently, at times risking a tentative transaction, but to no avail. Don Sindulfo kept an increasingly vigilant eye, left everyone except Benjamín in the dark about the work that consumed him, and gave full rein to his passion, with the illusory hope of victory.

One day, the completion of the machine, which coincided with the opening of the 1878 Universal Exposition, made it possible at last for several trucks to be loaded with all of its unassembled parts. Squeezed into a first-class car, the inventor, his friend, the niece, and that nuisance of a maid all suddenly departed for Paris, where the lovelorn tutor, free from the hussar's provocations, planned to realize his dream. This he never managed to do, as the reader who wishes to patiently follow the course of this incredible tale will see.

CHAPTER 5

Cupid and Mars

WHILE the ungainly contraption was being assembled at the site reserved for it on the Exposition Hall grounds, Don Sindulfo settled in with his family at the Concordia hotel on Malesherbes Boulevard. It goes without saying that during the hours the sage spent at the Champ de Mars overseeing the work, Clara and Juanita were kept under lock and key in their rooms; for our Spaniard, who was jealous as a Turk, was in constant fear of their escape or abduction. When he took the girls on an outing he always did so by coach, and they only attended the theater in curtained box seats.

The Time Ship

All of these precautions, along with the distance that separated them from Madrid, the thought of soon leaving the present age behind, and his nephew's unavoidable military duties, which prevented him from abandoning his post, suffused Don Sindulfo's mind with a relative calm. In this fashion almost a month went by and his fears were subsiding when, one afternoon, as he was returning alone from a meeting of the Scientific Congress and was coming up the left side of the Madeleine, he felt as though someone were tugging on his frockcoat from behind. He turned his head and then almost lost it when he suddenly found himself in the company of Pendencia, his nephew's orderly.

"Me da vu de la candel?" asked Pendencia, preparing to light his cigar stub from the flustered Zaragozan's own "medianito"[18] and translating his Cordoban vernacular into the language of Racine.

"The devil I will! What are you doing in Paris?"

"I'm bivvy-whacked, at th' Government's expense, with fifteen comrades on th' banks o' the Sane so that th' French can learn t' make soldiers as good as us."

And indeed, the War Minister had sent to the competition one individual from each branch of the Spanish army, in order to show off the men's uniforms and their enviable dapperness and valor.

"And is my nephew, too, among the company?" asked the sage, sensing his misfortune.

"He's th' one in command! They picked him fer his own merits."

"What?!"

"The Minister said, 'Soldier, go to th' Paris Disposition so they can see we're not all as ugly as yer uncle.'"

"Such insolence! I understand the scheme; but your wicked plans will fail. Woe unto my nephew if he dares declare war on me! You may go and tell him so from me."

And as they were just then reaching the inn, Don Sindulfo brusquely parted from Pendencia who, with an "Atcher service, Sir Pichichi," ran off looking for his master, in whom my readers will have already recognized the Captain of Hussars who had alighted from the omnibus near the top of the bridge at the beginning of this story.

Cupid and Mars

"Who has been here? Have you seen anyone from the balcony?" was the first question the distressed uncle asked as he entered his niece's rooms.

"Who do you expect us to see if you put locks on everything, down to the little glass shutters on the balcony doors?" replied Juanita with her usual brazenness.

Don Sindulfo thought it unwise to offer further explanation and headed for his room, adjacent to the prisoners'. But when he turned his back, some papers came into view that, dangling by a slender cord affixed to his frockcoat with a pin, Pendencia had hung upon him during their walk along the boulevard. Juana adroitly took possession of them while her mistress was opening the door, for both the kitchen maid and her young lady were certain that Cupid must have availed himself of the first opportunity that came along to communicate with them.

No sooner were they left alone than the letter reading began. The one from Luis contained a thousand declarations of love for his cousin, assuring her that soon she would be free of her implacable uncle's yoke.

Pendencia's letter was as terse as it was worth hearing. It read:

"My hart a waytz. Im all redy heer coma yorz til deth Rokego mez."

Juanita, accustomed to her soldier's epistolary style, understood it to mean:

"My heart awaits. I'm already here. Comma (that is, the punctuation mark). Yours until death, Roque Gómez."

By the next day, Luis had taken a room in the Concordia hotel. By a stroke of luck Don Sindulfo, who was walking at the head of the group, saw Luis as they were entering the dining room and, turning away before anyone else noticed him, he took everyone back upstairs and requested that from now on he and those with him be given their meals in a private room. Precautions were redoubled; whenever the tutor was away, Benjamín remained on guard. But all was in vain; Luis bribed whichever servant was on duty and the letters came and went, enfolded in a torrent of dinner napkins. Is it not true that they dispensed with the waiters and served themselves, in case anyone should spill the beans? Did Don Sindulfo not forbid Juanita from approaching the table to remove a dish or leaving her prison for any reason? None of that hindered the missives from coming, at times glued to the bottoms of the dressing-table ewers, at times wedged into the hollow of a pastry that, through a prearranged sign, Clara selected from among the rest on the tray, and finally from inside a nut carried by the hotel dog, which Pendencia had taught to come fetch treats for itself by slipping through Don Sindulfo's legs every time he opened the door.

In truth, that was not a pleasant way to live; Argos' one hundred eyes would not suffice to guard against so many ruses. Therefore, as

Cupid and Mars

soon as the Time Ship was ready for occupation, Don Sindulfo set up his household in it and, under the pretext of its safekeeping, acquired a permanent guard in the figure of two gendarmes who barred the approach of anyone not accompanied by the inventor. But though the guards' incorruptibility yielded neither to Luis's entreaties nor to his bribes, his orderly's mischief was increased many times over by the challenge. While the travelers were visiting Les Invalides, where he had established contacts, Pendencia might show up with a wooden leg and goat's whiskers, acting as a tour guide. Or he was just as likely to be wrapped in beggar's rags seeking handouts in the middle of the boulevards, something that—begging being against the law—would cost him a few hours at the police station. He was almost always found out, so Don Sindulfo decided that from then on they would venture out only for Mass and only by coach. Pendencia then disguised himself as a coachman; but he gave himself away when he was given directions to the Madeleine in French and he, whose forte was not languages, took them to the Père Lachaise cemetery instead. Having exhausted all other resources, one day Pendencia conspired with the Swiss honor guard at the church his compatriots attended and, taking the guardsman's place in front of the postulant who collects the offerings of the faithful during the ceremony, he prepared to deliver a letter to Clara. But burdened by halberd and baton and unaccustomed to circulating among the rows of kneelers, he became enmeshed in his rapier at such an inopportune moment that he toppled onto the sage, his wig landing on a gentleman's prayer book and his tricorne on the head of a female worshiper. The jig was up and Don Sindulfo immediately left the temple with his entourage, returning to the Time Ship, which, from then on, became for all its inhabitants a place of solitary confinement.

The days following this catastrophe were full of despair for the enamored Luis—who saw his hopes disappearing—and also for his orderly and their fifteen companions, who felt the hour of the journey to the past fast approaching and the fruits of their scheming unharvested. The captain's only consolation was to station himself with his men in the gallery of the Exposition Hall's central arch, whence they could gaze upon the Time Ship rising up one hundred meters away with the somber majesty of a massive tomb.

One afternoon when they were, as usual, occupied in this contemplative task—one fellow proposing to send a letter enclosed in an empty projectile, another suggesting the use of ballistics to launch a telephone wire—the clouds began to disgorge water, looking for all intents and purposes like the waterfalls of heaven being loosed upon the earth.

"Th' Disposition will be a mess if by chance there's a leak," the orderly said, listening to the flood as it rushed furiously down the large water spouts. "Don't worry," his master countered. "The drains may be the most remarkable piece of work in this edifice. Haven't you seen the plans on display in the Paris section? The sewers are higher than this dome."

"Wha . . . ?" cried Pendencia, his eyes starting from his head. "They got drains here?"

"No doubt about it. Look, the main one circulates almost at a tangent to the Time Ship."

"Huh! Full t' bursting with water and you stand there like th' cat got yer tongue?"

"I don't understand."

"You weren't born t' warfare like we military geniuses, Napoleon and me."

"Will you explain?"

"It's simple. If Don Sindulfo's got barrycades and counter-barrycades for his defense, we'll dig mines and counter-mines for our offense. Men . . . to th' sewers!"

An enthusiastic hurrah greeted the Cordoban's idea. No doubt, the sewer system was the ultimate stronghold of love. Studying the diagrams, they saw with pleasure that all they need do was dig a transverse tunnel a few meters long and they would find themselves beneath the mathematical center of the Time Ship. Bribing the janitor in charge of that section was the easier and more achievable task, given that the individual in question was from the Spanish border on

Cupid and Mars

the Canfranc side and moreover was fond of Charles IV's gold, which Luis did not spare in the pursuit of his goal.

Time was of the essence, but no obstacle is too big for seventeen Spaniards, half of them from Aragon and Catalonia, especially when they are soldiers always at the ready of General Daredevil.

Picks and hoes carved away, a tunnel was soon made by using struts, and finally, on the day appointed for the improbable journey, while Don Sindulfo was giving his lecture at the Trocadero accompanied by the ever-present Benjamín, the sixteen sons of Mars greeted their captain's arrival with the final blow of the pickaxe that placed them beneath the enemy fortress. When they emerged from the hole they found themselves in a rectangular room about the height of a tall man, a part of the vessel's hold designed to protect against humidity in the walls.

The invaders' plan was to take hatchets to the Time Ship's floor, but to their great surprise they found it open. The vessel had a floodgate that worked electrically by means of a horizontal guillotine device that, undoubtedly with an eye to increasing ventilation, no one had taken pains to close, oblivious to the fact that through it a subterranean attack could be made.

"Up and out!" was the unanimous cry, and by scaling ladders, crossing corridors, and storming rooms they reached the captives, who could not suppress a cry of fear when they saw so many men armed against whatever might come along.

Their show of gratitude need not be described. Feel it, those of you who know how to love.

"Darling, let's escape," was the first sentence that Luis, hounded by time and circumstances, managed to say to his cousin.

"Oh! Never," she replied. "Whatever be my fate, I'll resign myself to it before I go back on the promise I made my dying mother. I will always love you, but to run away with you . . . you mustn't expect it of me."

Pleas, exhortations, and tears were useless in the face of that dutiful and obedient daughter's steadfast resolve. All hope seemed to be lost when the crowd's applause, penetrating the compound, induced Clara to inquire about the source of such a din. When Luis explained that it reflected popular enthusiasm for her uncle's invention, the poor prisoners, who had been completely ignorant of the tutor's intentions, broke out in an indignant tirade against that monster who, through secrets and half-truths, was forcing them to go on a pilgrimage fraught with danger.

"That's impossible!" the orphan stammered.

"That devil of a scholar!" said the Maritornes. "We couldn't go backwards even if we were crabs!"

"True. Specially you, who've got so much up front."

"Let's flee!" Luis kept saying, realizing that the shouting was getting much closer. "Let's run, not to hide our love but to ask the courts for the protection the law owes you."

This judicious observation had its effect. Minutes were precious; the tyrant was approaching. A dreadful future could be the result of their hesitation.

"Very well," the pupil said decidedly.

And they all headed for the tunnel.

But when they tried to go through the opening, they found it was blocked.

A cave-in had cut off their retreat.

CHAPTER 6

The Vehicle as School of Morality

WHAT to do in such adverse circumstances? The fainthearted among them proposed staying in the hollow space between the decks and waiting until the Time Ship took off and allowed them to leave. But to be discovered, should the lady captives' absence be noted, was not as perilous as the prospect of being torn to pieces by any change in course the vehicle might experience during takeoff. The more determined opted for breaking down the door and forcing their way out. This plan was rejected on the grounds that it was violent and fruitless; therefore, the sensible idea of hiding and waiting for the best occasion to escape finally won the day.

Fortunately, the hold was well stocked with construction materials destined for future repairs and with all kinds of provisions, so hideouts aplenty could be found. A number of them holed up behind soup barrels, others squeezed in between bales of grain, some built walls with flour sacks and crates of canned food, several barricaded themselves behind piles of vegetables, and the rest turned the mummy's sarcophagus into a fort.

Clara counseled everyone to be very cautious and urged them not to move until she or Juanita returned to fetch them. Speaking for his companions, Pendencia gave his solemn promise to do just that and caused an outburst of laughter when he showed his face, which was all white from having brushed up against sacks of flour.

While this scene was taking place inside the Time Ship, outside it other events were happening which are worthy of recounting.

The lecture being over, Don Sindulfo, as we have seen, began his triumphant march from the Trocadero to the Champ de Mars, to the cheers of the frenzied crowd and between two rows of national guards that the City of Paris had provided to expedite his passage. Once inside the exhibition area, the mayor invited the sage to rest for a few minutes in an elegant tent that had been pitched *ad hoc* near the Time Ship. In the center of the tent was a table fit to satisfy the intemperance of Luculus and emulate the splendor of Cleopatra's feasts. It was the farewell lunch offered by the municipality of Paris to the illustrious inventor, since it seems to be a rule of nature, respected by custom, that in every public celebration the stomach must have the first word.

With the hosts, guests, and parasites (plants that spring up in every dining room) seated and all bodies duly rested, the jaws were free to begin their work. During the appetizers, all torsos formed a right angle with the table. As the digestive systems got loaded down with ballast, that angle became acute. The movable sides attempted to restore balance when the champagne glasses appeared, but by then perpendicularity to the tablecloth had been lost. Finally, with all shoulder blades propped against the backs of the chairs, the obtuse angle prevailed all down the line.

The Vehicle as School of Morality

Then the toasts began, some worse than others although all of them bad, since nothing hinders intelligence quite like praise. Therefore, sparing the weary reader, I will only extract from among that pile of perorations the good ones, which were precisely those that did not flatter.

Getting up from his seat and displaying an exquisite copy of the *Iliad*, recently published by the bibliophile society, the Sorbonne's librarian begged of Don Sindulfo that, as he passed through the era in which the father of the epic poem flourished, he ask Homer to sign his magnum opus, correct any typographical errors he could find, and solemnly testify as to whether it was in Chios or Smyrna where he had first seen the light of day.

"I suggest," an academic interjected, "that we substitute that last phrase with this one: 'where he was born.'" "Because," he continued, "supposing that logic in those fabled times was as demanding a science as it is now, we still risk being in the dark about the bard of Troy's hometown if, by asking him where he first saw the light of day, he takes it *pedem litterae* and answers us: 'nowhere,' being, as he was, blind since birth."

The amendment approved, it was the Agriculture Board President's turn, who, addressing Don Sindulfo beautifully, almost in verse—since the person caring for the country's agricultural interest was a poet—stressed the importance of combating the effects of the oidium and the phylloxera. He believed the safest method to deal with those diseases of the vine was to get hold of a few shoots from Noah's vineyard and grow them in France.[19]

This proposal was met with a storm of applause, since everyone knows that wine is one of the main treasures of the land beyond the Pyrenees which, despite its fabulous output, cannot meet demand in the event of a less-than-perfect harvest.

Many more ideas, all directed toward the betterment of mankind, were expounded over coffee and dessert and countless personal commissions of a ludicrous nature were asked of the doctor. A theater manager extended him unconditional credit to sign Molière up for twelve shows before the exposition closed; a typographer offered to transport himself back to Pericles' Greece, with the purpose of printing Socrates' lectures and publishing them in a political newspaper.

Don Sindulfo thanked each and every one; argued that his very first trip was dedicated exclusively to exploration; and, after offering to carry out as many of the different commissions entrusted to him as he could, he considered the ceremony over.

He had not yet reached the door when the police chief, who had just stepped out of his carriage, came into the pavilion and addressed the sage.

"May I have a brief word with you, Señor García?" he asked.

"It would be my pleasure, if it weren't already the anointed hour; I fear abusing the public's patience."

"I'm here in an official capacity. I represent the Cabinet."

One could hardly disregard such a statement. Their fellow diners withdrew discreetly to one corner of the tent while the two men maintained the following dialog in the opposite one:

"The government sends me to ask a special favor of you."

"Such trust does me honor. I'm all ears."

"Regrettably, as everyone knows, France is going through a period of moral decay that threatens to destroy its already dissipated family values, which are the very basis of society."

"Sadly, I am forced to agree with such an accurate observation."

"The government, having the most at stake in redeeming the country, has actively plumbed the depths of this frightful issue and believes the breakdown of society is caused by that scandalous sensual commerce that makes us outshine rather than emulate the infamous ancient cities of Sibaris and Capua."

"Obviously. But I don't understand what role I could play in said redemptive mission."

"That's what I'm here to explain. Rehabilitating women means creating the good mothers we lack."

"Not completely; you surely don't."

"You are very kind. I thank you on behalf of my own. Having mothers means assuring our children's proper upbringing. Well-brought up children result in model spouses and honest citizens. Therefore, one must sanitize the family in order to save our homeland."

"We agree."

"Well, now; out of all those poor women who drag their vices through our populous cities stridently hawking their merchandise, to everyone's shame, very few manage to make a profit that sustains them in old age. Their last recourse is usually to hospitals, theaters, and almshouses. And many of them, after losing their youth's first bloom, would ruefully retread the path of virtue were it not for the state in which excess and depravity have plunged them, making them unfit for the pure joys of family life. The Cabinet, then, after a special hearing, charged me to communicate their sentiments to you and commissioned me to make you a proposal."

The police chief brought his chair even closer to Don Sindulfo's and proceeded in this manner:

"Is it really true that with the wonderful vehicle you have invented one may regain youth as one goes back in time?"

"That's correct, provided one hasn't previously been subjected to the immutability current named after me, in which case one would see the centuries pass by without experiencing any change whatsoever."

"How quickly can you cover a space of twenty years?"

"In one hour."

"And, having reached that point, are you able to fix the age of the person at the point in time they are passing through?"

"With no problem at all."

"Well then. The government's strategy is to beg you to take along on your journey a dozen ladies bordering on forty—young enough that old age hasn't yet forced them to abandon their dreams, but advanced enough for women of their sort to harbor hopes of success—and offer them a return to their twenties in sixty minutes. It will follow that, enlightened by experience and having learned their lesson, when finding themselves again in possession of their charms they will take the path of moderation and abandon that of vice."

"That's a laudable plan. But, your honor, don't you fear—since every baby's bonnet eventually becomes a shroud—that when the good ladies see their faculties fully restored they'll want to tempt fortune once more?"

"I hope not. Anyway, this is only an experiment that we'll give up if we don't succeed and repeat on a large scale if we do. How will you answer the minister?"

"The mission honors me too much to refuse it, but I must warn you that I'm traveling with my niece and . . ."

"You needn't fear any scandal. The women will behave with dignity. We have already cautioned them, and fear of punishment will keep them in line."

"I would be glad of that, though I doubt it."

"I assure you; it's a fearsome threat."

"What is it, exactly?"

"Not lifting even one year from them should they overstep their bounds."

"You're right. I'm satisfied."

"Do we have a deal, then?"

"Absolutely."

"The government will know how to reward you for such a great favor."

"My prize will simply be for France to become supreme in moral dignity, just as it has conquered the world's respect in so many other matters."

The interview over, Don Sindulfo and his followers left the pavilion and met the happy lady explorers who were waiting in their carriages just outside the door. They got out, joined the official retinue and all headed toward the Time Ship.

Arriving at the foot of the colossus, they all said a last goodbye. The sage, Benjamín and the lady travelers went inside the vehicle which, hermetically sealed, held everyone's attention from that moment on.

After less than a quarter of an hour the murmurs of two million souls wavered in the air. The Time Ship was rising with the majesty of a Montgolfier balloon. No one applauded because no hand was free

The Vehicle as School of Morality

of an optical instrument of some kind or other, but enthusiasm was expressed in a silence more piercing than any sound.

Having reached the area where the journey was to start, the monster, now reduced to the size of a star, stopped as if to get its bearings. Suddenly, a shout erupted from the crowd. That spot, bathed in the glow of a midsummer sun, had disappeared out of the sky with the same abrupt haste as a shooting star changing from light to darkness right before our eyes.

CHAPTER 7

Away!

The Time Ship, as we have said, had a type of basement above which rested the floor of the hold and in whose thick wall were embedded steps that led to a large door, the vehicle's only entrance. This was rectangular in shape. In its corners stood four imposing tubes, the exhaust pipes that, with their openings twisted toward the four cardinal points, looked just like enormous blunderbusses bent to resemble the number seven. Running along the four sides of the main floor was an elegant gallery whose door, like all the other openings in the conveyance, remained hermetically sealed while in transit. Immense crystal disks, grazed by each puff of wind, enabled the travelers to contemplate the scenery from inside with the aid of powerful optical instruments and to correct the ship's heading while en route. Two pediments crowned each facade displaying the name of the colossus in their tympana and supporting with their gantries the deck that was sloped in preparation for stopovers. In this manner, while underway, navigating the void, one need not trouble oneself with the drains or take precautions against atmospheric diseases.

So then, from the outside, the Time Ship was a kind of keelless

Away!

Noah's Ark, all the more so because its operations had nothing to do with the liquid element and because, should it ever need to float, its big belly would suffice. As with ships of old, the hull swelled out from the floor of the hold and came together underneath the balcony, which it supported.

Now let us examine it from within. The ground floor was entirely taken up by the hold except for the small space—occupied by the vestibule and spiral staircase—that formed the entrance of honor to the upper chambers, whence one descended to the lower deck via another spiral staircase in one of the corners. In the opposite corner was the "García fluid" device, whose currents made bodies immutable (a precaution taken in advance with as much of the construction materials and food supplies as were on board). In front of this, the Reiset and Regnaut mechanism worked to produce breathable oxygen. Both this and the immutability device were prudently replicated in various places within the Time Ship, though their effects could be felt anywhere with the help of conductors. The effects of the electric batteries were also distributed throughout the vehicle in order to carry the currents to wherever movement was needed, because on that ship all activity was mechanical. To give an example: the hatch resembling a horizontal guillotine that, as we saw, provided access to the sons of Mars, was paired with another one of identical structure cut into the floor of the upper deck. Did one wish to load the Time Ship? All one need do was conveniently elevate it, place the materials underneath, apply a conductor to them and they would, on their own, rise up through the openings until reaching the isolators that paralyzed their ascent at the desired point. Cleaning was accomplished by the same process. Mechanized brooms swept the open spaces and positioned the debris over the main trap door. When this opened, the sweepings fell onto the lower deck and, after repeating the action, the guillotine's yawn swept them outside. In this way, one could begin sweeping on Monday and, a second later, find it finished on Saturday.

The upper story housed the powerful locomotive agent: electricity. Nothing would be more interesting than to describe its workings; but because this would lead us far afield and the reader, having accepted the principle, must absolve me from technical explanations, I will limit myself to saying that from the center of that zone the batteries launched their streams of current out to all the articulations charged with producing movement and to the pneumatic atmosphere-repulsing tubes. An elegant dial registered velocity and a simple needle regulated it. Located in the same room were the observatory and the laboratory with their lenses, containers, maps, compasses, libraries, aerometers, and chronographic tools. In the lateral gangways of the right wing and alternating with the system of berths were the ladies' cabin, the pantry, and the kitchen, where a live chicken sat on a plank being plucked by an electric discharge while a spark turned it into food 7,200 times faster than any ordinary grill.

The washing machine, located at the far end of the axis, was a marvel. The dirty clothes entered at one end and exited at the other washed, dried, ironed, and mended.

The left wing had been reserved in its entirety for the stronger sex and had nothing noteworthy about it except the clock room, where one clock marked the real time of actual existence and another, the time relative to the historical moment of the journey, expressed in century, year, month, and day according to Gregorian calculations.

After the association members had said their final enthusiastic goodbyes, the sages entered their fortress and the first precaution Don Sindulfo took was to put the dumbfounded new additions under lock and key in the collections room, warning them not to move from there until he came to get them because, no matter how earnest their pledges, he believed, and rightly so, that iron bars could only help enforce vows. Promptly and by means of one single electrical pulse he left the Time Ship hermetically sealed; this done, he administered to Benjamín a few discharges of immutability fluid and accepted the same from his friend in return.

"Time can no longer exert its influence over us," he exclaimed with an air of triumph once the operation was finished.

"Nonetheless, don't you think," objected his inseparable companion, "that we'd have lost nothing by waiting to inoculate ourselves until after the Time Ship had been under way for a few minutes?"

Away!

"I take your meaning, and no one would be more interested than I in losing a few years to see if, by making myself younger, my niece's standards would relax; but if any kind of accident happened to you or me—the only ones who know this machinery—what would be our fate, shot off into space with no set course? And what manner of responsibility would weigh upon us for leaving the most gigantic of scientific problems unresolved?"

The observation was so sensible that the polyglot had nothing to object to. And in truth, all would have been lost because, once they had been dosed, only the regular action of time would have had the power to destroy the action produced by the fluid.

Therefore, they went to the ladies' cabin, where Clara and Juanita had taken refuge just like little children who hide themselves when they think they have done something wrong; and after deviously leading the girls to the laboratory, while Benjamín cunningly managed to have them touch the conductors, Don Sindulfo rendered them immutable through a couple of discharges that made them writhe like snakes.

"Hey, you," said the lass from Pinto, facing her employer as soon as she could stand up and utter words, "unless you want to eat nothing but semolina soup from now on, do that one more time and you'll see teeth flying out of your mouth. Why'd you crank that handle and turn us into a pair of epileptics?"

"Quit shouting," ordered her master. "Here you are under my rule. My dominion has begun and there is no reason to question my conduct. Your duty is to be silent and obey."

"As for that, we'll just see," interjected Clara.

"What? You dare be insubordinate?"

"No, sir; but I protest your abusing our ignorance in order to trick us into taking a voyage that is without precedent in this world."

"And who told you . . . ?"

"For heaven's sake," said Juana, "who else could it be besides the same Spanish troops who have been making a fool out of you, though you know more mathematics than Montezuma?"

"What's this I hear? Has Luis found a way to deliver a love card to you?" asked the confused scientist without suspecting that, despite his tyranny, the captain had been able to serve as a living missive.

"A card . . . a card! . . . why, a whole deck of them, with you as the joker!"

"Try not to be insolent, else once we arrive in the Rome of the Caesars I will sell you as a slave to the first patrician I meet in the streets."

"And what will the patricians do to me? What? Don't I come from liberal stock? My father was stable manager for the volunteers."

"Hear our pleas."

"Never."

"I'm telling you, this Don Pichichi is the Calomarde of uncles."[20]

"These intrigues are over," shouted Don Sindulfo, livid. "These schoolgirl crushes are over and done with. And since you chose not to accept my hand of your own free will, I shall take you to countries and ages where the tutor's will is his pupil's law and, no matter how it may pain you, you will have to call yourself my wife."

"Never. First death, first torture. And if, having failed at persuasion, you take recourse in violence, I'll show you that I have the courage to face anything."

And directing a look of complicity at Juanita, she added, "We leave whenever you wish."

"Yes, sir. Giddyap, and the first time we stop to change the horses we'll get off to complain to the authorities."

The sage did not wait for the order to be repeated; he brought the contacts together and the Time Ship began its ascent, not without some emotion on the part of the captives, who saw the contours of the city disappear in seconds beneath their feet.

In the newcomers' room, the impression was stronger for their having been awaiting more impatiently the results of the journey. The silence in the lower deck was absolute. Only Pendencia, sensing the rocking motion, allowed himself to say quietly to his boss, "Cap'n, th' wine flask."

Suddenly the colossus set its course and began to displace atmosphere without anyone noticing that they were traveling at a speed of

Away!

twice round the globe per second, for since the propulsion was occurring in a void, the absence of layers against which to rub produced no discernible movement.

"We're under way!" Don Sindulfo cried, with the paternal pride his invention inspired.

"Full steam ahead," his niece resolutely proclaimed.

"All praise to the genius!" babbled Benjamín, embracing his patron.

"Jesus!" said Juana. "This is as bland as unsalted chick pea stew. There's not a bell tower to be seen, not a single head of lettuce, nothing that might cheer one's heart. I prefer the dullness of my hometown. Come on, Don Sindulfo . . . once we get to the Invalids, stop."

The poor thing did not realize that she had begun her sentence in Paris on the tenth of June, 1878 and was finishing it on the thirty-first of December of the previous year, high above the Andes mountains.

CHAPTER 8

Retroactive Effects

THE die was cast and it was impossible to go back or, I should say, forward, if we are to follow the logic of the situation. Clara and Juanita retreated to their room, secure in the knowledge that their defenders were near and ready to have them emerge at the very first stop. Having them come out of their hideouts while underway seemed risky to the ladies, as they were afraid that a vengeful Don Sindulfo would sentence them all to perpetual motion.

The sage, in turn, could not stop celebrating his triumph with Benjamín, and he truly had a right to do so, for never before had an experiment been so successful.

Retroactive Effects

"Eureka!" exclaimed in a sudden burst of passion that new Archimedes, who was moving heaven and earth without the aid of a screw.

"How high are we?" asked the polyglot.

"We left Paris twenty-one minutes ago," his friend answered, consulting the chronometer. "Therefore, we have un-done seven years and today's date is July the tenth, 1871."

"Shall we study the situation?"

"Let's."

"Course heading: east," said Benjamín his eyes fixed on his compass.

"Steady."

"Latitude 50° N."

"Correct."

"All we need do is tilt our telescopes one degree south and direct our gaze at our point of departure."

And aiming the lenses towards the southernmost disk, whose shutters opened automatically, both professors began to explore space. Naturally, they first turned off the electric lights that provided constant illumination to that hermetically sealed cloister, where it was always night. Since the vacuum effect was created only around the Time Ship itself, the atmospheric layers next to it conducted sunlight. As a result, if the vehicle had not been shuttered it would have been impossible to bear the dizzying alternation of light and shadow caused by the violent transition from day to night at a speed of forty-eight hours per second.

The time trekkers had spent few of those seconds in observation, seeing nothing but the gleaming vapor the cities breathed at night to announce their presence or their profiles bathed in sunlight and etched over the dark landscape by day. Then, unexpectedly, the two observers gave a cry that was as sudden as their feelings had been fleeting. Amid the shadows and above the Paris meridian, the reflection of a huge bonfire had just wounded their eyes.

"The commune!" they both shouted.

Indeed, what glittered below was oil from North American wells, pitting in vain its devastating New World influence against the civilizing sentiment of old, yet noble Europe.[21]

The sages did not leave their observation post until they found another clear fact to confirm their chronological deductions. In a few brief seconds they passed through spring and left behind that harsh winter, theater of one of the most horrifying international wars and fitting terrain for human madness. The land was a vast sheet of snow, as if the chill of terror sown in those fields had grown into a crop of ice. The king of all stars had nothing to shine on but deadly surfaces of steel and bronze, and the bullets' paths resembled arches of fire

Retroactive Effects

that had been raised in the night to keep the vault of heaven from crashing down. Hot air balloons entrusting the homeland's salvation to a current of air; carrier pigeons returning to the ark without the olive branch; Paris surrendering, Metz falling, Sedan leaving a crown orphaned . . . ![22] Why recall any more anniversaries? The calculations were correct. They were in the year of punishments.

Once the shutters were closed and the room was lit:

"Master, I have a question," exclaimed Benjamín.

"What is it?"

"Since we are bound for yesterday and will arrive in the past bearing the experiences of History, wouldn't we be able to change the human condition by avoiding the catastrophes that have caused so much turmoil in society?"

"Please state your thoughts more clearly."

"Suppose we were to drop by Guadalete at the end of the Gothic empire."[23]

"Well?"

"Don't you think that if we gave a course in morality to Cava and Don Rodrigo,[24] or if we showed Count Don Julián—by reading him Cantù,[25] Mariana, and Lafuente—the consequences of his treason, we would manage to change the course of events and avoid the Arab domination of Spain?"

"Not in the slightest. We may be present to witness facts consummated in preceding centuries, but we may never undo their existence. To put it more clearly: we may unwrap time, but we don't know how to nullify it. If today is a consequence of yesterday and we are living examples of the present, we cannot, unless we destroy ourselves, wipe out a cause of which we are its actual effects. Let's use a metaphor to illustrate my premise. Imagine that you and I are an omelet made with eggs that were laid in the eighth century. If the Arabs, who are the hens, didn't exist, would we?"

Benjamín considered this for a moment, and then replied:

"And why not? Even admitting the idea that we're all descendants of Muza the Moor,[26] stopping him and his men from coming to Spain doesn't preclude our existence. I don't destroy the hens; what I do is force them to keep on laying their eggs in Africa. Therefore, the omelet may survive, being different only in having the Atlas region, and not the Guadalete, for a stove."

Don Sindulfo bit his lip, not finding any way to refute his friend's argument, which he considered to be paradoxical. He cut the conversation short by opening his writing desk and jotting down notes about the defeat in his diary. Benjamín, in turn, went to the cabinet that held the most precious samples from his archeological museum and busied himself by going over the classification system.

Let us leave them devoted to such sensible tasks and see what was happening in the collections room, where the twelve daughters of Eve, in whom the French government was placing the nation's moral restoration, waited impatiently for their transformation.

Those of my readers who have visited France, and all of them probably have, will not need a description of the lady travelers' clothes. Having luxury as bait and the art of pleasing as their profession, one may easily gather that, in order to adorn themselves, such ladies had drawn upon the ingenuity of the entire silk industry of Lyon, exhausted the magnificent resources of the embroiderers of Cluny and Valenciennes, and had diamonds from Brazil, emeralds from Colombia, and pearls from the Gulf of Bengali all set in gold from California. A lady who looked like she had been an attractive brunette in her youth and who answered to the name of Naná—they all had stage names—asked a tall, slender blonde: "Hey, Niní! What's up?"

"Not much for now; but if the prefect's office makes me fifteen again, I swear I'll only marry a man who'll always vote government. A girl's got to be grateful."

"One of these days I'll get hitched," declared a fidgety one from her corner, where she was entertaining herself making paper birds.

"What do you intend to do, then, Emma?"

"Make them land in the court of Louis XV and ask them to introduce me to the King."

"As for me," said another named Sabina, "I'd sooner let myself get robbed by Romans than go back to Paris to dress in percale and sleep on a mattress."

Retroactive Effects

"But we've given our word," Niní insisted. "Remember, France's redemption is in our hands."

"In the hands of whoever trusts official promises," Emma argued. "As soon as they see us young and pretty, those same ones who now consider us instruments of salvation will be the first to want to disturb our domestic peace. Ah! Men! Men! . . ."

And as she kept playing with the paper bird, she noticed it had started to crumble without her fingers doing any crushing.

"Here's the proof," she added, explaining the phenomenon in her own way and putting the crowning touch on her thoughts. "They write their declarations of love on rotten paper so that they don't last."

"That's the fire of passion burning the paper," argued the optimist, Niní.

"Or the humidity of this place dissolving it," pointed out a new speaker. "The Time Ship isn't a shining example of cleanliness. Ever since we got here, I've done nothing but pick little tufts of wool and other fuzzy things off me that I'm sure are falling from the ceiling."

"That's true. I've noticed the same thing," said Sabina. "Don't move. Wait."

"What is it?"

"A butterfly's on your hat bow. It's a moth!"

"Ay! And there's a worm on mine!" cried another, running in search of a charitable hand to free her from it.

Emma meant to fly to her rescue, but stopped when she saw her fingers covered in a viscous substance that had taken the paper bird's place. Instinctively, she gave her arm a nervous shake, but when she looked at her hand again, the paste had disappeared and bits of rag and filaments of every size and hue dangled from her fingers instead.

A cry of amazement echoed in the room and the din became general when Sabina, who was looking at Niní for answers, saw a false tooth shoot out from her wide-open mouth as a brand new one took its place. At the same time, Naná's bleached blond hair, faded and missing the ribbon that kept it in place, fell to the ground as her head was covered over in silky tresses capable of making Faust's Margarita green with envy.

"Look at Emma," someone yelled. "Her crow's feet are gone!"
"And Coralia has lost her wart," blurted another.
"My complexion is so clear!"
"And my shoulders are so soft!"
"No more grey hair!"
"We're young already!"
"Hurray!"

And they checked their hand mirrors or looked at themselves in some other polished surface, all the while giddily hugging and kissing each other.

The cause of such wondrous effects is easily explained. Pushed backwards, time was achieving its deed of destruction. The ladies had not been subjected to the immutability current; nor had their wardrobes. As a result, with every passing minute retrogression was leaving its mark on their persons and on their apparel, since everything about them journeyed back towards its source. In this fashion, paper traveled from banknote to pulp to the original rag; satin metamorphosed into butterflies that reverted to larvae that shrank into seeds. Nothing charmed the senses more than those well-rounded forms half-covered by clusters of silkworms mixed in with fleece of extra fine wool, their delicate golden strands set against the mother of pearl of the half-open oysters where embryonic pearls lay. What an artistic grouping those minerals made surrounded by raw cotton, edged in green hemp and crossed by fragments of ribbons which, having been made before that historical moment, held on to their integrity as a fashion anachronism within nature's harmony of decay!

Bewilderment reigned; the enthusiasm was indescribable. But time was not stopping its course and the phenomenon was starting to take on alarming proportions. The products transformed into raw materials soon stopped adorning the shapes of those human sculptures. After each portion of matter had been torn from its place, the fractions began to depart in search of their roots. Fleeces vanished into sheep; oysters, called by their beds, ran to rest under the coasts of Malabar; cotton fled to bury its roots in the North American plains and the kidskin of lace boots, freed from its tanning, flew to cover the

Retroactive Effects

bones of the innocent Alpen goat once more. Meanwhile, the empty spaces such desertions were leaving behind revealed features that could coax nudes from the classical chisels of Michelangelo, Praxiteles, and Phidias.

When the ladies saw their nakedness they covered their faces with their hands, since modesty is an inborn quality in humankind's more beauteous half, and then burst out in such ear-splitting screams that Don Sindulfo abandoned his notes and Benjamín his classifications as they ran to find out what the commotion was.

"You can't come in," some of the women said when they realized the sages were trying to open the door.

"We've had enough," others cried.

"Ay! My corset . . . !" bawled another.

The sages briefed Clara and Juanita on the situation the moment they arrived. They entered the room in distress and, frightened by the unwonted sight, came out again begging science to help them.

"For pity's sake, man! Those ladies are going to catch cold!" bellowed the Maritornes.

At this point, Benjamín, having grasped the meaning of the situation, arrived with a few immutability fluid transmitters and, passing them through the half-open door, instructed the excursionists to grab on to them tightly. The women did just that and, with a couple of turns of the contraption and a few dozen moans from the victims, the latter were firmly stabilized and the damage redressed.

"Lend them some of your clothes," Don Sindulfo said to his ward and to Juana. Then he and Benjamín returned to their work in the laboratory, chatting about the incident and laughing their heads off. The polyglot had just sunk into his seat when, his hair on end and with a heartrending scream, he jumped back up as if a galvanic jolt had yanked him out of his chair.

"What happened?" asked the sage, coming to his aid.

"Look . . . Just . . . Look!" stammered poor Benjamín, pointing to the famed commemorative medallion they had bought at auction from the Madrid archeologist and that the catalog said was attributed to Gaius Servilius, prefect of Pompeii, in honor of Jupiter.

The Time Ship

Don Sindulfo picked up the gleaming metallic disc from the table. The article in question had not yet been fixed in time, since they had been waiting for the chronological instant that might confirm its authenticity. But that moment had arrived, time's effects had been erased, and the lettering stood out against its polished background with a terrifying eloquence.

SERV C   POMP   PR
JO . . . HONOR

Etched in brass was an advertisement for a funeral parlor that had been founded in Paris around the time they were passing through. Its integrity restored, the medallion now read:

SERVICE DE POMPES FUNÈBRES
RUE D'ANJOU SAINT HONORÉ.

CHAPTER 9

The Gradual Reduction and Ultimate Elimination of the Army

Having repaired the damage that retrogression had done to their clothing, the lady travelers hurried to the laboratory in search of Don Sindulfo and began giving him ample proof of their gratitude.

The two sages had not yet recovered from the astonishment caused by the medallion's metamorphosis. In truth, they had abundant cause for renouncing their faith in science, which on that occasion had treated them so shabbily. Nevertheless, they plucked up their courage, concealed their anger and, shutting the cabinet doors, chose to devote their energies to contemplating that assortment of mankind's more beauteous half. The collection was complete: one would think one had been transported to Mohammed's paradise or the Paris Grand Opera's *foyer de la danse*.

Although the lady passengers' conduct was beyond reproach, Don Sindulfo, fearful of any imprudence, wished them not to come into contact with Clara, whom he begged to retire to her cabin with Juanita.

"There's no way we're going to stay locked up in there," said the lass from Pinto, "now that we've found out the house is full of *captive*-ating ladies."

"It doesn't matter," replied the tutor, swallowing his anger. "You don't know each other; you don't speak the same language."

"The missy speaks French, and these ladies know every tongue. They've already told us they travel for pleasure, even though they're going the wrong way."

And so it was. In the few minutes they had had to confer, not only had Juanita apprised the women of the situation, she had also won the troops over to her side. They would employ their wiles to force Don Sindulfo into making a stop that would allow them to extract the soldiers from their hiding place and flee together; for it must be said that, once the twelve daughters of Eve had seen their youth restored, they had only one goal: freedom.

Realizing that the fight was unequal and reassured by the flawed notion that, once returned to the age of relative candor, the Parisians would harbor only pure and innocent feelings, the tutor forgot that "every baby's bonnet eventually becomes a shroud" and let all the women remain together, though under the watch of his inquisitorial eye.

"At this moment we are entering the year 1860," exclaimed Benjamín, consulting the navigation display.

"*Ay!* The very day I lost my fiancé in Constantinople," Niní cried, putting emotions into play to sway Don Sindulfo's heart and aid Clara's plans.

"And that's when I left my mother's home in Bona because of my stepfather's extreme harshness," offered Sabina, moistening her eyes with saliva to feign tears.

The sage reclaimed the floor just in time, for a few seconds more and all those young ladies would have turned out to be natives of Algeria.

"Slow down," Don Sindulfo protested. "Your tender feelings are as yet premature. I beg you to recall that we are traveling backwards and that for us the year begins on the thirty-first of December; or, to put it another way, we are entering the year when the real world is exiting it. So you still have three minutes left before you must give yourselves over to your painful anniversary."

"All the better," Niní cried joyfully. "That way I'll be able to see him alive. Ask me whatever you want, but put me back in his arms again and an age of happiness will begin for me, who's known only disgrace."

"Have mercy," Sabina said. "Since you've made it your job to rehabilitate us, let us owe you for the complete cure."

"What you ask is impossible. When we come back from our journey I shall return you to France, but time is money and I cannot allow myself a stop. If I were to make one in Africa, it would be over Tetouan, so I could be present for the memorable campaign that brought such honor to the Spanish army."[27]

"What!" reproached Juanita, playing her part in the scheme, "We're going to pass by the Riff, where my uncle, bugler for the mountain brigade, died of a gunshot wound before I was born, and you'd be so cruel as to not let him hug his favorite niece?"

"Didn't you just say you'd never met him?"

"That doesn't matter. At home we have his portrait done in *guerreotype*."

"I think," stammered Clara, using all her powers of seduction, "that my uncle holds the Castilian name in too high a regard not to render this just tribute in honor of our compatriots' heroism. And he's too kind not to give in to his ward's pleas."

"So be it, since that's what you want," the vanquished tutor replied. "We will be present for that epic event; but without disembarking."

The Time Ship

"A bird's-eye view?" asked Juanita, trying to push the issue, but at a gesture from her mistress she understood that, once Don Sindulfo had started down the road of concessions, he would not be long in surrendering.

The sage changed the heading to 35° N and, after the chronometer marked the twilit evening of the fourth of February, 1860, he reduced the speed to a cart's pace and allowed the Time Ship to glide over Tetouan, out of projectile range but close enough to the theater of war to be able to appreciate the smallest details of that memorable battle.

All hearts born betwixt the southern slope of the Pyrenees and the tip of Tarifa beat violently. With the disk open, everyone trained his or her optical aid on the field of operations, and a shout of enthusiasm resounded throughout the room.

"You can make out the combatants over there," exclaimed Naná, fussing with her hair in case some staff officer should happen to glance up, while Juanita spluttered in astonishment, "Good Heavens! It looks like a puppet show."

"But it's strange...!" adduced Clara, focusing on the scenario that was playing out before her eyes. "I can't understand their movements."

"Yes, that's true," they all broke out, consumed by the odd goings-on.

"What is?" asked the sage.

"Look for yourself. They're doing everything backwards."

"Ah! Yes, of course," replied the learned man, acknowledging what for him was of little importance, given that he had foreseen it. "What's happening is that, since we are traveling backwards in time, we begin to see the battle at its end."

"It figures!" broke in Juanita, "Just your style, starting everything at the tail end...!"

And in effect, the travelers watched the battle of Tetouan in reverse chronological order, just as the hero of Flammarion's *Lumen* watched the battle of Waterloo while ascending in spirit to the star Capella, having first to pass through the luminous rays of Earth, which in space illuminated past events.

Gradual Reduction of the Army

"Observe," continued Don Sindulfo, "how the first thing one notes is that the dead bodies arise."

"True," agreed Benjamin. "And then they fire their muskets."

"And then they load."

"*Load*, as in *burden*? Well then, they must be sages," retorted the Maritornes, not wasting any opportunity to bring her victim down a notch.

"What's this? Are they fleeing?"

"No, they're going backwards, because we're traveling toward the moment when they occupy the positions they hold before they advance. That is, we're just now reaching the start of the battle proper. So, if we stopped we'd be able to witness it in order."

"Well then, w*hooa!*," said the country lass, generating a feeling of mirth in those present, whose repeated pleas the sage had not the strength to resist, pricked as he was by his own patriotic pride. The Time Ship was then made to float in the atmosphere, thanks to a slight movement of the graduator.

These lines, written as they were twenty-one years after that memorable event and with pen flying across the page, strike me nonetheless as not lacking appeal for the generation now replacing us. I therefore copy here the narrative from Don Sindulfo's diary, which must have inspired the painter Castellani to capture that day with his brush[28] and must also have been of service to the Royal Press in describing the panorama on display in front of the Mint in Madrid. It reads:

> We are in the center of the Moroccan camp of Muley-Ahmed. The Spanish troops are approaching in close pursuit of the enemy, all the while holding them to their position. In front of us is the sea, behind us, Tetouan, to the right the Martil river and to the left, Geleli Tower and Casablanca.[29]
>
> General O'Donnell sends his troops to surround the Muley-Ahmed camp, with the objective of attacking it from two different points with Generals Prim and Ros de Olano's troops. The artillery is stationed between them, protected by the engineers.

Cannon fire explodes from forty guns that slowly advance, until setting up position some forty meters from the Moroccan trenches.

In the foreground, the Commander-in-Chief can be seen on horseback with his staff officer; he is giving orders to Commander Ruiz Dana, with Colonel Jovellar and the Chief of Staff, General García, at his side. To the rear, the Spanish artillery fires its cannons upon the strongholds. In the distant background, the sea and the fleet.

To the right, General Ros de Olano is giving instructions to his son and directing the movements of the Third Battalion, First Division, commanded by General Turón. He gets his soldiers to breach different points in the trenches. The Albuera regiment with its Colonel Alaminos; Rodrigo City with Lieutenant Colonel Cos-Gayón; Brigadier Cervino heading up the Zamora and Asturias battalions. All invade the camp at the same time, in spite of the fierce resistance of the enemy, one of whom, in the throes of death, finds enough strength in his fanaticism to drag himself to an abandoned cannon and fire it, wreaking dreadful havoc upon the first ranks of our troops.

To the left, General Prim attacks the trenches, followed by Colonel Gaminde; he gets in through a narrow embrasure, surrounded by Catalonians, soldiers from Alba de Tormes, Princesa, Córdoba, and León. He closes ranks, forming a confusing throng with the enemy and enduring bitter, man-to-man combat. At his side I see Commander Sugrañes and Lieutenant Moxó fall mortally wounded, the former waving the flag of the intrepid Catalonian Thirds. Don Enrique O'Donnell vigorously reinforces the attack by his superior, General Prim, and then heads toward Muley-Abbas's camp in the Tower of Geleli, which the Moors hastily abandon.

Muley-Ahmed tries with vain but stalwart courage to stop the flight of his soldiers, who abandon Casablanca and flee in terror before Prim's bellicose host. Terrified, they are deaf to their leader's command; they drag him along in their flight and

Gradual Reduction of the Army

leave to our troops' control, as a trophy for so decisive a victory, the camp, with its eight hundred tents, eight cannon, weapons, ammunition, camels, horses, and equipment.

In the background, near Tetouan, the sultan of Morocco watches in dismay the defeat of his large army.

While our soldiers march, the enemy threatens to attack the rearguard. But General O'Donnell unhesitatingly dispatches to Tetouan two Third Company battalions under the command of General Mackenna. Mackenna, rapidly moving up the Martil river under cover of General Alcalá Galiano's cuirassiers, repels the enemy in their own stronghold after a brief skirmish and cripples their plan.

The fearsome enemy forces, coming down *en masse* from the Tower of Geleli, make as if to attack our right flank with their infantry and three thousand cavalry; but the General-in-Chief, alert to all the vicissitudes of combat, orders Count Balmaseda's lancers to advance. The troops, their movements protected by General Río's reserve corps, which is based at the Estrella redoubt, lustily charge the enemy and send them headlong into flight.

The day's work is over. It will not be long before Tetouan opens its doors to the victor, and the emperor of Morocco must already regret having stirred up the just wrath of the Spanish nation.

The enthusiasm on board knew no bounds. Everyone pleaded with Don Sindulfo to let them disembark and embrace the heroes; even Juanita did, for she claimed to have recognized her family's lungs in the call to arms her uncle blew upon the trumpet. The sage, although possessed by that general feeling of admiration, had a vengeful nature inconsistent with his intellectual lights. He saw in this a chance to unburden himself of his grindstone of a kitchen maid and agreed to the demand, resolving to resume the journey as soon as Juanita crossed the Time Ship's threshold in search of her alleged relative. He therefore chose for the descent a small grove of trees that would protect them from stray bullets and, to everyone's great contentment and with the simplest of maneuvers, the vehicle touched down.

But, alas! No man commits a bad act without sooner or later getting his just punishment. Each one was savoring the success of his or her scheme when Benjamín, up at the disks studying the horizon, gave a cry and took an involuntary step backward.

"What is it?" asked his other half, running to his side.

"Great Scott!" replied the polyglot, turning pale. "We have undoubtedly fallen into an ambush the Moroccans set for our troops."

A cold sweat crossed every traveler's brow.

"Let's get out of here!" was the general opinion.

"Look at the Kabyles[30] heading this way."

"There's nothing for it but to take recourse in flight," judged the sage, rushing over to the regulator and putting the machine in motion, while Benjamin closed the disks and reconnected the electric lighting, crying, "Hurry, they're catching up to us."

He had not even finished saying this when:

"A Moor!" cried one of the lady travelers in a strangled voice.

"Two!" squealed Juanita, shielding herself behind her master.

"Twenty!" shouted the others, overcome by terror and sheltering in a tight group in the corner of the laboratory.

They were, in fact, two dozen fugitives from Muley-Ahmed's camp who, seeking salvation in the forest, witnessed the vehicle's descent; and believing it to be a weapon of war, they had determined to attack it. But finding no obvious entrance, they availed themselves of its protuberances, scaling them with the strength that comes of fanaticism and managing to breach the exhaust tubes before the colossus could get under way.

After the first moment of shock, when no one dared raise eyes to those strapping six-foot-tall super-Muslims armed with Moorish daggers and muskets and with faces etched with the vengeful scowl of the defeated enemy, Naná resolved to ask Don Sindulfo:

"Tell us, sir—will they do anything to us?"

"*Our* throats they will slit. But you ladies will be carried off to their harem as concubines."

Gradual Reduction of the Army

"With the eunuchs? Horrors!" whispered the ladies in question.

"Well, as far as the harem goes," Juana interjected, facing her master, "I think you could come along, too."

"Such insolence!"

"To keep us company and teach us science in our leisure time."

According to Benjamín's translation of the invading chief's orders, the tutor was not mistaken about their intentions. The voyagers were surely lost. Nevertheless, a bright idea blossomed in the tormented Don Sindulfo's brain.

"If we can buy some time," he said to the polyglot, "we're saved."

"How so?"

"By running the vehicle at maximum speed and making those Kabyles, who have not been rendered immutable by the current, shrink until they wind up disappearing once they've crossed beyond the instant of their birth."

"A brilliant idea!"

The Time Ship

And by forcing the regulator, the machine was made to run at a vertiginous speed.

"Get them!" shouted the Muslim chief.

The Moors rushed to execute the order. But the *ayes* and lamentations of the weaker sex were so frequent and piercing that, unable to restore silence, the invaders gagged everyone's mouths with linen cloth and, pinning their arms down with strong bindings, dragged them behind so they could take the slaves to the refuge of the scattered camp.

The Rifeños spent a quarter of an hour searching in vain for the exit, to the great satisfaction of the captives who, though unable to call for help or flee, bound as they were, could nonetheless see the change in their oppressors as they rapidly became younger, and they nursed the hope of finding themselves free of the yoke before long.

But the Mediterranean character is impulsive and does not consider patience a virtue. Suspecting they were the prisoners of their captives, the little patience the sons of the desert did possess ran out, and they settled for leaving the ship by the way they came in. Convinced, however, of the impossibility of doing so with their booty, they adopted the extreme measure of deciding to exterminate the travelers.

By then they were in the ship's hold, and the women despaired to think that, where one voice alone would have been enough to call out to their saviors for help, they found themselves reduced to speechlessness. With their prisoners placed in a corner of the storeroom, the Moors occupied the center and prepared their muskets. By now those unfortunates had no doubt about the sad fate destiny had in store for them. Pressed together and confused, the wretches wallowed in the despair born of impotence. The gun barrels were already pointing at their chests when time, exercising its powerful influence, suddenly changed the cord binding the tutor into slender hemp filaments that left him free to move his muscles. Perceiving such a providential advantage and employing it to unite the conductors that hung down from the wall nearest him was but the act of a moment. Instantly, the

Gradual Reduction of the Army

hatch doors flew open and the sons of Agar vanished forever into endless space.

The joy that followed those moments of anguish was indescribable. Restored to freedom, they embraced one another without distinction of sex or station; not even Juanita could resist saying to her master, in a sudden outburst of gratitude:

"If you weren't so ugly, I'd marry you."

The sage was savoring his victory, quite convinced that by it he had won a favored place in his pupil's heart, when she, fearful of seeing new hardships arise, exclaimed, "The time has come to tell him everything," looking to Juanita for advice.

"Absolutely!" responded her resolute counselor. And adding, "Help, brave men!" she roused the Spanish soldiers to leave their hideout, laughing openly at the good uncle's astonishment when he instinctively perceived the trap that had been set for him.

"What! They are here?" he shouted, livid with anger.

"Forgive us," Clara said repeatedly.

"Neither you nor them," fumed the jealous tutor, striking everything within range.

"All right, then," Juanita said. "War to the death; and let any sage who is man enough come out and fight. Don Luis, Pendencia, soldier boys: Down with Mathematics!"

A frightful *aye* followed upon that spirited declaration. The seventeen sons of Mars suddenly appeared in the hold, clambering over the sacks of flour and supply barrels. But as none of them had been treated with the immutability current and the oldest of them had seen fewer than twenty-five Springs, the twenty years undone in time since their departure from Paris had reduced them to tender little toddlers.

"This is dreadful," murmured the French ladies, who had had high hopes about Spanish gallantry.

"I'm fainting!" the pupil managed to say, not believing her eyes, while an enraged Juanita, a veritable basilisk, raised her fists furiously to her master and exclaimed:

"You are the most savage sage I know!"

The tutor was well pleased at seeing the vengeance that chance was serving him up on a platter. Meanwhile, the vehicle kept traveling and the infantry shrank so much that they could no longer stand on two feet.

"But good God, man, can't you see they're dissolving before our eyes like salt in water?" the Maritornes remonstrated, foaming at the mouth.

"All the better," answered Othello's twin. "That way we'll be finished with them for once and for all."

And the little angels were lying on the floor waving their arms and legs about in their newborn immobility and crying at the top of their lungs. Moved by compassion at their plight, each daughter of Eve took one in her arms and strolled about the hold with him, and they watched each infant diminish while the implacable uncle rubbed his hands in satisfaction and grinned devilishly.

"My darling Luis!" said Clara over and over, flooded with tears and offering up her caresses to what was left of her Captain of Hussars.

"Don't you have a little mischief for your Juanita?" the Pinto lass asked of her microscopic Pendencia.

And that rascal of an aide-de-camp, as though still wanting to give proof of his roguishness, bit her dress at the place where children his age nurse.

Suddenly the women turned pale, their arms crossed over their chests: they no longer embraced anything at all. The army had dissolved out from under them.

CHAPTER 10

In Which a Seemingly Insignificant Yet Greatly Important Incident Takes Place

Losing a loved one is among the most terrible trials that a human being can endure, and one goes through several stages of distress according to the circumstances surrounding the event.

"At least he died in his sleep in the company of loved ones," those in charge of consoling the distraught relative tell him.

"And you have the satisfaction of knowing God allowed him to reach a ripe old age," add others.

And, indeed, all these remarks do soothe the pain which, as the product of a constantly thinking and talking machine, lets itself be felt only moderately, reserving its highest intensity for greater calamities.

Now then, let the reader imagine what the travelers' mood was by the fifth act of that tragedy for whose denouement there was no possible *deus ex machina*. Indeed, a fiancé means more than a relative in the eyes of the beloved and, added to the bitterness of being forever separated from theirs, the enamored maidens suffered the humiliation of seeing that, although love is a deity that enhances all it touches, in their case it was the reverse: everything shrank in their hands instead.

Clara fainted upon seeing the immensity of her misfortune and had to be carried to her cabin by her female traveling companions. Juana, more composed but no less wounded, voiced her distress by railing against the oppressor and calling the guards to come to their aid.

But Don Sindulfo's situation was graver still. Bad-tempered, mean-spirited and narrow-minded he might be, but he was far from evil. And the death of the twenty-four Moors, although carried out in legitimate self-defense, were two dozen daggers piercing his heart. Besides, the appearance of the sons of Mars meant to him not only that his orders had been disobeyed, but also showed the futility of having drained his science and his resources just to get rid of a rival. Hence, one may easily understand how his deranged mind had induced him to let time devour those wretched men without lifting a finger to help them. We have seen him take this first step on the path of crime while in the grip of jealousy, madness, and desperation. But let us not get ahead of our story.

The Mohammedans, despite being men, were enemies of God and had made an attempt against his life; therefore, they deserved to die. But those seventeen youngsters toward whom he had acted the cold-blooded Herod, what harm had they done him? Had their childish prank deserved such cruel punishment? Was not one of the victims his own nephew? Would it not have been more humane, since they had not been subjected to the immutability current, to head back to the present and, once restored to their natural sizes, let them all disembark more or less at their right age?

Don Sindulfo pondered these and many other questions, but the

An Important Incident Takes Place

thought of his unrequited passion and his own wounded dignity won out in the end. As a result of such bitter struggles, he fell into his friend's arms delirious and convulsing.

But had his body not been rendered immutable? one may ask. Certainly, but the action of the fluid, which penetrates both skin layers and permeates the muscle tissue beneath, stops at the bones, petrifying them as it does every surface it touches. This way, the skin of the subject affected by the current does not lose its youthful suppleness nor does it suffer any spots, blemishes, or inflammation caused by atmospheric activity. And yet one feels hunger and thirst, suffers from lack of sleep, and is not safe from internal complaints caused, more often than not, by a moral system that science has not yet managed to callus.

Benjamín carried the inert body to his bedroom with the idea of provoking some reaction by putting it to bed. But when he passed by the laboratory, he remembered they had set the Time Ship at a vertiginous speed during the Moroccan invasion. Fearing a catastrophe brought on by carelessness, he pushed the lever and reduced the speed to what he thought was average.

How small incidents can be the cause of the greatest events!

Don Sindulfo, curled up in his bed, continued to shiver and from time to time managed to give Benjamín a good whack.

"Juanita," said the latter as he came out and encountered the flounce-skirted lass. "Heat up some water for a tisane for your master, who isn't feeling well."

"Who, me? Well, if he doesn't want me to scald him raw, he'll have to wait until I've lit the fire."

"Come, now! Let go of your anger and think: if he dies, no one will be able to lead us to safe harbor."

"Don't you know how to use the machinery?"

"Not really. Besides, charity counsels you to be compassionate. Go light the stove while I get the tea and sugar from the pantry."

Be it from fear of remaining forever in space or the compassion inherent to those of her sex, Juanita did not answer back and headed for the kitchen.

"You know what to do, right? With a couple of electric sparks you can light a bonfire before you can say Jack Robinson."

"I won't be using any of those *telegraphics*, thank you. I'll manage the old-fashioned way."

And so saying, she reached the stove, placed some charcoal in it and began to strike matches on sandpaper one after the other without managing to ignite any. But the remarkable thing was that no trace was left on either the striking surface or the match head.

"Of course. Don Sindulfo's drool must have softened everything up," she mumbled. And she went to look for another box and a few wood shavings and rags to aid in the lighting process. Having found nothing suitable, she stumbled upon some bits of cloth and leather of seemingly rich origin but rags nonetheless and very appropriate for such pressing circumstances. She placed the scraps in the stove and tried to light the matches once more, to no avail.

"Let's see if you're any better at this," she told Benjamín, who came in bearing a cone of sugar and a tin of Oolong tea.

"This is faster," the polyglot declared as he touched the electric spark to the burner. This made the rags catch fire but not the coals. And it should be noted that, though neither of them detected the fact, the substitute shavings had started to take on strange shapes that resembled ribbons, dress sleeves, boot heels, bits of fabric, and buttons and such.

"Break off a bit of the sugar," Benjamín ordered Juanita as he poured boiling water over the leaves in the tea pot.

"Not even the devil could crack this Egyptian pyramid! It's as hard as a sage's head," Juanita said while hitting the cone over and over again with a hammer and not managing to make the slightest dent in it.

"Leave it. There's some loose sugar here," replied her conversation partner, taking another packet from the kitchen cabinet, adding a teaspoon to the cup and pouring the beneficial liquid into it.

"Do wait a minute . . . the tea isn't ready yet! It hasn't even changed color."

A cold sweat ran down Benjamín's brow. The sugar's resistance, the

An Important Incident Takes Place

coal's incombustibility, and the water's immutability had given him the key to the puzzle. Seized with nervous agitation, he began to stir the sugar into the tea and, raising the teaspoon to his lips:

"Horrors!" he said turning pale.

"What is it?" asked the maiden, staring at him and fearing he would begin to diminish in size like the others.

"What else can it be? We made our household goods immutable in order to preserve them, and now we find they resist all physical influence."

"Meaning?"

"Meaning that the sugar doesn't sweeten, the coal doesn't ignite, the sugar cone doesn't break, and no one will be able to bite into a potato."

"So we're going to starve?" stammered Juanita, her eyes popping out of their sockets.

"No, but we'll have to stop before every meal and partake of the fare native to the time and location. You've seen what happens if we stabilize our foods. And yet, if we were to abandon them to the retrogressive action of time, in three minutes bread would revert to wheat stalks and wine to grapes."

"And where should we eat our grub today?" answered the country girl, pleased by the idea of a stopover because of the liberating promise it held for the prisoners.

"In hell," Benjamín mumbled as he left the room with the cup of hot water in his hands which, once administered to his friend, had an emetic effect that plunged him into a sweetly pleasant drowsiness.

Meanwhile, Juanita had rushed to give an account of events to her partners in misfortune who, gathered around the pupil's bed, were witnessing a scene no less wondrous than the previous one.

It just so happens that while the women applied themselves to consoling the poor orphan, Niní, who had sadly seen the two beautiful pearls she was wearing disappear from her earlobes before she was stabilized, cried out with joy; for when lifting her hands to the disinherited cartilages, she found her precious jewels restored.

"Look! This is a miracle . . ."

"Indeed it is," they all exclaimed. And, casting her startled eyes around, her sense of wonder grew exponentially: every object that had been snatched away by time's backwards motion was being restored to them without explanation. A shred from Naná's dress, covered in larvae, took the shape of cocoons and then metamorphosed into a finely woven piece of Lyon satin. A strip of calfskin, suddenly tanned, was shaping itself around Sabina's foot and covering itself with stitches and lace, making it as chic as a Charles IX half-boot.

"My shawl!" cried one.

"My lace!" said others.

And all gave themselves over to the most unreserved enthusiasm until the most rational one among them cautioned:

"Slow down. Temper your joy. It's true that we've recovered our wardrobe, but who's to say the restoration won't be complete?"

"What?"

"Aren't you afraid this same phenomenon, which we cannot explain, will win us back a pearl and with it, the wrinkle we thought we'd lost?"

The observation was so pointed and the fear of losing their charms so deep, that a unanimous cry for help burst from every lip and, leaving Juanita behind in charge of Clara, the ladies bolted from the room and went in search of the sages. Luckily, in the laboratory they found Benjamín, who had a hard time silencing the rebellious mob.

"What's the meaning of this?" asked the boldest among them. "Are you trying to make us old again?"

"We want a free say in this," argued another. "We're already well over forty."

"We aren't lepers!" they all shouted.

Benjamín, who could not make head or tail of what was going on, pondered the situation with eyes fixed on the ground. Noticing a shiny object, he instinctively picked it up and found it to be a Moroccan coin.

"One of the Kabyles must have dropped that," said Niní, refocusing his attention on the pressing matter at hand. "Don't you pay it any mind."

An Important Incident Takes Place

"But if this coin belonged to a Moroccan, how is it that, not having been subjected to the immutability current, it's still here? Since we're traveling backwards, it should have disintegrated."

"Maybe it was minted before the year we're in."

"No. It's dated 1237, and since the Arab calendar starts in 622, the year of the Hijrah, its date translates to AD 1859, that is, the year before we were attacked by the Rifeños. We must have passed that year three minutes after the invasion."

"And . . . ?" was the question in every astonished lady's eyes.

And Benjamín, turning his own towards the clock room:

"Damnation!" he said after checking the relative time chronometer. And he immediately brought the Time Ship to a halt.

"Why did you do that?"

"Because when I tried to reduce our traveling speed a while back I must have crossed over the midpoint and we were actually advancing. We've undone the progress we had made and are now flying over Versailles on July the ninth, that is, on the day before we left Paris."

No one can describe the joy that lit up the ladies' faces once they were convinced they had been returned to their theater of operations without losing their youth. They all begged Benjamín to let them disembark and, although he feared Don Sindulfo's ire, the idea of how ridiculous he would look when his colleague learned of his incompetence got the better of him. And so, believing his secret was safe, since neither Clara nor Juanita had witnessed his defeat, and persuaded of the benefit of abandoning the lady associates, he resolved to do as they wished, which earned him an abundant and enviable harvest of hugs and kisses.

The vehicle descended majestically onto the park next to the Trianon theater. The lady travelers sneaked out and Benjamín, turning the speed all the way up, took off into space, his mind set on trying to make up for lost time.

"Now, on to China to search for the secret of immortality."

The next day, Parisian newspapers carried two stories: one was commented on by every leisured person in the boulevards; the other one touched only the scientific world.

The Time Ship

The first one told how twelve young women, who wanted to exploit the public's credulity by pretending to be Time Ship travelers, had been carted off to prison since they showed no sign of being the ladies chosen by the Prefecture. There they had had their personal data recorded and been issued passports, which the impostors could not produce when they returned.

The second piece of news was shorter but more significant to science, in whose annals it still counts as an article of faith. It merely related that at nine forty-five A.M. the astronomical observatory had witnessed a huge meteorite plummet to Earth somewhere around Versailles.

That's how History is written!

CHAPTER 11

A Bit of Tiresome, Though Necessary, Erudition

On the fourteenth day of the ninth month of the year 604 BC, in the village of Li in the feudal state of Ch'u, now Ho-nan province, the great metaphysician of China was born after eighty-one years in the womb (so say his disciples). Because he was born with white hair he was called Lao Tzu, that is, "the old child."[31]

Until he appeared, the Celestial Empire's most arcane philosophy had been distilled into the I Ching, an encyclopedia organized by Fu Hsi, in whom historians believe to recognize Noah after he left the Ark and made his way to Shansi province near Mount Ararat on the opposite side of Bactriana. Its fundamental purpose is to teach the origin of things and the transformations undergone with the passing of the ages. In it, God is considered the cornerstone upon which everything rests. It is both Li and Tao (reason and law) and as such it reveals itself to human intelligence.[32] Lao Tzu, guided by a peaceful sort of wisdom, taught the spurning of passions and the elevation of oneself above all earthly interests, grandeur, and glories, recommending self-denial for the benefit of others and humility as a path to exaltation: language that calls to mind the humbleness and charity of the Savior's doctrine.

He enshrined the whole treasure chest of his intelligence in his work called the Tao Te Ching. Ching means that the book is a classic: Tao and Te are the words used to begin the two parts which make up his treatise and that, as happened with the Pentateuch, gave it its name. Together, the two titles mean Book of Supreme Reason and Virtue.[33]

Here is a fragment that confirms that, when faced with the spectacle of his country's misfortunes, Lao Tzu isolated himself instead of striving for reform, as Confucius did later. He exhorted man to seek in ascetic solitude supreme goodness, which consisted of absolute calm: "Man," he says,

> must strive to attain the highest level of incorporeity, so as to remain as unchangeable as possible. Beings appear in life and fulfill their destinies: we contemplate their successive renewal through which all things return to their original state. To return to your original state means to attain stillness; attaining stillness is to return to your destiny; returning to your destiny is to become eternal. He who knows how to become eternal is enlightened; he who does not becomes a victim of the error and of all calamities.

This set of morals, which we can call passive, was exaggerated by his disciples, who called themselves Tao-sse, or celestial doctors.[34] And in effect, although Lao Tzu believed the public and private good to reside solely in the exercise of virtue and in identifying with supreme reason in order to dominate the senses and achieve impassivity, his followers took advantage of this inaction to abandon themselves to a rigid asceticism. And declaring that wisdom engenders disorder, they recommended to the people the most complete ignorance, all

Tiresome, Though Necessary, Erudition

the while reserving for themselves the cabalistic and divining arts so they could use them to swindle the masses when, with the appearance in China of Buddhism, the Tao-sse mixed with the Bonzes.[35]

The two sects, the Yang and the Me, are but branches from the same trunk: their differences are so insignificant that they deserve not to be reviewed but rather described as the basic principle of the Tao-sse's religion, whose consequence was to elevate sloth to dogma among the ignorant classes.[36]

In the year 551 BC, nearing the winter solstice in the twenty-second year of Lingwang's reign, there was born in the village of Ch'u-fu, feudal domain of Lu (in today's Shan-tung province), the great K'ung Fu-Tzu, or Confucius, as we call him in Europe.

This philosopher, as far removed from blind credulity as from the magical fictions of the Tao-sse, never concerned himself with human nature or divine origins or, in short, with metaphysics. His nature was not that of an innovator; he cared only about restoring the bases of the moral practice of primitive societies.

"What I teach you," he would say,

> you can learn on your own by making legitimate use of your spirit's faculties. There is nothing as natural or simple as the morality whose healthy customs I seek to foster in you. Everything I preach to you has already been put into practice by the sages of old and can be reduced to three fundamental laws—the relationship between vassal and lord, father and son, and husband and wife—and to the exercise of five capital virtues. These are humanity, that is, the love of all without any distinction whatsoever; justice, which gives to each what is his; the observance of ceremonies and established uses, so that all who live together follow the same rules and experience the same advantages and inconveniences; rectitude in judgment and feelings to seek and desire that which is true in everything, free of selfish delusions for oneself and impassioned ones for others; and sincerity, that is, an open heart that keeps falsehood and dissemblance from both word and deed. These are the virtues that have earned the

first founders of the human race the title of "venerable" while alive, and have rendered them immortal afterwards. Let us take them as models and strive to imitate them.

This, in essence, is Confucius' moral system, whose distinctive character lies in making all duties derive from the familial and reducing all virtues to one: filial piety. Its dogma is obedience to the superior by the inferior.

As for metaphysics, here is what a Mandarin disciple of Confucius said to Father Pedranzini:

> We are very careful not to pass judgment about things that are not apparent and that the wise men of old considered uncertain. The axiom of holy men consists of the particle "if," for they say if there is a paradise, the virtuous will enjoy a thousand delights there; if there is a hell, the wicked will be thrown into it. But who can confirm whether they exist or not? To abstain from evil and do good is the important point. The Tai-hio counsels that virtue is what is foremost; riches and well-being are secondary. The Liun-in charges us not to do unto others what we do not wish done to ourselves.[37] Everything comes down to this. Proceed thusly and it will suffice. The joys of paradise, if there is one, will follow as a result.

This moral system was dominant among the enlightened classes, whose followers, hostile to the obscurantist precepts of the Tao-sse, took "the scholars" for their name and "the academy" for their communion.

Among the disciples of Confucius, the most notable was Meng Tzu or Mencius, who died in 314 BC.[38] Distressed at seeing the triumph of the two Tao-sse sects, that is, the Yang, who preached self-interest as the principal regulator of human activities, and the Me,[39] who maintained that love should be spread equally among all, without regard to bloodlines, Meng Tzu popularized a generous philanthropy based on Confucian morality that can be summarized as: He who follows virtuous reason serves heaven well. His book, together

Tiresome, Though Necessary, Erudition

with the three apothegms of Confucius, are even today required reading for those who aspire to civil service.

We see, then, two large groups fighting among themselves for dominion over consciences: Lao Tzu's metaphysics, which held sway over the ignorant, lazy masses and was leavened by the magical doings of its followers, the Tao-sse; and Confucius' moral teachings, cultivated by the scholars, bringing light to privileged intellects and serving, in a sense, as the state religion, endorsed and followed by emperors who are indifferent rather than tolerant of all other practices and beliefs. Nevertheless, there was a time when the cabalists threatened to take over everything. It was in the second century BC when the Tao-sse, breaking away from the pure doctrine of Lao Tzu, began giving themselves over to strange speculations. They claimed to have discovered the secret of immortality in some mysterious and unpleasant brew. The Confucians tried in vain to unmask them; protected by Emperor Wu-ti, the scholars would no doubt have succeeded had one of them not taken the cup his rivals had destined for the monarch and downed its contents in one gulp. This provoked the august one's wrath and, in his blindness, he condemned the man to die in his presence.

"If this elixir's power is real," the Confucian told the emperor, "then the order you have just given is futile; if, on the other hand, it is false, then with my death you will obliterate your mistake."

The deception uncovered, Wu-ti restored his allegiance to the scholars. The Tao-sse went on exerting their influence over only the idle and the ignorant, the former, as has been seen, practicing the religion of the spirits and the latter preaching skepticism and indifference and proclaiming that death has no greater object than to make the soul pass on to another body or dissolve in thin air, so that nothing remains of a man except his blood in his offspring and his name in his homeland.

In spite of this and because, in his books, Confucius maintains that he is only trying to reestablish the original doctrine and that he was nothing more than *the precursor of an illustrious person who would come from the West*, in the first century of our era King Ming-ti sent a fleet there in search of the great reformer. The ships traveled quite a distance, but not daring to go farther they docked at an island where they found a statue of the Buddha. It was transported to China in the year AD 65, where since then it has been venerated under the name of *Fo* and continues to be worshipped by Lao Tzu's disciples and the scholars.

Back then, some Christians who were fleeing Nero's persecution reached the Celestial Empire. But, restrained by their scant numbers and by the conditions in the country, they remained in the shadows until AD 635 when, during Tai-Tsung's rule, the Nestorian priest Alopen of the Tatsin (that is, of the Roman Empire) was received in Chang-an.[40] The emperor sent his leading dignitaries to meet him and bring him to the palace; he had their sacred books translated and, convinced that they contained a true and wholesome doctrine, decreed that a temple to the new religion be built and twenty-one priests consecrated to its service. This event was recorded on a monument raised in Hsingan-fu that succinctly sets forth the Christian doctrine.[41] It is said that the missionaries summoned by Alopen arrived at the court of Tai-Tsung in 636; that the latter published an edict in support of Christianity; that Gao-Tsung had churches built

Tiresome, Though Necessary, Erudition

in every city; that Wu Zetian persecuted believers and that Kuo Tzu always went into battle accompanied by a Christian priest.

The political upheavals that shook China at the beginning of the third century of our era (when this story will take place), could not avoid transmitting their energy to the religious skirmishes that between them the three founding tenets of Lao Tzu, Confucius, and Fo (or Buddha) stirred up.

Emperor An-ti was the first who, in the year 120 (AD as will be all that follows), granted the palace eunuchs honors and privileges to the detriment of the favored status the scholars had enjoyed at court until then. They continued squabbling over power until the year 187, when the eunuchs caused the monarch to become suspicious of the academy, whose company of educated men posed a threat to his tyranny. Emperor Ling-ti exiled the learned men and threw the most illustrious to the law courts for sentencing, proclaiming himself a friend of science for having had the five classic books of the *I Ching* engraved upon forty-six marble stones in three different types of characters.

Although the Tao-sse appeared to make common cause with the eunuchs, they took advantage of circumstances and did not wait long to use them to their benefit. The plague had ravaged the empire for eleven years; a Tao-sse named Chang-kio found a surefire remedy for it in some water prepared with mysterious incantations. This charlatan easily won credit among the masses. Followed by an unruly throng of empiricists, he trained them and in short order found himself at the head of a large band. His doctrine was that the Blue Sky, that is, the Han dynasty, headed at the time by Emperor Hsien-ti, was reaching its end in order to make way for the Yellow Sky. His purpose discovered and aware that his downfall was certain, he launched into open rebellion. Fifty thousand men rallied to his cry and, taking up the yellow turban as their insignia, they rushed to lay waste to the country.[42] Their forays were helped by the rising up of many ambitious men who hoped to divide China into numerous states; but the prudence and valor of general Tsao Tsao, head of the band of scholars the emperor had called to his aid, put down the insurrection and the vanquished pledged their allegiance to his banner. Hsien-ti named

The Time Ship

him his prime minister; but swollen with pride over his triumph, Tsao Tsao was soon seen putting on the twelve-pendant hat adorned with fifty-three gemstones—a distinctive royal emblem—and having himself driven about in the golden carriage pulled by six horses. He would soon have appropriated the imperial seal had death not cut him off at the pass. Nevertheless, his work was consummated by his son Tsao Pi, Hsien-ti's prime minister, who usurped the throne in the year 220, putting an end to the Han dynasty and beginning that of the Wei.[43]

But let us not get ahead of events, since we are going to have our readers attend this memorable event. Let us state here, for the readers' greater edification, that in the year 220 the Time Ship arrived at Henan, court of the Chinese empire under the reign of Hsien-ti during the time when the revolt had been stifled. Tsao Tsao was dead and his son Tsao Pi had been elevated to the honorable post of prime minister. Power had been wrested back by the scholars, who mercilessly persecuted both the disciples of Fo, for the novelty of the Buddhist religion imported from Indostan, and the Tao-sse, for the vulgarity of their empiricism.

CHAPTER 12

Forty-eight Hours in the Celestial Empire

THE saying "Nothing lasts forever" lies like a dog, because Don Sindulfo spent well over sixteen centuries on his sickbed, from the moment he hurled the children of Mohammed out into space, and those of Mars out into the void, until the Time Ship landed in the vicinity of Henan, then center of the Chinese Empire.

In the three-and-a-half days the trip lasted, Benjamín, taking advantage of the sage's drowsiness and the girls' sleep, made all the corresponding stops and stole out of the vehicle in order to stock up on necessary provisions since, as we have already seen, those he had on board were worthless. He owed their first feast to the pious munificence of Queen Isabella of Castille; incidentally, the episode almost cost him his life because when he got to the Santa Fe camp, where the Castillian army despaired over the stubborn resistance of the Granadian Moors, he was taken for one of Boabdil's spies, mainly because his costume of suit jacket and flared pants seemed very strange for the time.[44] Fortunately, the polyglot kept his wits about him and, remembering how valuable the knowledge he had acquired during his History studies could be, asked to be brought before the queen so he could disclose important revelations to her. Doña Isabella was accompanied by her husband Don Ferdinand, Cardinal Ximénez, and his first captains. And all of them except the grand lady were in favor of lifting the siege that was exhausting the besiegers' patience as well

The Time Ship

as the royal treasury, when Benjamín burst into the tent and asked, prophetically:

"What's this I hear about lifting the siege?"

And, whispering in the queen's ear, he added:

"Today, on January the second, 1492, a Friday (just like the one when the Savior of Men spilled his precious blood during his ordeal), at three o'clock (the precise hour when the Word Incarnate exhaled his last breath), the banner of Santiago and the royal standard will fly from the tower of Alhambra."

Doña Isabella turned pale; the courtesans around her, fearing foul play, reached for their swords. And the master of languages would surely have had a rough time of it if the Moorish horns, mixing with the Castillian trumpets, had not stopped for a moment and provided a life-saving pause.

"What's happening?" asked the king when he saw Count Cifuentes come into the tent with a joyful look on his face.

"What is happening, my Lord," said the noble gentleman, "is that Boabdil has just surrendered. And so that the victors may enter Granada in safety, the conquered king sends his sons as hostages of the Castille camp along with six hundred armed men and two of their most distinguished captains."

A cry of surprise broke from every throat.

"Who are you?" asked the queen almost kneeling in amazement before he whom she, in her holy faith, regarded as a celestial apparition.

"A poor mortal," answered Benjamín, "who in return asks only that you let him go on his way with a bit of bread to placate his hunger."

Such a small price sealed the impression Doña Isabella had formed of the prophet and, not daring to tempt him with human gifts, she herself prepared a couple of saddlebags stuffed full of tasty cured ham from Alpujarras and the best white bread from Castille, plus a flask of wine from Aragon that the camp stewards kept in store for Don Fernando's table.

Benjamín was ready to exit the tent when the sovereign called him to her side, her hands crossed in a pleading gesture:

Forty-eight Hours in the Celestial Empire

"What can I do," she asked, "for the happiness of my vassals and to ensure my place on the throne?"

"Lend your ears, my Lady," answered the polyglot, "to a Genovese who will come to offer you a world."

"To Columbus?" asked the queen in amazement. "I've already seen him, but everyone declares him a madman! Besides, my coffers are exhausted."

"Sell your jewels if necessary. He will repay their value a hundredfold by creating vices for mankind."

And so saying, he handed the queen a Breva de Cabañas cigar that the poor lady turned end over end, perplexed as to its nature and purpose.

"What is this?" she finally brought herself to ask.

"Smoke!" cried Benjamín, then disappeared.

And, indeed, two years later, after searching for another route to the Eastern Indies, Columbus returned from America with a new world for Spain and an army of tobacco shops for poor military widows.

The Time Ship

The second stop for provisions Benjamín made, twenty hours later (that is, when the eleventh century was drawing to a close), did not offer anything worth mentioning. This was not the case with the landing that, after a like amount of time, he made in the year 696 in the city of Ravenna, late on a Sunday afternoon.

This town, as everybody knows, was then the residence of the exarchs who controlled the destinies of the Italian territories under the rule of Byzantium. Governed by the local institutions of the Late Roman Empire, the city had schools for the urban militia, but a barbaric custom was practiced there. On holy days, the young and old and women and children of any social class would leave the city, group themselves into different camps and freely engage in rock fights that always resulted in several wounded and dead. Benjamín was on his merry way back to his vehicle from a convent where he had received supplies aplenty, on account of the beggar's rags on his back, when the ear-splitting cry from a fleeing crowd made him understand—reconciling dates with what he had read in Agnellus—that he was witnessing that historical moment when the Tigurian gate's defenders, having defeated those of the Sommovico sally port, chased them until they finished off half the opposing camp.[45]

"This is none of my business," the traveler told himself, and he started to run across country. But the pebbles were raining down in such profusion that, hoping to speed up his pace, he quickly grabbed hold of a Lombard donkey grazing in a field and, clinging to its back, rushed off. Unfortunately, a stone from a Tigurian sling hurt his mount so inauspiciously, by hitting it smack on the hock, that it sliced the whole leg off. The rider, picking himself up after the fall, could not even find the severed limb; he wanted to keep it as a souvenir of that tragedy which, by the way, ended as follows. After being defeated, the sally gate defenders faked reconciliation and, having invited the Tigurian faction to a feast, they slaughtered each and every one and threw their bodies down the sewers. The traitors were hung, their furniture burnt, their dwellings razed, and the area was thenceforth known as the brigand's quarter.[46]

Benjamín miraculously reached the Time Ship, where he shared

Forty-eight Hours in the Celestial Empire

his food with Clara and Juanita, who had not left their room since the army's disappearance, confined there by grief. He made them drink some beneficial herbs he had gathered for Don Sindulfo and resumed their journey toward the Celestial Empire. But when he opened his cabinet to jot down a few notes in the logbook, what do my readers think he found? Nothing less than the hairy, blood-stained donkey's leg replacing the famous bone the wretched man had bought in Madrid and paid an exorbitant price for, having mistaken it for the fossil of a human shinbone found in the vicinity of Chartres.

Finally the year 220 came up on the Relative Time quadrant. After the colossus landed in the suburbs of Henan, the hope of possessing the secret of immortality erased the anthropological disappointment that Benjamín never, ever mentioned to his traveling companions.

Don Sindulfo, recovered now from his attack, though his mind was not all there as the course of events will show, and the girls, resigned to passive obedience, indifference being a symptom of grief, all prepared themselves to enter the court of Hsien-ti. They did this after the polyglot explained the vanishing of the French ladies by saying that an insurrection on board had forced him to let them disembark, as had been their wish.

Nobody had anything to say about the matter.

Clara and Juanita's hearts ached too much for them to care about anything other than their own troubles, and the sage for his part kept as silent as a post, his mind focused only on his mission, which was to disembark in an era of obscurantism and autocracy where the arbitrariness of the law would allow him to force his ward to become his wife.

The city was deserted. The first empress had passed away the night before and the emperor's prescribed national mourning prohibited every son of the Celestial Empire from leaving his house or opening any door or window for the next forty-eight hours.

When the travelers reached Henan's walls they were interrogated by the officer of the guard about the purpose of their visit. Benjamín, as the expedition's interpreter, conveyed their wish to be granted an audience with Emperor Hsien-ti. The trekkers' clothes, their European features, the strict security around the emperor. and the suspicion that the Time Travelers might be Lao Tzu's disciples—so persecuted then by the Scholar's Party in power—brought the official up short and, believing he was serving the monarch's cause, he ordered the guards to escort them blindfolded for an audience with the emperor.

Once permission from the emperor was granted, the travelers—anxious but somewhat reassured by Benjamín's attempts to persuade them, based on his erudition, that the officer's behavior stemmed not from malice but from following the Chinese court's rituals—found themselves before Hsien-ti.

This ruler was a corrupt man of dissolute nature whose thirst for pleasure was not quenched by the offensive luxury that surrounded him, won at the expense of his wretched vassals. The palace or *yamen* where he lived, copied by prince Tsao when he built his a century later, was indescribably opulent. Its walls were made solely of marble and the sun's rays caressed the shiny lacquered surface of the rooftop tiles. The little bells on the entablature were made of gold, the columns supporting it were silver, and every kind of precious stone embellished the heavy curtains hanging on the doors.

The most beautiful women from the Mandarin and plebeian classes lived in the palace. Astrologists and artists, among many others, formed the emperor's ten-thousand-person retinue. A thousand maidens mounted on richly harnessed steeds were his personal guard and often accompanied him during his outings. At other times he would travel in a light carriage drawn by trained lambs that stopped whenever one of the five thousand actresses destined for Hsien-ti's sensual pleasure offered fresh grass to the ruminant beasts so she could claim the great honor of having the monarch rest in her arms.

When the travelers entered the room where he awaited them, Hsien-ti could not suppress a gesture of surprise brought on by Clara's beauty. Nevertheless, he controlled himself, as the decorum his status as widower demanded, and he merely exchanged an intelligent look with his prime minister, Tsao Pi. In return and perhaps wishing to flatter his master, Tsao Pi made a meaningful gesture while staring at Juanita, as if to say: "This other one isn't half bad, either."

Forty-eight Hours in the Celestial Empire

Describing both the ceremony and the strange oratory style used for the interview would take us so long that, just to give an idea, we will summarize what the historian Cantù and other sinologists have said about it. And let us note, by the way, that these customs are still practiced in China today, almost to the letter, since it is well known that stagnation is the basis of the country's character.[47]

The artificial politeness of the Chinese, say those who describe these ceremonies, manifests itself in every aspect of their lives: the regulation-filled visits, the role one plays in them according to status, the manner of walking and the interminable compliments. They never use the first person "I" in conversation but rather "your servant" or, if the rank calls for it, "your unworthy and humble servant." They do not address anyone except as "Most Honorable Sir." Their country is vile, wretched, and abject, just like their gifts, no matter how splendid they make them. And everything that belongs to the "noble gentleman" to whom they are speaking is "worthy of the highest esteem." Every aspect of their visits is regulated by an etiquette code that has the power of law, and anyone who overlooks the tiniest of its stipulations would be dishonored and even warrant punishment. European ambassadors used to go through forty days of training and then were examined by the tribunal of rites. Afterwards, were they to commit an error before the emperor, the tribunal members would answer for them.

They say that a duke of Moscovia begged the emperor in his credential letters to forgive his envoy if the latter, lacking in practice, committed a small blunder, and the Son of Heaven, returning the diplomat's documents, answered the Moscovian sovereign: "Legatus tuus multa fecit rustice."[48]

But it is not only in court that this happens. Every Chinese person who wants to visit another, be it a scholar or a merchant, introduces himself via a servant who goes before him bearing a card (tie tsee)[49] with his name and his compliments. On it one may read, for example: "Your Lordship's tender and sincere friend," or "The perpetual follower of your doctrine presents himself to bow deeply before you."

If the host receives him, the chair or litter passes through several courtyards before reaching a reception hall. Once there, ceremony dictates which greetings should be performed, the precise left and right head movements, the mutual insistence that the other be the first to enter, the bow the master takes before the seat of honor that has been destined for the guest, a seat that will not be occupied until the former cleans the dust from the latter's garments. Finally they both sit down with heads covered, for to do otherwise would be irreverent, and the conversation begins, host and guest taking special care not to call each other old, a sign of politeness and exquisite good manners. Tea is served right away, and for this operation there is also a prescribed way of offering it, accepting it, bringing the cup to one's lips, and giving it back to the servant. When taking leave, a good half-hour is wasted in idle palaver, of which they have an endless supply. If one of them gives a compliment, the other one says *fei sin,* meaning "you are profligate with your heart." The smallest service earns one a *sie putsin,* "my gratitude knows no bounds." Asking a favor is always followed by *te-tsui,* "what a great sin it is for me to take such a liberty!" Praise is not accepted without protesting *ki can,* "how could I believe it?" And at the end of every meal the host says the following: *Yeu-tau, tai-man,* "We have received you badly, we have treated you poorly."

The master of the house goes to the door to see his friend enter his sedan chair. The latter assures him he will never do so in his noble presence. And, after an exchange of entreaties and refusals, the former leaves and the latter climbs into his litter. But he has not yet taken his seat when the host rushes out to wish him a good journey. The guest returns his good wishes, insists he will not depart until his friend leaves and, although the friend says he will remain rooted to the spot until he disappears from sight, good taste dictates that he be the one to yield. Finally, after raising many objections, the host withdraws. The guest is just about to leave when the person who invited him steps out of the door to bid him a last farewell, which the other one acknowledges with gestures, his head out of the window, until he finally manages to get home. After a couple of minutes, one of the host's servants arrives to inquire after his health on behalf of

Resurrection of the Dead before Judgment

his master, thank him for the visit, and beg him to come back again soon.

Now that we know all about these particulars, let us relate in our usual style the interesting interview the four travelers had with Emperor Hsien-ti and his prime minister in the palace at the court of Henan.

CHAPTER 13

Nineteenth-century Europe Meets Third-century China

THE spectacle of so many accumulated wonders could not help jolting Clara and Juanita out of their catalepsy, especially the latter who, though not quite recovering her good humor, at least began talking again.

"Hey," she asked her master, "Isn't it true that Chinese people wear pigtails? So how come these ones are bob-tailed?"

"Because the Celestials," answered Don Sindulfo, "retained their capillary integrity until the seventeenth century, when they were conquered by the Manchurian Tartars, who forced them to grow something resembling a dog's tail on their heads as a sign of their enslavement."

"I'll have to make a study of it," said the Pinto lass gravely, taking the seat that was offered to her.

The ritual of greetings over, the emperor questioned the travelers about their origins and the purpose that had brought them into his presence. Benjamín said they were from the West; that they lived in a time six hundred years after the emperor's; and that, possessing the secret of traveling backwards through the centuries, they had to come to Henan to inquire after the principle of immortality the Tao-sse preached of, so that once they had perfected it they could open the doors of the future to mankind, just as they had already done with those of the past.

Hsien-ti and his minister exchanged a conspiratorial look. They had no doubt that the voyagers belonged to the vanquished sect of tricksters who, with similar unbelievable tales, sought to bamboozle the court and the people in order to restart the wars with the Yellow Turbans. At that moment the travelers' death sentence was tacitly decreed, although the rapture with which Hsien-ti and his minister beheld the features of the two young ladies seemed to presage a favorable commutation of their capital sentence.

"And what proof can you give us that you are being true to your word?" challenged the monarch, in order to discover by what artifices the imposters planned to back up their claims.

"My Lord," replied Benjamín. "It will be an easy task for us to convince Your Majesty. We need only present you with some small example of the progress civilization has made in the sixteen centuries that separate us. The empire can then benefit either by appropriating the achievements of other nations, or by hastening the discoveries China will make in centuries far beyond the one through which we now traverse."

"Indeed," said Hsien-ti with an incredulous smile. "If it is as you claim, it deserves to be taken into account. Make us admire those marvels of civilization."

Benjamín hastened to comply. Reaching into an overnight bag, which he had had the forethought of supplying with a number of trinkets, he began emptying it. He did so as a proud son of the nineteenth century who, puffed up with the conquests of his times, thinks he can freely make sport of his ancestors to whom, when all is said and done, he owes the very foundations of the knowledge he usually has done little more than fine-tune.

"Here you have a bronze vase," he said with paternal solicitude. "An imitation of the Greek amphora. An alloy unknown to your empire about whose uses you'll be gratified to learn."

"Not so fast," replied the emperor cutting off his speech and leading Benjamín over to a door, before whose pilasters stood two immense urns of the same metal.

"What!" exclaimed the astonished polyglot. "Not only do you know about fusion, but you know how to apply it in the making of monumental works of art?"

Hsien-ti could not suppress a hearty laugh, and laying his finger on some Chinese characters that ran along the decorations he added, "Read here."

The beleaguered traveler took a step back in surprise when he saw the following maxim on the neck of the vase: *Purify yourself every day, thus to improve your health.* This motto corresponded to all the implements used by the emperor Chang, founder of the second dynasty and whose authenticity was clearly established by the seal of his kingdom that was placed smack in the middle.

"See here!" Benjamín shouted to his companions, "These urns were cast in the year 1766 before the Christian era."

"Meaning," interjected the tutor, "that by our count, they are almost thirty-six-and-a-half centuries old."

Benjamín was still biting his lip in archeological despair when, upon recognizing the curtain material partially hidden by the precious stones, he asked: "What's this? Are you also familiar with the art of weaving silk?"

"Your ignorance astounds me," the minister responded. "Don't you know that discovery occurred in the sixty-first year of the reign of Huang-ti,[50] the era when, for the educated, the history of China begins, along with the cycle of sixty years divided into 365 days and six hours, which is the basis of our computational system?"

"And I'll bet," said Juanita when she heard the translation, "that that Don *Juan-Tea* was already old in Jesus' time."

"Indeed, since he was in the flower of his youth 2,698 years earlier," Don Sindulfo replied.

"As I just said; your contemporary, sir."

"Let the bronze be and may the silk rest in peace," insisted Benjamín, who could not adjust to getting beaten in the contest. "But I'll wager Your Majesty won't know what this is for."

And unfolding a piece of paper, he presented the emperor with a compass.

Hsien-ti exchanged smiles with the minister, and leading the polyglot to a window that overlooked the river he asked, "Do you see those boats?"

"With steel hulls!" he cried in astonishment, noticing the sheets of metal plating in the evening light.

"Yes; it's been over six hundred years since we used wooden boats, and for more than twelve centuries we have equipped our boats with the device you present to us as a marvel. Heaven only knows who invented it."

The sages were thunderstruck and unable to make sense of what they were seeing, when they were jarred out of their bewildered trance by a turbulent crowd rushing about and shouting to make way for some strange-looking covered carts.

"What's going on?" inquired Don Sindulfo.

"Nothing of importance," replied Tsao Pi. "A fire somewhere. Those are the fire engines that will extinguish it."

"Fire engines!" everyone cried.

"They should aim a shot at you," said the Pinto lass to her master, "to see if they calm that youthful ardor of yours."

"But that invention," put in Benjamín,

still in denial of the evidence, "along with the artesian well, porcelain, the suspension bridge, playing cards, and paper money, do not appear in China, according to our historiographers, until the eighth through thirteenth centuries, and we are just at the start of the third. For although it is true that in 1847 the learned sinologist Stanislas Julien[51] reported the dates of certain Chinese discoveries to the Paris Academy of Sciences, the periods he cites seem so fantastical that European pride cannot accept them."

"And what does that good man say about us?"

"He theorizes that by the tenth century of our era you already had knowledge of engraving and lithography."

By way of an answer, the emperor merely showed him his portrait and that of his dead wife, both made using those two procedures and hanging on the walls seven centuries before Julien's hypothesis.

"And what else does he say?" added Hsien-ti.

The polyglot, lowering his voice, replied: "That in the twelfth century you possessed Gutenberg's marvelous invention."

And so saying, he handed the monarch a newspaper, all the while explaining to him the mission that the press came to fill.

"Ah! Yes. My predecessor tried to allow the publication of a gazette intending that all his vassals might become censors of the abuse of power. But instead of using it as an instrument of censorship, they turned it into a forum for diatribes and insults and it was necessary to rescind authorization and limit the right to print to the publication of our sacred books."

And he directed the travelers' attention to a richly bound copy of Confucius' analects that lay on top of a small table.

The two sages threw themselves at it with rabid bibliomania. But the night's shadows were already so heavy that they would not have been able to examine it if Tsao Pi, giving the order to light the lamps, had not commanded some slaves to enter. Using sponges soaked in a flammable substance, they filled the place with light simply by applying the flame to some gas burners protruding from the wall.

"Gas!" was the unanimous cry.

"Yes, gas," said the emperor calmly.

Europe Meets Third-century China

"But where do you extract it from?"

"From the bosom of the earth; from fecal matter, whose emanations we transport wherever we wish by means of underground tubes."

"Julien mentions that as well, though he attributes it to the eighth century. Sir, do not be surprised by our astonishment, for although we had vague notions of your advances, these are so many and in such open contradiction to the decadence and backwardness of nineteenth-century China that we dared not give much credit to the civilization of the past because of the stagnation and even regression of the present."

"All nations that achieve a high level of development tend to see their greatness disappear, usurped by other emerging states," stated Hsien-ti, believing it imprudent, given the plans he harbored, to accuse the travelers of being vulgar impostors who wanted to pass off as miracles of some supposed future age the most rudimentary notions of contemporary science.

"So one must take as an article of faith Julien's claim that, along with ink and rag paper, gunpowder belongs among the discoveries of the second century BC?"

"Gunpowder?"

"Yes. That composite of seventy-five parts sodium nitrate, fifteen-and-a-half parts carbon and nine-and-a-half parts sulfur, attributed in the Middle Ages to the German monk Schwartz, which the sinologist in question believes was brought to Europe from China, where potassium nitrate already occurs naturally."

"If you aren't talking about cannons, I don't know what you mean. Let's see if this is it."

And, taking from a collection of arms an arrow coated in black powder (which was nothing other than gunpowder), to whose lower end a rocket had been tied, the emperor lit the short fuse that hung from it, notched the arrow against the bowstring and shot it through the window. The sky was lit up like a tongue of fire, the arrow's trajectory increasing with the new impulse force lent it by the firecracker's explosion in the atmosphere.

From that moment on, the German monk was relegated to the ranks of imaginary beings.

"I do not doubt," continued Hsien-ti, "that all of these processes will be perfected over the centuries; but you can see that, in essence, you cannot teach us anything new. And the proof is that you come to our realm in search of the secret of immortality that is held as dogma among the disciples of the spirits of the Celestial Empire. Very well; I do not wish your journey to be fruitless. I will reveal to you that arcane mystery upon one condition."

"What is that?"

"Yesterday I lost my companion, the empress. The law allows me to take a new wife once forty-eight hours of national mourning have passed. Tomorrow that period ends. Permit me to share the throne with this lovely young lady."

And saying this, he took Clara's hand in his own. She withdrew it, startled, asking them to explain the meaning of such a sudden assault. Benjamín's translation of the monarch's demand incensed the pupil and exasperated Don Sindulfo, who in vain had placed in the empire's legal authorities his hopes of becoming his niece's husband.

"Tell him we don't cast pearls before swine," said the Maritornes. And everyone except the polyglot prepared to vigorously oppose the emperor's proposal, when the notion of losing their lives if they stood their ground made Don Sindulfo come up with a conciliatory plan.

"Let us pretend to give in," he said in a low voice to his companions, "and once we're back in the Time Ship, where we shall ask them to take us to dress for the ceremony, we'll get underway. Just let them try to catch us then!"

The girls agreed to the plan, but Benjamín resisted because fleeing would deprive him of the coveted secret of immortality. Nevertheless, he quickly appeared to consent, as he was secretly planning the scheme which shall soon be revealed.

Meanwhile, the emperor and his minister plotted the way to rid themselves of the swindlers as soon as the head of the family's authorization (so unavoidable in China when it came to matrimony) granted him the honor he sought.

The Chinese ritual requires the bride to remain in her house until the nuptial party goes to escort her to her husband's. It was therefore decided that the travelers would return to their dwelling, whence the imperial retinue would fetch her on the evening of the following day.

They said their farewells to Hsien-ti and his minister and, accompanied by an honor guard to protect the Time Ship from the outside, and by a horde of slaves laden with gifts and provisions, the time travelers walked to the vehicle, the door being opened by Benjamín, who contrived to enter first.

As soon as the servants had withdrawn and the sentries were scattered around the colossus at a respectful distance, Don Sindulfo, taking hold of the regulator, said with a burst of laughter, "They won't say we didn't make monkeys out of them."

But suddenly he paled; the monkey in this case was he. The electrical system did not work. They had been reduced to prisoners.

CHAPTER 14

An Unexpected Guest

SAD as the night Hernán Cortés spent before the Battle of Otumba was the night the explorers spent on board the Time Ship. Clara, being no doubt the most worthy of compassion, did nothing but weep and ask herself in desperation what crime she had committed to deserve being the scapegoat for every whim of an inexorable destiny. The tutor claimed he had acted in good faith, since his plan all along had been to foil the emperor's plans by fleeing. But his good intentions, stemming from a selfish motive, were powerless before a stronger force that kept them at a standstill, every forecast of his scientific calculations notwithstanding.

"A continuity fluid is not the cause of this paralysis, since the currents are circulating freely," held the sage on the basis of the inspections of the vehicle he and Benjamín had made on several occasions, having no idea his friend could betray him.

"I bet your lordship's head," claimed Juana addressing her master, "that if we call a Chinese blacksmith, he'll tell us at once what's causing the cart to be jammed. So much for your cutting a good figure before his majesty. Fire up your brains, sir, since, as the emperor has shown, you're carrying a gas factory inside yourself."

Don Sindulfo looked to his friend for advice, but Benjamín remained mute, just like those who have an unrepented crime on their conscience and try to evade paying for it by keeping silent. And indeed, the polyglot was solely to blame for the situation. It is true he was not aware of Hsien-ti's plans for the male crew members and trusted that some kind of subterfuge would return Clara to the Time Ship so she could escape as soon as the ceremony was over. But science is so selfish that it thinks about everything in *anima vili*[52] when it comes to an experiment, and the idea of losing the secret of immortality if they left third-century China had more power over him than the unforeseen events to which he would expose his companions in misfortune if they stayed. Therefore, he boarded the Time Ship first, as we have seen, and cunningly placed a porcelain cup between the fluid conductors and the steering mechanism, causing the electric current to stop and the vehicle to break down. Each time the unsuspecting Don Sindulfo performed a check-up, Benjamín, assuming a helpful attitude, would go before him and conceal the cup with a skillful sleight of hand, only to put it back the moment the sage, convinced there was no obstruction, went on ahead and activated the machinery.

Having exhausted all technical means, they gave desertion serious thought, but it was impossible to do so successfully, since the guard on duty had orders not to abandon the travelers for a single instant. But even assuming it were possible, escape would not improve the travelers' situation since, once their absence was noticed, it would not be long before the fugitives were caught. Besides, there was another powerful reason to object: they could not leave the Time Ship without the risk of being stranded more than one thousand and six hundred years from their own era, a fact that would have benefited Don Sindulfo if the local circumstances had allowed him to fulfill his desire of forcing the marriage yoke on his ward.

They all resolved to wait for Providence to send them a ray of hope along with the light of the new day, and laid down on their beds worn out with fatigue.

The night was as long as if spent in pain. Every fifteen minutes the sentry's cry split the monotony of silence that was also broken at intervals by hollow thumps like those of a hammer on a nail. The noise seemed to be coming from the hold and, fearing the celestials might break in, Don Sindulfo and Benjamín went down to the cellar. They stayed there for fifteen minutes without hearing any more hammering sounds, though these resumed as soon as they returned to their rooms.

"I'm sure they're coming from that other side," exclaimed Benjamín.

"Yes, they must be building an arch of triumph for us," interjected the sage.

And they remained absorbed in their own thoughts waiting for dawn, which came before long and greeted them with an encouraging smile. But the day, not stopping in its tracks, followed its course without bringing any means of salvation, and each minute that elapsed devoured the travelers' hopes.

The forty-eight hours of national mourning prescribed by law expired at nightfall and immediately afterwards the new empress would have to go to the *yamen* and share the throne with the sovereign.

Hsien-ti's servants had been visiting the Time Ship since daybreak bearing sumptuous delicacies, extravagant presents, and Chinese-style wedding dresses. Presiding over the servants was King-seng, court master of ceremonies and a pleasant young man of dashing good looks to whom everyone took an instant liking, owing perhaps to his sad countenance or to the kindness he showed the captives.

Finally the female slaves and the eunuchs arrived at dusk. They were in charge of dressing and coiffing both the bride and her attendants, which meant that the hour of abandoning all hope had arrived. Desperation, the last bastion of the impotent, took hold of the voyagers. Clara and Juanita, clinging to one another in a corner, heroically stood their ground and refused to hand over their bodies to what they considered funeral attire. Don Sindulfo, his eyes aghast, urged his friend to speak out against that cruelty in the language of Confucius, just as he himself was doing in energetic Aragonese. Benjamín, not quite regretting his actions, was beginning to feel a certain compassion for his companions. Grief, confusion, and chaos reigned supreme, when the master of ceremonies ordered the servants to leave the laboratory and, calling the travelers aside, told them: "You poor wretches! Don't worry. I will save you."

Imagine the surprise and delight of all four when they heard King-seng's words as Benjamín translated them. Clara clasped his hands, Don Sindulfo thanked him in Latin just in case the liberal arts had already made their way to the Celestial Empire, and Juanita threw him a Pinto-style hug that almost floored him.

"Silence, fools!" continued the guardian angel of the dispossessed. "Don't let them hear you. The emperor thinks you're Tao-sse's supporters coming to Henan to restart the struggle of the Yellow Turbans and he intends to eliminate you as soon as the nuptial ceremony is over. He's only going through this wedding to satisfy his vulgar appetite, since a recent law prohibits him from increasing the number of his concubines."

"How horrible!" the prisoners murmured.

"Yes, but I am here, and I know everything about it."

"About what?" inquired those present, tightening the circle around him.

"Some ten full moons ago a fugitive came from the West. While hiding in Henan, he found a way to contact Empress Sun-che, the oppressor's martyred wife. I am not privy to what he told her, but the noble lady honored me with her trust and led me to understand that the fugitive was the one Confucius refers to in his apothegms as the one who will bring the revelation of his doctrine from the West, and that, indeed, he had offered her immortality."

"Immortality!" repeated everyone as they listened intently to a tale that vindicated Benjamín's fixation.

"Yes," continued King-seng, "for her and her family. The empress asked me to recruit converts and ordered the mysterious individual to bring a few families over from his far-away land to help spread his

The Time Ship

wisdom. You are no doubt the first ones to answer the call and I offer you my protection."

The proposal was too important for anyone to dare disabuse the master of ceremonies of his assumptions. Therefore, seeing their salvation in what he believed, they conspired to go along with him, especially the polyglot who saw his goal within reach.

"And where would we find this Westerner?" asked Benjamín.

"Misfortune hounds you," declared King-seng. "He is dead."

"Dead!" they all cried, pretending to be deeply upset.

"But you will continue his work. Two days ago the emperor, already believing his wife to be a Tao-sse partisan and taking a dim view of her, surprised the foreigner talking with the empress. When the emperor heard him offer her the secret of immortality, it convinced him that they both belonged to the swindlers' sect. Tsao Pi, his chief minister and leader of the scholars party, called for vengeance. As the Westerner was being sawn in two in the execution square the people, for whom everything that happens in the palace is a mystery, were told that Sun-che had suddenly succumbed. But the poor empress had been buried alive in the *yamen*'s dungeons by order of her callous husband."[53]

"How barbaric!" declared all his listeners except for Benjamín who seemed to be absorbed in deep thought.

"Everyone partial to the empress has cried out in indignation. And she may still be alive, because that type of death is a slow one. But whether dead or alive, we will bring her out of her tomb. And to do just that my followers, once reassembled, will start a rebellion right in the middle of the wedding banquet. Cast aside all fear. I will protect you with my troops, but help me with my plans by preparing for the ceremony, since the slightest suspicion may ruin us. Place your trust in the people I have brought along to serve you. They obey me absolutely. Now go. Time is of the essence."

The idea of engaging in a fight whose outcome was unknown was not that attractive to peaceful people with no vested interest in the empire. And yet, their particular situation seemed so fraught with insurmountable dangers that they did not hesitate to choose the side of the dilemma that offered them some probability of success.

They called in the servants and let themselves be dressed in all the splendor of their rank. They even spiced up this task with a few jokes, lest we forget that the people who found themselves in this predicament were Spaniards.

Once they were ready they caught a glimpse of a multitude of whimsically shaped lanterns through the open disks of the vehicle and heard an infernal noise of tambourines, cymbals, and the obligatory gong or Chinese bell heralding the arrival of the imperial retinue. When the entourage reached the doors of the Time Ship it stopped, since ritual prescribes that the home of the maiden bride not be violated.

"Come in," exclaimed King-seng as the emperor's representative, taking Clara's hand in order to lead her to her litter.

"Come in," cried everyone else in their hope-induced enthusiasm.

They were just crossing the cellar and nearing the main door when several raps made the retinue stop in the middle of the room.

"What was that?" asked the master of ceremonies.

"Did you hear it?" replied Benjamín.

"Yes. It would seem someone is calling."

And since everybody was paying attention, the thumps could be heard again, this time more insistently.

"Don't you see? They're coming from this side," Clara pointed out.

"From the box," added Juanita, consulting the antiquarian with her eyes.

"What? From the one with the mummy in it?" stammered Don Sindulfo, as shocked as his companions.

Meanwhile, Benjamín, who had struck a meditative pose, declared: "Yes. That's it," striking his forehead with the palm of his hand.

"What is?" was the unanimous response.

"We've been going backwards in time and have arrived in the period when the empress was buried alive; my mummy is none other than Emperor Hsien-ti's unfortunate consort."

He was just about to approach the sarcophagus when a new thump, more formidable than the others, made the hinges of the box fly through the air and a beautiful woman at the peak of youth emerged from that death bed.

"Sun-che!" cried all the Chinese, as they recognized the marvelous apparition and bowed before her.

"The empress!" repeated the travelers in their astonishment.

Juanita said nothing. But she was secretly beginning to suspect that the sages were not as stupid as she thought.

CHAPTER 15

The Resurrection of the Dead before Judgment Day

"Vengeance!" was the first word the empress uttered upon finding herself surrounded by her allies.

"Vengeance!" they echoed in tribute to Sun-che.

"Let me kiss the feet of him who watched over me," continued the illustrious lady.

And her eyes, shimmering with tears of gratitude, came to rest on King-seng.

"Alas, mine is not the honor of having saved your precious days," replied the master of ceremonies who, unable to explain the empress's presence on the Time Ship any other way, assumed that its crew, more fortunate than he, had been cunning enough to spirit Hsien-ti's innocent victim from the dungeons.

The travelers knew that the mummy, though encased in an age-old, camphor-soaked sarcophagus that let it scoff at the backward action of time, owed its resurrection to being free of the immutability current. Still, they did not disabuse the mandarin of his belief, because it seemed rational and suited their plans.

"What then, are these the ones?" queried the empress when she was brought up to date. And she kissed Clara and Juanita in paroxysms of joy, to the great contentment of the latter who, for the first time in her life, witnessed herself made the object of a sovereign's affections.

"Yes; it is they who broke your chains. Unfortunately, they arrived too late to save your Western brother from death. As you know, his torment preceded yours."

"Poor martyr!" Sun-che managed to say in sad tribute to the man who had been her best friend.

But suddenly, raising her beautiful dark eyes and fixing them on Don Sindulfo and Benjamín who, with archeological glee, were savoring that triumph of science:

"How strange," she said. "I have seen you before. Your faces awaken in me a vague and confused memory that I cannot pin down."

"Ha! Don't you believe it, Your Highness," interrupted Juana. "These pesky Don Juans never leave our side. They're two malignant pimples that have infected my lady and me."

The polyglot, seeking a logical explanation for such an extraordinary phenomenon, supposed, and said as much to his friend, that the mummy had caught sight of them through some chink in the box when she had come back to life in the hold. But because she was fading in and out of consciousness before being fully restored to life, she had lost all sense of time and thus attributed recent events to the distant past; a gross mistake, as will be shown in the course of this incredible tale.

"But what is the meaning of this music? What do these festive preparations herald?" Sun-che asked when she heard the sounds of a gong that announced to the gathering that time was passing and the emperor's patience running out.

Then King-seng related what had been going on. He told the

sovereign lady how Hsien-ti had circulated a false account of her accidental death and was preparing for his second marriage to the foreigner, whose relatives had given their consent in exchange for the secret of immortality.

"The scoundrel is lying," thundered the empress. "What he is planning is your extermination, but he shall not succeed."

And instinctively she embraced Don Sindulfo, as if to defend him from all traps.

"Will wonders never cease; he's hooked her," Juana said to her lady. "Now let's see if that'll make the pest stop tormenting you."

"He shall not succeed," repeated the master of ceremonies, "for, sensing that you had not yet expelled your last breath, your supporters are merely awaiting the start of the marriage ceremony to launch the rebellion."

"Very well then, let us go. I shall lead you into battle."

"Half a minute," objected Benjamín, for whom the august lady's bellicose zeal meant fewer chances of success if, vanquished in the fray, he could not take possession of the coveted talisman. "Prudence dictates that we think things over carefully before plunging into a dangerous adventure."

"Agreed," said King-seng. "Your Eminence must not expose herself to risk. Everything is set to be sprung upon the tyrant when he least expects it. Let us not anticipate victory and, by so doing, turn it into defeat."

"Let's wait until he reveals the secret of immortality to us."

"Immortality?" the empress asked with a touch of pride. "And what does he know of that? He has lied to you. I alone possess the evidence the Westerner gave me, and I have known how to hide it from Hsien-ti's inspections by secreting it in the most remote parts of the palace."

"All the more reason for you to proceed with caution if your goal is to recover it. I imagine you don't want to leave such precious evidence under wraps."

"Oh, no! You speak truly. It is vital to clear up that mystery whose solution seems to lie in the West."

"How?" they all asked.

"This is not the time for explanations," Sun-che went on. "Night is falling and the tyrant must be impatient. Follow the envoys; pretend to yield to the emperor's plans. I will arrive at the palace before you and will retrieve the evidence; as soon as the ceremony begins in the Dragon Courtyard I will reveal myself to my followers. After a brief struggle, you must overpower Hsien-ti and, once I have liberated the people from an oppressor, I shall tell you who should be my companion on the throne of Fo-hi."

And so saying, she cast a glance at Don Sindulfo that froze the blood in his veins and prompted his servant to whisper in his ear:

"Good luck isn't for the seeker, it's for the finder. Long live Don Pichichi the First! What a plucky King of Clubs you'll make!"

Everyone was set to burst out in applause, but Sun-che, urging silence, dressed herself in a slave's tunic so she would not be recognized and, followed by two eunuchs she could trust absolutely, departed the Time Ship. King-seng led Clara by the hand to the litter. Once this had been closed and locked, music pierced the air and the wedding retinue slowly wended its way through the pressing crowd to the *yamen*.

It was necessary to cross fourteen courtyards to reach the imperial rooms; the one called the Courtyard of Honor was located right next to the main part of the building. In the center was the sacred dragon, a monster cast in bronze with its open maw parallel to the floor and its coiled tail disappearing heavenward. Countless kiosks bordering the area served as spectators' galleries for the mandarins and high-level dignitaries and also formed a type of bodyguard for the imperial pavilion, to which only the monarch, his family, and his prime minister had access.

All of these structures, like the imperial residence that was open to the four winds and stood at the far end above a sumptuous marble staircase adorned with blood-red jade, were richly illuminated by thousands of lanterns of every shape and size: here, a tulip and a rose that stole their colors from nature; there, dancing figures showed through an enormous globe whose walls were made of rice as trans-

Resurrection of the Dead before Judgment

parent as crystal. Beside a fish made of light that waved its tail and fins back and forth were two cocks fighting a huge battle. Here, two watermelon halves hung from an architrave, displaying their reddish flesh; there, a lobster crowned a pediment, flexing its joints. Incense burned in hundreds of censers; floral shields that looked like butterflies and winged insects perfumed the air. The entrance was guarded by the sentry gods: two gigantic figures with sinister faces and titanic muscles, whose rich dress was equaled only by their artistic candor. The Maidens' Guard surrounded the emperor's pavilion; the remaining military forces were deployed on the second level, bows across their chests and pikestaffs at their sides. The palace's lesser servants overran the gallery.

"Are you certain of what you say?" the monarch asked Tsao Pi in a low voice to avoid being overheard by his three official concubines, who were taking their seats behind him.

"The evidence will soon convince you. The rebellion is to break out this very night in the *yamen*, but it will be put down, I swear it. I know the rebels and have taken precautions."

"So, the imposters really were members of the Yellow Turbans?"

"And supporters of the empress."

At this point in their conversation the wedding party arrived and, with solemn steps, began to cross the Courtyard of Honor. When the call to attention sounded, everyone hurried to take up his or her post. Lanterns and banners formed the backdrop for this procession that ended at the betrothed's litter, at whose door walked the master of ceremonies appointed by the august consort for the presentation. Don Sindulfo, Benjamín, and Juana took advantage of their right as family members to surround the litter. The courtesans and servants followed behind, and the cavalry made up the rear.

Once the precious cargo had been deposited in the center of the courtyard and the ritual genuflections performed, King-seng delivered the palanquin's key to the monarch, who came out to meet his future bride and lead her to the pavilion. After that, the leader of the scholars read aloud Confucius' precepts about a wife's duties to her husband. While he was congratulating Hsien-ti on behalf of the academy, a melancholy song with a singular rhythm made those attending the wedding turn their heads; stunned, they saw the empress emerge from the open jaws of the sacred dragon.

Resurrection of the Dead before Judgment

"Sun-che!" exclaimed the entire court, prey to a range of emotions.

"Treason!" shouted Hsien-ti upon seeing his victim's resurrection.

But the Celestials' astonishment at regaining their empress was child's play compared to what Juanita experienced when she felt her arms gripped as though by pincers. It was Don Sindulfo and Benjamín who, with eyes popping out of their heads and their hair standing on end, were stammering between nervous spasms:

"Mamerta!"

"My wife . . . !"

Juanita thought they had gone crazy, but, no; the sages had recognized in the song's rising and falling pitch the famous and unintelligible refrain with which the banker's daughter—that mute girl of the garbanzos and inventor's wife who had drowned with her father while bathing off the beaches of Biarritz, as my readers will recall—had shattered their eardrums while she was still alive.

In vain did they search the empress's features for some trace that would proclaim kinship with the deceased. Starting with the fact that she could speak, everything about her was the complete opposite; and yet, could that rare melody possibly be reproduced with such surprising fidelity in pause and inflection by a human being born over three thousand leagues and sixteen centuries distant from the earlier example?

The two friends did not have time to rectify or ratify their impressions because the rebels' impatience, overcome by zeal, made them break out in hurrahs for Sun-che. And before the emperor's henchmen could prepare for combat, the rebels had turned their arms against them. To the misfortune of the generous liberators, Tsao Pi's foresight had seen to it that the bowstrings were coated with a corrosive substance, so that when the archers readied their bows the strings broke and the arrows fell lifeless at their feet instead of zinging through the air.

"After them!" the prime minister shouted to his men, and with no regard for hierarchy or position, the empress, the time travelers, and the insurgents were bound up with cords and their cries stifled with leather gags.

"Do you have any more accomplices?" the emperor asked Clara, who with desperate efforts was protesting her innocence.

"Understand," Hsien-ti added, "that my wedding was but a pretext to uncover your plot. Only confession will save your life. Answer me."

Clara shook her head.

"Your orders?" asked Tsao Pi of the tyrant.

"Do your duty," replied the latter after a brief pause. "And so that my people can see that nothing makes me flinch where the health of the state is concerned, begin the sacrifice with the rebellious empress and the disguised Yellow Turban sympathizers."

And while they forced the prisoners to kneel before the dragon, a column of archers broke off from the imperial forces and volunteered to carry out the slaughter.

They indeed took aim; but when the emperor gave the order to fire, they turned their weapons against him and the ferocious Hsien-ti fell lifeless to the floor, riddled with arrows and bathed in blood. His terrified soldiers, in the grip of the superstitious belief that when the leader dies his troops will never see victory, scattered in flight, Tsao Pi's forces powerless to stop them. Sun-che's defenders, whom the archers had freed of their bonds, hastened after them to finish off the job.

Meanwhile, the innocent victims, restored to life, were hugging one another and weeping with emotion. Gesturing because their voices were caught in their throats, they gave thanks to their saviors.

"To whom do we owe our lives?" Clara at last managed to ask.

"Long live Spain!" shouted seventeen voices. And the archers, removing their outfits, showed themselves to be the sons of Mars in all their glory.

"It's them!" their fellow Spaniards cried upon beholding that wonder, even more phenomenal than the previous ones.

"You! And life-sized!" repeated Juanita, never tiring of looking at Pendencia and taking the measure of his chest with her arms.

"What, didja think my heart shrinks in th' face of danger?"

Clara, in her joy, was on the brink of fainting; but as women have a talent for seizing opportunities, she lost consciousness only to the degree strictly necessary to require resting her head on Luis's shoulder for support. Benjamín was rambling on about the phenomenon's causes and Don Sindulfo was foaming at the mouth and bellowing:

"How is it that you all are here?"

"Well hey, didn't we all travel together?"

"I shall explain," said the empress. "When I made my way to the palace, I saw them patrolling near the postern gate. I knew by their clothing that they were with you and they, understanding my intentions through my gestures, prepared to carry out my plans, which were to watch over you."

"But that isn't what I mean," the tutor shouted, growing more and more heated. "How is it that after evaporating en route you reappear whole in China?"

"This isn't the time for explanations," Benjamín declared, fearing some new complication. "Did you bring proof of immortality?"

"Yes," Sun-che replied.

"What matters most, then, is to get out of danger."

"To the Time Ship!" they all proposed.

"But it doesn't work!"

"Who knows? We'll find out when we get there," argued Benjamín, certain of what awaited them. "The main thing is to batten ourselves down in a safe place."

And the empress, cozying up to Don Sindulfo, said, "Let us go," adding: "Free of the monster, she who once possessed an empire will now be able to abandon herself to the irresistible attraction she feels for you and will be proud to call herself your slave."

All it took for the sage to lose the rest of his marbles was to hear that declaration at point-blank range. And he might well have done something regrettable, given the state his mind was in, had not the clanking of arms announced the enemy's nearness and the need for flight. So they flanked the ladies by columns formed of the strong sex and, some of them giving in to rightful pleasure and others to despair, they took the path to the Time Ship, which they reached without further mishap.

In order to finish the account of the civil conflict between the Taosse and the scholars, we can say that Hsien-ti's followers recovered from their stupefaction and wound up defeating Sun-che's supporters, who were discouraged by their sovereign lady's disappearance and by the lack of a captain to lead them into battle. Tsao Pi, seeing the orphaned throne, climbed its steps, placed the imperial hat on his head, and founded the seventh dynasty, known to history by the name of *Wei*.

CHAPTER 16

Where All Is Explained and All Is Entangled

THE situation on board had changed completely. The young women danced for joy when they saw the crew had expanded in, for their taste, such a pleasant manner; and even the empress made no secret of how much she was enjoying her widowhood. The soldiers, lulled asleep by Cupid, were beginning to forget their past misadventures; and Benjamín, so close to achieving his goal, thanked the situation that had brought him so near to finishing his work, now that all obstacles had been removed from his path since he was, for all intents and purposes, the head of the expedition.

And to be sure, from the moment they entered the Time Ship, Don Sindulfo, who had not opened his mouth once during the trip, collapsed onto a chair in an alarmingly dejected manner. One moment he would stare at the floor as if in meditation and another his wild glossy eyes would wander from one person to the next as if in menace. Hundreds of confused thoughts vied for attention as they crossed his overheated brain; the veins on his forehead pulsated irregularly, now formulating a theory to find a scientific explanation for so many inexplicable events, now ranting and raving in blind jealousy, demanding revenge.

"Looks t' me like Don Pichichi's got a screw loose upstairs," said Pendencia who, like the others, had noticed the state of the tutor.

"Your own hat holder's in no better shape," retorted Juanita, addressing Benjamín. "To think that just now, when the Chinese wanted to stick it to us, these two gentlemen thought they recognized Don Sindulfo's deceased wife, may she rest, etc. etc. Can you believe such nonsense?"

"We'll discuss that later," answered the polyglot, somewhat peeved. "Not knowing the causes doesn't allow us to negate their effects."

"What?"

"On this implausible trip what seems absurd may in fact be rational. Let's give ourselves some time."

Just then they heard a piercing scream and saw Sun-che trying her best to release her arm from Don Sindulfo's tight, trembling grasp. The poor woman, led by her instinctive love for the sage, had tried to offer him a caress and the wretched madman had treated her as some sane men treat their wives just because they are wives. But, overcome by a nervous convulsion, the victim was waving her free limbs around so forcefully that the unlucky presumed husband got more than a few kicks in the shins, plus a collection of double punches from his mouth to the nape of his neck. His nose, being the most prominent point, was not exactly spared, either.

"It's her! It's her!" shouted Don Sindulfo releasing her at last and running to join his family. "It's Mamerta! Do you remember how we couldn't go against her will without suffering the consequences of her anger, and how she always managed to do as she pleased?"

"Calm down, my friend, calm down," Benjamín kept saying, no less interested than the tutor in the similarities the sovereign shared with the Zamoran banker's daughter. "As long as we can't explain rationally or scientifically how a run-of-the-mill Spanish woman who drowned in the nineteenth century can also be a Chinese empress in the third century, we should consider the whole thing to be pure coincidence."

"For pity's sake, mister," argued Juana, "that's just what happens to every woman. It's written in the dreary rulebook of our sex. Why, if you hadn't been my employer, the minute you took us out of Paris I would've flown into a rage and smashed that noggin of yours."

"And she's got th' paws t' do it!" added Pendencia, pointing to Juanita's clenched fists.

"Would the deceased by any chance have a more distinctive feature so that we could assess how the empress compares with her?" asked the Captain of Hussars, who was as baffled as the rest of them.

"Try to think," insisted Clara.

Don Sindulfo collected himself for a moment and, after thinking hard for a while:

"That's it," he exclaimed, smacking his forehead, and from the back of his lapel he pulled out a threaded needle he was in the habit of carrying in case he needed to attach index cards to the catalog. And before the present company could ask about his intentions, he approached Sun-che, who was resting after the incident.

"Please stitch this back on for me," he asked roughly tearing a button off his frock coat and presenting it to the empress while eyeing her closely so as not to miss a second of the experiment.

Not being able to follow what was going on around her, the good lady was starting to get bored so, considering it a curiosity, she picked up the button. But when she noticed the sewing utensil she let out a sharp scream and, dropping her head onto her chest, fell swooning into her chair. As an astonished Benjamín told the amazed travelers, this particular exploit was, as we said at the beginning of this tale, typical of the mute lady's nature.

"There is no doubt indeed!" Don Sindulfo, writhing like a snake, kept shouting. "It's the same horror before threaded needles that never let her mend even a pair of my socks."

"One can tell the banker held a professorship in laziness," said the maid under her breath while the troubled Don Sindulfo, muttering incoherent phrases, hitting everything in his path, frothing at the mouth and with his eyes shooting flames, walked wildly to his study in search of a solution to the problem.

They all hurried after him but stopped before the slammed door. They then resolved to help the empress, a precaution that proved useless since the noble lady—one would think someone had whispered it in her ear—had recovered her perfect health the moment the needle vanished.

The Time Ship

"I assume," said Luis to the polyglot, "that in the state my uncle is in, you won't tell him where the expedition is headed."

"Heaven forbid! He could take his anger out on us," said Clara.

"With that mule driver steering th' cart, we're sure t' tip over."

"Don't you worry," argued Benjamín. "I'm too interested in the matter to entrust victory to a madman."

"What? Has he lost his mind?" asked the others.

"I'm afraid so. And yet, I haven't given up hoping to save him. Trust me."

And asking Sun-che to come near the immutability machine while the travelers commented on the situation, he gave her a few shots of current, which must have upset her, too, judging by the nervous blows she rained down on the antiquarian's skull. Immediately afterwards, he removed the object that impeded the wheel's action and, after elevating the vehicle to the atmospheric zone where movement could take place, he suddenly stopped the Time Ship and proclaimed:

"Let's decide where we're headed."

"To Paris!" was the unanimous cry.

"Egg-zackly. To Paree t' shut th' genius up in a nuthouse and get a priest t' throw his nupshell blessing our way."

"Before we do that," Benjamín argued, "let's see if the main goal of our expedition has been achieved."

"And what would that be?"

"Obtaining the secret of immortality the empress offered us."

Pressed to explain herself, she produced a parchment scroll where an expert hand had drawn the map of a city.

"What's this?" asked the anxious archeologist fearing some deception.

"Some old skin from the drum a shepherd used to celebrate Jesus' birth at Bethlehem," said Juanita.

"But, the formula!" insisted Benjamín impatiently to Sun-che.

"The Westerner didn't have the chance to initiate me in that mystery, since he was taken by surprise by my tyrannical husband. But when he guaranteed the effectiveness of the active ingredient, he told me that one of his ancestors had buried the proof of immortality in

All Is Explained and All Is Entangled

Pompeii under an emperor's tomb that was marked on the scroll by a red circle."

"Yes, here it is," interrupted Benjamín pointing to a circular stain on the papyrus under which one could read in proper Latin: *Nero's stone effigy.*

"It seems," the empress continued, "that this information was passed down through several generations without anyone daring to validate it, until the fearless martyr whose death we all regret decided to unveil it. But, having been accused of desecration when he was caught just as he was about to dig up the statue, he narrowly managed to escape prison and get as far as my dominions, where I was lucky enough to meet him. A secret expedition to his homeland to retrieve the mysterious talisman was already in the works when the end you all know of came about to destroy our plans."

"There are still people alive to put those plans into action," said Benjamín, his eyes sparkling with excitement. And addressing his companions he added: "To Pompeii!"

His cry caused a few protests, but happiness is so accommodating and the traveler's wish to tour the past so natural, now that they were free from the perils they had suffered up until then, that once the grumbling stopped, Benjamín started up the vehicle and directed it towards the pampered, happy daughter of the merry Gulf of *Neapolis.*

The seven hours that it would take the time travelers to cover the one hundred and forty-one years separating the start of the third century from the latter part of the first was not long enough to bore people who had so much to tell each other and so many wonders to admire. Led by Juanita, the neophytes proceeded to make an inspection tour of the Time Ship while Benjamín, once things settled down, looked for the cause of those extraordinary occurrences.

The first thing he tried to explain was the reappearance of the once-vanished soldiers. Thus he thought back in time and, trying his best as a logical man, told himself that if the consequence was anomalous, its origin must of necessity also be out of the ordinary. Now then, what extraordinary circumstance had taken place during the voyage? Im-

The Time Ship

mediately he remembered the retroactive impulse he himself gave to the Time Ship right after the Rifeños disaster when, thinking he was traveling to the past, he had in fact been going toward the present up until their arrival at Versailles on the eve of their departure. Light had been shed, darkness conquered: his logic was perfect.

And, indeed, if my readers remember the incident of the Moorish coin (the one that was lost by a Kabyle and disappeared as soon as it reached the instant it was minted, only to show up again when the Time Ship, on its way to the present, went beyond the minute it was issued), they will understand how the phenomenon of the resurrection of the sons of Mars had the same explanation. Having evaporated when going backwards in time, they had lost their human form; yet, their immortal spirit had not abandoned the Time Ship, just as the wheat kernel hiding in a clod of earth, though invisible, remains in the soil until the time comes for its germination. That is why, as the vehicle traveled towards today and the hour of the soldier's birth came, the flesh answered its chronological call and the kernel, breaking through the earth, revealed its stem to become a strong reed and turn once again into an ear of wheat.

How they escaped a second vanishing after Benjamín, noticing their absence, found the right path again can be easily explained. The soldiers, having seen themselves shrink and expand by turns, once they recovered their own size were keen on not losing it again, so, bent on imploring science to give them shelter, they went up to the laboratory. But once they got to the hall they heard the explanation about immutability Benjamín was giving the Parisian women and, since the Captain of Hussars knew a bit of Physics, he gave himself and his companions a few jolts of the fluid. He, very wisely, thought that if they were to remain hidden they would serve the cause of the imprisoned maidens better than if they showed themselves and were exposed to any eventuality the tutor's jealousy might cause. And, hidden in their rabbit holes, they arrived in China just in time to avert a catastrophe.

Benjamín jotted down these observations in his personal notebook, but carefully refrained from making them known, preferring

All Is Explained and All Is Entangled

instead to let everyone believe in a magical explanation rather than confess his own ineptitude.

The second problem had a more difficult solution. After sixteen centuries, how could a Chinese empress appear before his eyes so physically different yet so evidently similar in structure to that Mamerta who had drowned on the beach at Biarritz? The polyglot was enthralled by such metaphysical concepts, and the trip was drawing to a close without him having been able put two and two together when some terrible howls coming from Don Sindulfo's cabin snapped him out of his reverie.

"The madman! The madman!" shouted the travelers who, having heard all the noise, rushed in looking for Benjamín.

"Yes. What could be the trouble?"

"Some type of brain cramp," said the Andalusian.

And they all instinctively turned towards the room. But they had not yet moved any further when the door opened and Don Sindulfo, suit crumpled, hands tense and face flushed purple with rage, ran into the laboratory screaming at the top of his lungs:

"Damnation! Now I see how Sun-che may be my dear departed Mamerta."

"How?"

"Through metempsychosis!"

Those not in the know failed to understand a single word, but the polyglot remained still, thoughtfully weighing faith against doubt.

"What in the world do you mean by that?"

"Metempsychosis!" continued the sage dismissing all comments. "The transmigration of souls, through which the spirit of those who die goes into the body of another animal, one rational or foul according to the person's merits in life."

"Ay!" said Juanita. "Then, since you've been such a pest to us, you two will end up at the Madrid flea market."

"Do you mean," asked his already interested nephew, "that because of a series of transmigrations the empress became your wife in her last incarnation?"

"Exactly. And when we go back in time she shows herself in the real body she occupied at this time, just as we could have met her as a vegetable or a pack mule among the luggage when we made our stopover in Africa."

"Allow me to disagree," said Benjamín. "We are Christians and our dogma rejects those theories, but she is Chinese and a Buddhist, therefore she may be able to transmigrate as her religion prescribes. Because who is to say that Providence doesn't impose its punishments according to one's particular beliefs?"

Everyone except Sun-che, who seemed oblivious to what was happening, understood that the poor doctor had lost his mind. Only Benjamín, who as a scientist was excited about the discovery of that kind of experimental metaphysics, ended up agreeing with the madman, which essentially meant almost losing his own mind in the process.

"That's just it. Eureka!" he screamed, Archimedes-like, and hugged his friend.

"But Mamerta didn't speak," insisted Juanita, "and this one gives speeches like a congressman."

"Not really; 'cause if her husband can't figger out what she's saying, she might as well be moot."

"Besides," said Luis with a smile, "if she lost the power of speech back then, it might have been a punishment sent by the god Buddha for having abused it during an earlier existence."

"So," argued Clara trying to use the situation to break out of her chains, "you'll just have to stop chasing me, because you are joined in holy matrimony to that lady. You won't dare marry me, since our religion forbids bigamy."

The doctor, feeling pressed on the very point that had worried him ever since he had discovered the affinity between Mamerta and the empress, flew off the handle when provoked by Clara's arguments and his mood changed from single-minded serenity to dizzy fury.

"Me, give up the love to which I've dedicated the full force of my life, my actions, my intellect?" he kept saying, clenching his fists and rolling his eyes. "Oh, never!"

"Watch out fer his bite!" interrupted Pendencia carefully stepping to one side of the raving sage, who came after them all saying:

All Is Explained and All Is Entangled

"No. If Providence is against me, I'll fight it. But you will be my wife even though I have to become a criminal to achieve it."

"It's no good," said the daring Maritornes. "Even if you cut our throats, the dead come back to life here."

"Well then, we will all perish. We need to put an end to this situation."

"How?"

"There are ten barrels of gunpowder in the ship's hold. I'll put a match to them, and there will be no trace of the Time Ship left."

"Don't be such a monster!"

"Calm down, everyone," cried Benjamín remembering the episode that forced him to land a few times in search of supplies while traveling from Africa to China. "The provisions, once rendered immutable, become useless, as I myself have experienced."

"You idiot!" barged in the madman recovering his wits for a minute.

"What?"

"If you squirt more fluid over the bodies so that the previous currents come into contact with the new and become one, you need only rotate the transmitting disk counterclockwise to collect them all and, once neutralized, the provisions will get their natural properties back."

"That's good to know, but it's a lost cause."

"We have to sink the Santa Barbara."[54]

"Let's run for it."

"No, don't be afraid," said the tutor switching from threats to pleas. "A blast would kill us all, and I don't want her to die. I will respect her life. But you," he said looking at the soldiers and the empress and returning to his previous frantic mood as fiercely as ever, "prepare to suffer my revenge. You are obstructing my happiness and I will destroy you so I may see my plans through, even if I have to cross rivers of blood in order to get Clara to the altar. Oh! I've got it now! . . ."

And with this, he headed for the ship's hold at a furious pace. His companions, clearly leery of imminent danger, ran after him intent on restraining him.

Leading his men, Luis was the first to reach the hold. But reveling

The Time Ship

in his plans, the doctor had cunningly already hidden himself, and as soon as he saw the sons of Mars and his nephew enter the room, opened the cleaning hatch. The seventeen heroes then disappeared into space, followed by cries from the enamored ladies and Benjamín who, running after them, could only witness the ghastly disaster.

"Let's save ourselves!" was the general cry, no one daring lose courage while facing such a serious situation. And they all rushed for the stairs. But Benjamín, having noticed that Don Sindulfo was trying to head them off by going up the rear spiral staircase, told the three deathly pale women to wait there for him. And, climbing like a monkey up the outer ridges of the machine, he went through the laboratory skylight, stopped the Time Ship dead, cautiously replaced the insulator, went back down the same way, opened the door, and he and his comrades in misfortune left that deadly place behind before the madman could find them missing.

Amid so many setbacks, luck was on their side. They had arrived in Pompeii.

CHAPTER 17

Bread and Circuses

Titus, succeeding his progenitor, had only been emperor of Rome for a few months. In his mercy this generous prince, who considered the day lost if he had not performed some good deed, was beginning to erase the bloody memory of Nero and the sordid avarice of his father, Vespasian.

The victor in the Siege of Jerusalem, "the delight and darling of the human race,"[55] as he was called, Titus had outlawed the persecution of the Nazarenes begun by Tiberius and eclipsed by Agrippa's son. Despite this, the torments did not entirely cease.

The provinces, governed by arbitrary prefects armed with supreme authority and hiding behind total unaccountability, indulged in blood sports, at times to satisfy the natural instincts of the plebian class, at times to aid and abet the praetorians' secret plans. This was the state of affairs in Pompeii.

The Pompeians busied themselves not with political squabbles but with beautifying their city, the summer residence of the patrician families of Campania and Lazio, in order to attract the floating population that was so profitable to them. And such was their mania for preserving public ornamentation that, when all Italy set about demolishing statues of Nero upon that monster's fall, Pompeians respected, without deifying, the ones on their streets that had any claim to artistic notoriety. But the more the dark and misty breath of summer blew the levantine citizens of Naples and Salerno toward Vesuvius's slopes, the more passions ignited, and for four months Pompeii outdid the city of Rome in civil discord.[56]

In those days the Pompeians' prefect was a senator who had sold out to Domitian's cause. Two years later Domitian, that second Caligula, would hasten his brother Titus's death, enshrining him among the gods while at the same time vilifying him among mere mortals. Pretending to submit to the emperor's plans, the conniving prefect wasted no opportunity to stoke the fires of disobedience so as to favor the ambitious plans of his Cain-like benefactor.

The grape harvest festivals had begun, celebrated throughout the farmlands of Italy from the third of September to the third of October. The time of the major games was approaching and with it came public discontent, not only because the games' end signaled the summer vacationers' resentful return to everyday tasks but also because, under Titus's reign, the circuses were no longer the lugubrious hecatombs where the Romans guzzled down their bloodthirsty inspiration. Scaled back to running, jumping, discus throwing, and boxing, they lacked the gladiators, beast fighters, chasers, and swordfighters with their dust, roars, blood, and corpses.

But there were other circumstances as well. A fire in Rome had consumed the Capitol, the Library of Augustus, and the Theater of Pompey, along with other monuments of lesser importance.[57] Titus promised that everything would be rebuilt at his expense; to keep his word, he even sold the furniture in his palace, refusing the donations offered by his imperial cities and allied princes. Public enthusiasm knew no bounds and celebrations were held everywhere to honor the emperor's largesse. But Domitian's henchmen, taking advantage of such an auspicious chance to ridicule the sovereign's mercy, incited the masses to demand so insistently that their favorite blood sports

Bread and Circuses

be reinstated that Titus had to give in to the general uproar. At the inauguration of his celebrated amphitheater, he made gifts of gladiators, naval battles, and some five thousand wild beasts. Egged on by the prefect, the Pompeians contributed a great deal to this painful reconquest.

It was twilight on the seventh of September in the year AD 79. The ceryx[58] in charge of maintaining order was hurrying around to each post urging the sentries to maintain public safety without stopping the torrents of people who, streaming out of the baths, the Basilica, the temples of Jupiter and Hercules, the shops on the Avenue of Plenty, and the shabby dwellings along the Street of Good Fortune, were trooping toward the praetor's house carrying fiery torches and shouting like in Caesar's Rome:

"*Panem et circenses!*"

The prefect, wishing to conceal his handiwork behind a veil of legality, showed up at the palace door surrounded by his praetorian guard. He was preceded by six Roman *lictors* wearing short cloaks, who propped their *fasces* against their left shoulders and with their right hands cleared a path through the groups with their staffs.

"To the forum," the prefect said, and he headed towards the general assemblies, followed by the crowd that kept shouting:

"*Panem et circenses!*"

In that sanctuary of public opinion, an orator stated their demand in the name of all the citizens of Pompeii.

"You do know," argued the prefect, "that the laws forbid it?"

"Hear me," replied the magistrate who had the floor, "if the people become languorous and soft, when the time comes for battle they won't have the strength to open the Janus temple gates."

"No more *quadriga* races!"

"No more discus."

"We want fighters!" was the unanimous cry.

And since their exasperation was threatening to turn into mutiny, the prefect granted them the *andabates* who, fighting blindfolded or with their eyes covered by armor, presented less risk.

"No! Gladiators!" insisted the fevered crowd.

And the besieged prefect, pretending to bow to circumstances, gave in to the cries of the populace. But as weakness from those in power signals the downtrodden to press their advantage:

"*Bestiarii!*"[59] cried a few, and before long it had become the general chorus. And between one concession and another, the Pompeians regained not only the *laquearii* (who hunted and ensnared their adversaries with skillful throws of a slippery lasso) and the *retiarii* (who, with trident in one hand and throwing net in the other, entangled their antagonists to finish them off once they had been defeated), but they also got back the fierce wild beasts that tore the flesh off prisoners of war to the applause of the abominable crowd or used their teeth to rip a pathway to glory for the sublime martyrs of the Christian faith.

Because of the people's impatience, the following day was set for the renewed spilling of blood in the amphitheater. Since the urgency of the demand left no time for the furloughed state gladiators—whose upkeep was paid by the Treasury—or for *postulatitii*[60]—preferred by the public for their greater skill—to get in shape, they had to resort to fighters maintained by private businesses that rented them out for profit.

As for the *bestiarii*, since there was a shortage of war prisoners and criminals condemned to this type of fight, they decided to substitute them with slaves and people either accused of impiety or suspected of following the doctrine of the so-called Imposter from Galilee.

With the prefect restored in triumph to the praetorium and all hails to the emperor having been drunk, the inebriated crowd retired to their homes to await the morrow. Pompeii remained sunk in that calm that presages all terrible storms.

That was the instant when the fugitives from the Time Ship entered the city, sliding like shadows across the volcanic pavers of its straight and elegant avenues.

Benjamín pursued his scientific ends with the mulishness of an Aragonese sage, even in the midst of the greatest calamities. In preparing for flight he had provisioned himself with a pickaxe, and now he strode under the light of the waxing moon consulting the map of his theater of operations. Sun-che, who in addition to having witnessed the tragic disappearance of the soldiers had, thanks to the polyglot, been caught up in the doctor's madness, leaned against her interpreter's left arm, tired to death and consumed by sad thoughts. Hanging from the sage's right arm and dragging herself along rather than walking came the one most worthy of compassion: the hapless pupil who, for a few brief hours, had touched the seventh heaven of her dreams only to be pitched from the highest heights to the lowest depths of despair.

Juana was the only one who, despite the gravity of the situation, did not lose heart.

"Just you wait," she said, "maybe we'll see them reappear someplace dressed like Jews on a Holy Week float."

"No, this time we've lost them forever."

"Huh! Those guys are like that bird, the *Felix*, that they say gets reborn after being burned to *asses*."

"Here at last," exclaimed Benjamín, stopping at a *quadrivium* or four-way intersection. In its center rose the statue of Nero that faced the gate of Hercules at the far end of the Street of Domitian.

The Time Ship

The impatient sage invited the travelers to rest while he went about his excavations. Clara and Sun-che lay back against a stone bench near a fountain that flowed with a gentle murmur; lost in thought, each was soon, if not quite asleep, then dozing off.

Juanita, hoping to see Pendencia appear in the form of a centurion or draconarius,[61] kept the archeologist company, making his work lighter with her caustic jibes.

The treasure's location was so perfectly indicated on the map that within a scant half hour of breaking the earth the pickaxe struck a resistant body.

Benjamín, his heart in his mouth, unearthed a small, uninscribed metal box that proved to be merely the case for some precious object. Opened at last in an atmosphere of tremendous anxiety, the polyglot drew forth a handful of slender cords that were knotted every so often. A glance sufficed to show that the pattern of knots was not random. The sage gave a shout of surprise.

"Shoelaces!" said Juanita. "Gosh, don't they make you want to hang yourself?"

"Be quiet, you ignoramus."

"At least use them to credit yourself a dozen disciplinary lashes."[62]

"Do you know what this is?"

"Now you're going to say it's a pound of noodles from the days of Solomon . . ."

"This is the first form of writing used by man, a legacy given to humanity by Fo Hsi, as the Chinese call him, or as we say, Noah, when he left the ark. This is the prototype of the written word revealed to the erudite by the paleographer Shuckford in the Academy of Inscriptions."

And with true scientific furor, Benjamín prepared to decipher the puzzle. Unfortunately, a thick cloud eclipsed the slender ray of light from the moon as it was preparing to slip beyond the western horizon. Mere touch being inadequate to the task, he had to postpone his project.

"But tell me this, what kind of inkwell did those *pototripes* use? Haven't people always written in the same way?"

Bread and Circuses

"Not in the least. To the best of our knowledge, there are three known ways of writing: along a perpendicular line; orbicular or round; and horizontally. But these three great branches can be subdivided into many variants."

"Lord! And here am I, who can only write a letter on lined paper or I get all twisted around."

As the cloud still insisted on leaving him in the dark, Benjamín, as much to distract himself from inaction as to give in to his natural inclinations, began to lecture as though he were in a paleography course: "Carrasco's Mythology says the Indians from Trapobana Island, according to Diodorus of Sicily, write using straight perpendicular lines.[63] Du Halde[64] states that the Chinese and Japanese, though also using the perpendicular, write like the Hebrews, from right to left; therefore, their books begin where ours end. The northerners or Scythians carved in rock their letters—called runes—using curved lines and joining them from the top downward and vice versa, but obliquely or in spiral form. According to Nienhoff, the Tartars, whose consonants are similar to the Ethiopians' because they are linked to the vowels, write along the perpendicular from right to left; the Mongols go from top to bottom, in Trevoux's opinion. The Giro del Mondo[65] says the inhabitants of the Philippine Islands and Malacca begin in the opposite direction, from bottom to top and from left to right. And Acosta claims the Mexicans used a perpendicular line that ran the entire page, from top to bottom. They also knew the use of slender cords dyed assorted colors and knotted and tied in various ways, according to the importance of the event they were describing; this custom was common among all the savages of the American continent. The great Peruvian civilizations, says Baltasar Bonifacio, used the aforementioned cords like the North Americans did. They were stored in archives arranged and tended by the learned and were consulted for all events worthy of being transmitted to posterity."

"Wait a second," Juanita interrupted. "Is this parade going to be very long?"

"If it bothers you we'll stop."

"Not at all. It doesn't bother me because whatever I don't understand just goes in one ear and out the other. But if you don't mind, I will sit down. Ok, so we'd gotten up to the savages of incontinent America."

He looked at her with pity and continued: "Moving on to the second system, then. Pausanias and Bimard de la Bastie claim the Greeks were familiar with orbicular writing as known through the inscription on Iphito's shield,[66] said to postdate the siege of Troy by 300 years. Maffei says the Etruscans or ancient Tuscans also used it. The most remote northern peoples linked their writing from the top down and vice versa, but also in oblique lines or spirals. And the lack of difficulty in accepting those characters as true runes legitimates the inscriptions that Pausanias himself cites as having lines very similar to those of the northern tribes. The Greek inscriptions on the monument erected in Olympus by the Cypselids were difficult to read because of their multiple curves."

"The same thing happened to me with Pendencia's letters, and they were written on lined paper. Every line was like a station of the Cross: if it were in Latin, you'd mistake it for *articular* writing."

"Let's take the horizontal," resumed the sage.

And Juanita, thinking it an order that was starting to flatter her, stretched full out along the streambed as if she were on the softest of mattresses.

"I'm not falling asleep, no sir," she put in when she understood by Benjamín's odd twitch that she had misunderstood. "You go on, if I get bored I'll tell you to stop."

Benjamín searched for the moon; but as it was still concealed, he halfheartedly resumed his dissertation.

"Well, then. Writing along a horizontal line encompasses various traditions: the first-period boustrophedon, right to left; the second through fourth periods, left to right; and the aratory, which combines its predecessors, back and forth along parallel lines with all margins aligned with the starting point."

"Such drama! You know, one of those texts would look like a military drill."

"Orientals have always written from right to left, like the Etruscans, excepting the Armenians and the inhabitants of Indostan, who do it from left to right. Pelasgo's, Cecrope's, and Cadmo's methods have all shown that the Greeks follow the Oriental of the two styles, because when they write several lines they go from right to left. That's the direction the Huns used."

"And the Huthers?"

"I am speaking of the Huns, known today as the *zikulos* on the Transylvanian side."

"Oh, right! Go on, I don't know about them."

"The Ethiopians or Abyssinians, the Siamese, and the Tibetans write from left to right; these last ones, almost horizontally. Two notable inscriptions show us boustrophedon writing from the first period, known among the Gauls and the Franks as well. The first was found in the ruins of the temple of *Apollo Amyklaios* in Amykles, a Laconian city, around AD 1400. The second, mentioned by Muratori, consists of the Nointel or Baudelot marble discovered in 1672 in an Athenian church; the marble fixes the date at around 457 BC.

Throughout history and even today, characters have been written upon a range of materials: the pelts of four-legged beasts, prepared in diverse ways; fish skins; the intestines of snakes and other animals; linen and silk cloth; the leaves, bark, and wood of trees; the leaves and stalks of plants; bones, marble, common and precious stones; metal; glass; wax; brick; pottery and plaster."

"Well, as for characters, although mine isn't among the worst, if Don Sindulfo doesn't get our soldiers back you'll see how maidservants use fingernails to write on sage hide."

"Marble, bronze, and metal sheets or laminates were in common use by the Greeks and Romans; using animal hide dates from the time of Job. Du Halde says that, before the invention of paper, the Chinese wrote on wooden slabs and bamboo tablets. According to Flavius Josephus, the pyramids and obelisks and the columns of the Babylonians' astronomical observatories were made of marble, stone, and brick. Solon's laws were inscribed on wood; those of the Romans, on bronze; three thousand of them were lost when the Capitol burned. Northern tribes recorded their runic inscriptions on stone and rock.

Lead writing appears during the time of the Flood. Writing on marble has been preserved in diptychs or two-paneled tablets—politychs exceed this number. According to Pliny, people also wrote upon the leaves of palm trees and certain malvaceae. Similarly, claims Alfonso Costadan, in some regions of the East Indies they write upon macaranga leaves, which are six feet long by one foot wide. Michael Boim says the inhabitants of Fort Mieu, near Bengal and Pegu,[67] do the same thing using the areca, a species of palm tree, and the bark of a tree called the avo. Those who live in the kingdom of Siam and Cambodia, along with the Philippine islanders (although this latter group follows the Spanish method) use a bodkin or knife to scratch their characters onto palm or banana leaves or the smooth part of sugarcane. The Syracusans did it on olive leaves and the Athenians on shells. In Athens, relates Suidas, the names of the brave who had fallen in defense of the homeland were inscribed on Minerva's veil."

"Oh, *that* must make the poor dear's shawl look good. Come on! That veil must have been made out of dark glass and the writing done on the inside."

"According to Philostratus, the Indians wrote on their *sindoni*, as they called their cloth or garments."

"Ay! I've always seen them naked; in pictures, I mean."

"The Jews were particularly skilled at joining together the sections of a parchment so one could see no seams at all. This is why, adds Flavius Josephus, Ptolemy was filled with admiration when the seventy elders, sent by the high priest, unfurled the law scrolls before him, all written out in letters of gold. Nevertheless, drypoint engraving, without the aid of ink or other colors, seems to have been the first process. The Chinese mountain people of *Kuei-cheu* use that method on tablets of very soft wood. The Parthians inscribed letters onto their garments with a needle, not using the papyrus they could have found in abundance in Babylonia."

"Since you're driving me crazy with so many foreign names, at least explain some of those overblown phrases that are making my head feel as lumpy as a cobblestone street."

"Papyrus is a species of cane that resembles the typha that thrives

Bread and Circuses

in low, wet places. Its woody roots are usually ten feet long; its triangular stalk, while under water, measures no more than two codos,[68] though altogether it can reach four or five. Through various processes it was made into paper, never exceeding its stipulated length of two feet. The tools used for writing have been, with minor differences, the same ones we use today, namely ruler, compass, lead, scissors, penknife, sharpening stone, sponge, stylus or punch, feather or cane, inkwell or writing box, lectern, and little glass bulbs or bottles, one containing a thinning agent for the ink and another the vermilion or red used at the beginning of chapters. The stylus, stylus graphium, and the burin, cœlum celtes, were used for dry or inkless writing; they were later used on marble, metals, and on tablets of various shapes and sizes prepared with gypsum and wax. Arundo cane, juncus rushes, and calamus fronds were used for writing with ink before the use of feathers was known. The juncus or calamus could be found in profusion in Egypt, Knidos, and Lake Amaya in Asia, says Pliny. The Greeks had them brought from Persia. Gathered in Aurac in the month of March, they would leave them to harden for six months in the muck or manure, by this fashion acquiring a beautifully marbled varnish of black and deep yellow."

Just then came the sound of a snore, but Benjamín, drunk on oratory, did not stop until he had finished his account. "The use of goose, swan, turkey, and crane feathers," he resumed like a shot, "seems to date from the fifth century. The Siamese used the pencil. The Chinese, then and now, use a rabbit-hair brush, finding it softer and superior. The only attributes that ink from remote times has in common with ours are the color and the rubber that went into making it. It was called *atramentum scriptorium* or *librarium*, to distinguish it from *atramentum sutorium* or *calchantum*. Black was made from resin smoke, from fish, tartar, burnt marble, and ground-up charcoal, whose ingredients, in fusion, were subjected to solar action. The peoples of the Orient used poppies and alum, which Africans sometimes substituted with cuttlefish or squid ink. Allatius tells of having seen ink made from burnt goat hair that, although a bit red, had the properties of color fastness, shine, and excellent adhesion to parchment, which made it quite difficult to erase. Chinese ink, discovered 1,120 years before Christ, is extracted from a variety of materials, especially pine or burnt oil. Among Indians, the practice of decocting the limbs of what they call the dragon tree provides them with that liquor that is so...."

Benjamín had reached this point in his inexhaustible flood of words when a "Kill the sage for me," from Juanita, who was dreaming, made him realize his erudition was for naught and he brought his disquisition to an end.

That was when a man, lantern in hand, turned the corner and stepped into the *quadrivium*.

"It's the madman!" shouted Benjamín, recognizing Don Sindulfo, who had come in search of the fugitives. Upon hearing Benjamín's voice, the three sleepers awoke as though they had been violently shaken.

"Mercy!" shouted the unfortunates, hugging each other in mutual defense.

But Benjamín, for whom that beacon was like a lightning bolt to the walker lost in shadows, ran to his friend before the latter sensed his presence, shouting just like the scholar from Syracuse who, so they say, ran naked from his bath when he discovered the principle of displacement, crying out "Eureka!" again and again.

"What is this? Has my rival come back to life?" asked the lunatic, persecuted by his mania.

"No. I have found the secret of immortality. Shine your light so we can read."

And consulting the short lengths of cord, his chest puffed up when he saw that the placement of the knots corresponded to the Armenian writing style about which he felt he could pontificate.

"Well, then. What does it say?"

Benjamín, not without difficulty, read as follows: *If you wish to become immortal, go to the land of Noah and . . .*

"Damnation!"

"What is it?"

"I cannot interpret the meaning of the remaining characters. It doesn't matter," he continued in his delirium. "We shall fly to the region of the Patriarch and crack this insoluble puzzle."

"When it comes to tongues, you only know the one that comes in a stew," the imprudent Juanita allowed herself to say. Upon hearing her voice the madman, staring fixedly at the Three Graces, clenched his fists. Turning to Sun-che he said, "You, too, are in my way. But soon you'll be no more than a corpse." He was starting to leap at her when he tripped against one of the stone benches and fell flat on his face. Benjamín came to his aid while the female trinity retreated in fright to the fountain.

"This sort of thing doesn't happen among Christians," shouted the girl from Pinto with all the force of her indignation.

"She said Christians," the ceryx whispered to his followers. Attracted by the lantern light, he had been spying on the voyagers and, thanks to the links binding Spanish and Latin, was able to deduce that dire fact.

"What's going on?" everyone asked when they found themselves surrounded by guards.

"Arrest them."

Widespread terror ensued.

"I'm innocent," declared Clara.

"Respect the empress," Sun-che ordered in Chinese.

"Get that one, Señor chili pepper!" spluttered Juanita, pointing at the tutor.

But even as their cries increased in intensity, the guards bound and gagged them. They brought them thus into the presence of the

Prefect, who in an orgiastic state was savoring the delectable booty, so favorable to Domitian's cause.

"Mercy!" cried one and all, free of their bonds and falling at the intoxicated senator's feet.

"Don't excite him with your *ayes!*" said the polyglot. "He only understands Latin."

"Fine, then. *In nomine Domini nostri Jesu Cristi,*" said Juanita, scared to death but remembering the salutation with which her village priest greeted the faithful.

Bread and Circuses

"Who here speaks the name of the Imposter of Galilee?" roared the prefect, barely able to keep himself in check.

"These Christians, who have just profaned Nero's statue."

"Who is their leader?"

"This guy, the oldest one," answered Juanita, after hearing Benjamín's translation.

"Take him up to the crater and throw him into Vesuvius's entrails."

An explosion of tears and lamentations followed the savage order, but before the travelers could say a word of consolation to Don Sindulfo, he had vanished among a group of sentries charged with carrying out the decree.

"The rest of you," continued the toga-clad drunkard, "prepare to be the ones fighting the beasts in tomorrow's circus."

"Horrors! They're consigning us to the circus," translated the archeologist, covering his face with his hands while Clara fainted and Sun-che vainly sought explanations, her eyes agog.

"To the circus? Well, just hang on," put in Juana, "because if it's the Price circus, I have a cousin there who works as an usher."

"No. They're condemning us to be devoured by wild beasts."

Tied up once more, no one could utter a complaint. The guards removed the prisoners from the praetorium and the prefect, unsteady on his pins, went back to the festive hall shouting with fierce joy to his fellow revelers: "The people will have their wild animal show! The peace of Pompeii is, for now, secured."

And so it was. A few hours later, in the light of dawn, the poor tutor, feet bloody from the climb up Vesuvius, tumbled down into the volcano's deep abyss, while at the same time his traveling companions entered the amphitheater's dungeons to serve as supper for wild animals and entertainment for the basest commoners.

CHAPTER 18

Sic Transit Gloria Mundi

I will not stop to describe the amphitheater because everyone in Spain, except those blind from birth, has seen its perfect analog: a bullring. Suffice it to say that, since early dawn, the twenty thousand spectators Pompeii's arena could hold had been filling the seats in the *cunei* (the sections marked out by the *designatores* or masters of ceremonies that the *locarios* had assigned to them in accordance with their rank or position).

The *podium*, which was a kind of raised bullpen with ascending seats, extended all around the arena and was reserved for high-ranking civil servants. Presiding over it was the *cubiculum* or prefect's box, akin to the *suggestum*, the Roman emperor's throne, which was covered by a pavilion-like baldachin. This same feature, though less

Resurrection of the Dead before Judgment

lavish, was shared by those boxes occasionally occupied by a vestal virgin, a senator, or a foreign envoy.

The raised seats destined for the knights were located next to the podium, and behind these were the *popularia* or sun-facing lower tiers for the masses, although the comparison with our bullrings is not exact, since the rays of ruddy Phoebus did not bother people a bit. And not because the sun was covered by clouds, since it shone smack in the middle of the sky with such force that, though it was the eighth day of September, the air still had to be cooled like during the dog-days of summer, with a fragrant solution made of water, wine, and saffron. This fluid was piped up to the highest part of the building, a covered space reserved for women, whence it was made to mist down softly over the crowd. Nor was the eclipse due to the whim of some self-serving, class-leveling enterprise such as Casiano's who, in the year of our Lord 1874, had the gall to post this famed public notice in Madrid on the eve of an extraordinary bullfight: *By order of the authorities, it will not be sunny tomorrow.* It was simply due to the fact that canvas canopies, which in the great Roman circuses were typically made of purple silk embroidered in gold, were drawn over the spectators' heads.

Underneath the podium and circling the arena were the *caveae*, the low vaults or stalls, with their *posticoe* or gates closed by means of the *ferries clathris* or cast-iron griffins. Here they put the gladiators and wild animals destined for combat. In front of them was the *libitinensis* gate through which the dead animal fighters were carried off to the *spoliarium* where they were stripped of everything they had on.

The echoes of the bugles announced the impending arrival of the gladiators and, indeed, shortly afterwards they entered the arena in a group, saluting the audience who greeted them with a round of applause that made one think Frascuelo and Lagartijo[69] had changed clothes and that Madrileños from every barrio were summering in Pompeii. For one must remember that in every era people have chosen to either applaud or whistle in order to express their satisfaction or disapproval. And when the latter form of expression took place in the theater, the actor who was its target was obliged to take off his mask and acknowledge receipt of the disapproving sounds.

Once the parade was over, the bullring cleared and a new bugle call announced the *essedarii* who fought on chariots in the manner of the Franks and the Bretons. Afterwards came the *hoplomachi*, armed from head to toe, ready to fight their opponents, the *provocators*. Neither managed to draw blood, the whole thing coming down—to the great displeasure of the crowd—to a few minor bumps on the head. Next on show were the *myrmillos* using their Gallic lance and shield to fight the *retiarii* who, holding net and trident, chased after them shouting: "*Galle, non te peto; piscem peto,*" which means: "Gallus, I don't want you, I want your fish." This referred to a fish their rivals sported on their metal helmets. Whether the rooster had lost his spur,[70] or the fisherman was more adept on shore than at sea, the point is that during one of their scuffles, as a pair took a crack at one another, they both had the bad luck to stumble and fall at the same time. This earned them more booing and jeering than when the president spares a bull from being pierced by the picador's lance.

At last came the time for the *meridianis*, gladiators who fought at noon and offered a spectacle which, to speak technically, was called the beast of the day or specially chosen fifth bull.[71] An exceptional circumstance highlighting their importance was that both fighters were *rudiarii*, meaning that having served for three consecutive years, they had won the *rudis*, a thick, gnarled club. This was a symbol meaning the combatants were retired and did not have to report to the circus except of their own free will, as was the case on that occasion.

The applause over and the governor or prefect having given his consent, the competitors took up the *arma lusoria*, wooden swords won as prizes for various performances, and began to warm up by crossing them repeatedly in a kind of prologue called *proeludere*, as the picadors do when testing their lances against the wall. But they had to be on their toes during this operation, since as soon as the bugle sounded they would have to put down their toys, grasp their real killing gear and strike each other such divine blows as would be a blessing to see.

Those two did just that; and since both were famous matadors, it was with a great deal of effort that the luckiest one—not necessarily the strongest—gave his opponent a toreador's thrust that toppled him like a piece of lead and left him writhing on the sand.

At the sight of blood, the populace roared enthusiastically. The winner lifted his eyes to consult the audience who held the right of life or death over the loser and could pardon him by showing the palms of their hands with their thumbs hidden. But such was the bloodlust that those judges, making fists and showing their pollices, erupted in cries of *"recipere ferrum,"* "finish him off." Now the only thing missing was the prefect's endorsement of the people's cries. But the president, be it out of pity or an authoritarian whimsy to contradict, this time waved a white cloth to signal *missio*, or pardon in the name of Augustus. Such clemency was wasted, however, since the wounded man had just become a corpse. After his body was attached to hooks and dragged out of the arena by four slaves, two officials came out to offer the victor the silver palm for his valor. The spectators, believing the reward miserly, began to shout:

"*Lemnisci! Lemnisci!*"

And the prefect, so as not to offend sensibilities, conceded to their demand and arranged instead for the gladiator to be presented with the flower garlands laced by woolen cords that were the symbol of the *lemniscati*. With that, the lucky man was emancipated from slavery, joining at once the category of the *libertos*.

A murmur of satisfaction which, along with settling back in one's chair is the prelude to every crowd's favorite part of a show, signaled that it was time for the *bestiarii*.

Clara and Sun-che, overwhelmed by the horror of the situation and too low-spirited to walk, were practically carried in by some of the soldiers. Benjamín, feigning a strength he did not possess, tried to appear manly and composed by advancing at a calm pace. Juanita alone was the one who, adopting a stance unsuited to the circumstances entered the arena imitating the ease of those young men who throw themselves into the ring to run before the polled bullocks. Having escaped from various and imminent dangers, she thought herself *impermeable*, if we are to use her own expression to translate the idea of invulnerability. The success her bearing had can only be compared to the ovations bad comedies get in Madrid.

The prisoners wore short tunics and trousers, their arms and legs wrapped in leather bands like primitive Lombard warriors. In their right hands they brandished short swords and in their left a red cloth intended to excite the beasts, which may be the origin of our manner of killing in the art of Pepe-Hillo.[72]

Once brought before the prefect's cubiculum, they were made to chant three times "*morituri te salutant*". But Juanita, fond as she was of joking and wishing to show off her knowledge of Latin, mimicked a bullfighter's stance and, pretending to tip an imaginary hat with her free arm:

"*Dominus vobiscum*," she told the senator. "*A toastus so that you may blowem up like a dogus from blood sausagem indigestisbus. Salutem and scabiesum.*"

Once the speech was over and the fighters had dispersed around the ring, the guards retreated and the prefect signaled for the beasts to be released. Juanita, planting her heels before the *caveae*, readied herself as the doors opened on their hinges. But instead of desert lions from Libya, Luis and Pendencia, along with their fifteen companions-in-arms, flowed into the circus brandishing their revolvers, which had been restored by the system of dis-immutability whose use the unfortunate Don Sindulfo had shown them during his earlier fit of madness.

Seeing them and throwing themselves each at her own man, including Sun-che despite her not having one, and Benjamín who liked them all, took but an instant.

"Didn't I tell you?" cried the lass from Pinto. "They're just like asparagus spears, begging your pardon; you cut off their heads and they soon grow another."

But it was not the most auspicious of occasions for entertaining themselves with metaphors. The spectators, their expectations frustrated and realizing they were being tricked, cried out:

"That's cheating!"

And leaving their seats, they unsheathed their weapons and hastened toward the arena to take revenge with their own hands.

Luis, who had thought of everything, formed his troops into a square and, placing the women in its center, had his men fire a round before the mob reached the podium, making good use of every last bullet. There was a pause born of surprise but, since the Pompeian's valor was beyond question and they had not yet come up with an explanation for the incident, they charged on ahead vehemently, only to be met by a second volley. The fainthearted stopped; the bravest had but a single cry:

"Onward!"

And they were already climbing down into the arena when Luis ordered his men to fire over their heads as though in some sort of hunt whose outcome left them in disarray. Those modest war tools that were sending death from afar in a nonstop hail of bullets assumed a supernatural quality in the Romans' eyes that they quickly ascribed to their gods' ruthless anger. Panic and a general dispersal broke out. Such is the power of progress that granted a mere handful of men the sight of twenty thousand, world-conquering legionnaires running away from them!

The Time Ship

The amphitheater emptied. Subsequently, everyone relaxed and began to lament the tutor's misfortune. Any attempt to rescue him was deemed useless, since his death sentence must have been carried out by then. They ended up swapping explanations, especially regarding the reappearance of the sons of Mars. And that one could not be simpler.

My readers will no doubt remember the hammer blows Don Sindulfo and Benjamín heard while they surveyed the Time Ship the night they spent in China. Well, the blows came from the military men themselves who, wanting to continue their voyage in a safer hideaway than behind barricades of staple goods, had used some tarred canvas they found in the hold to build themselves a huge pouch or hammock that covered the entire space between the upper decks. These were connected to the hold through an opening disguised with its own hatch door, which was located next to the discharge chute where breathable air came in via a rubber tube through a simple hole.

"So then," Pendencia summed up, "when Don Pichichi, may he rest in peace, thought he'd hurled us into space he'd only opened th' front door to our own house."

And, after thanking God and laughing at the remark:

"Now, let's make our escape. Noah's land awaits us," said Benjamín, while removing the cords he had kept in his chest pocket throughout all of these tribulations.

Giddy with happiness, they all naturally followed him; yet, when they reached the arena door they found it shut and, judging by the screams and shouts of the mob outside, concluded that forcing it open would be unwise. Indeed, the entire populace was carrying furniture, baskets, timber, and every other device handy to build a barricade with, and was busy erecting a colossal one around the building where the time travelers were to be starved out.

The situation was dire. They returned to the bullring and had just begun a family powwow when a horrible blast reverberated in every corner of the city and a reddish purple light brightened the sky. This scared them out of their wits because, overlooking the chronological

Sic Transit Gloria Mundi

error, they assumed the blast was caused by gunpowder from mining explosives that the natives were using to blow up the building.

"Consider today's relative date," said Benjamín. "What calendar day do you think this is?"

"For us it's always Friday the thirteenth," answered Juanita.

A second commotion frightened them further. The archeologist turned deadly pale and, sniffing the slightly sulfuric odor in the air, screamed "Damnation!" while tearing at his hair.

"What's going on?" asked the travelers.

"Yes. . . . Today is . . . September the eighth in the year AD 79. . . . The year Vesuvius erupted! . . . We are witnessing the last day of Pompeii!"

He was caught in mid-sentence by a geological spasm, a volcanic aftershock that gutted the circus, brought down most of its walls and sent everyone rolling about on the arena floor. Luckily, none of them was caught under the rubble. Lava came pouring down; ashes smothered their breathing.

"Let's get out of here!" shouted Benjamín as soon as he managed to stand up. And they all rushed to get through an opening, stepping over corpses scorched by the eruption, ignoring the cries of the dying and the despair of the living.

The Time Ship

Since the immutable state they all shared made them immune to any physical influence, they were able to reach the Time Ship unhindered, burning substances sliding right off their flesh without sticking.

Once inside, Benjamín raised the vehicle up to the flight zone. A noise similar to that of a stone thumping against a drainpipe made a chime-like sound, but the oversized machine had already begun its dizzying journey and, devouring time, was on its way to enriching science with the discovery of the past while leaving behind a painful lesson for the future.

CHAPTER 19

Shipwrecked in the Sky

The temporal distance they had to travel was the longest they would cover in the entire journey, for they had resolved to make no stops. They were now in the year AD 79 and as everyone knows, the Flood took place in 3308 BC.

Although the zone in which the Time Ship traveled was far above the region where storms form, and consequently they had nothing to fear from the cataclysm brought on by mankind's wickedness, they felt it best to err on the side of caution and agreed to come to a halt in a later period, historically speaking. In terms of time travel, this meant setting down before reaching the great catastrophe.

Their objective was to meet up with Noah, and as this repopulator of the world was still alive 350 years after leaving the ark, not only could they avoid the ravages of the Flood, they could possess the secret of immortality all the sooner by disembarking in 2958 BC, the year of Noah's death. That would be 3,037 years before the destruction of Pompeii, if they added the 79 carried over from the first century.

However, since it was not a question of distracting him with such matters at the end of his life, time not being of the essence, they decided on ten or so extra years just in case, and set the landing for the same date in the year 3050, when the patriarch was 937, that is, thirteen years before his death[73] and 258 years before the world would go berserk.

Rounding off to a pace of five centuries per day, they calculated it would take seven days (including stops for mid-atmosphere meals) to gobble up the thirty-and-a-half centuries in question. But they were not lacking in good spirits—the occasional memory of Don Sindulfo notwithstanding—and had supplies enough to last for two months; so by paraphrasing the axiom, "nothing is longer than a week of hunger," they figured nothing would be shorter than one of happiness.

The expedition began in the best of circumstances. They killed time explaining the marvels of the Time Ship to Sun-che and recounting their hazardous journey (leaving out references to the inventor, so as to spare Sun-che the heartache of widowhood) and making plans for the future, all of them, of course, rosy-colored and perfumed with the incense of wedding vows.

They were about halfway through their journey when, at noon on the fourth day, as the vehicle was slicing through the cleanest and most transparent of atmospheres, the apparatus suddenly stopped working.

"What's happening?" they asked each other, puzzled.

"Maybe they're changing the horses," said Juanita.

But Benjamín's alarmed expression kept all from savoring the joke.

"Perhaps a continuity solution . . . ," he said meditatively.

"So, we're going to plunge to Earth if the current isn't restored," Luis surmised.

"And yet," the polyglot objected, "we're not moving."

"Eh? This isn't going up or down?"

"No."

"Well, that does us a load of good!"

And led by Benjamín, the travelers set about examining the equipment without finding a single flaw that would explain the mystery.

Shipwrecked in the Sky

The afternoon was spent in vain undertakings and, with the shadows of night heightening the danger, their alarm reached considerable proportions. Only a few among them were able to nap; to sleep, none. They repeated their inspections in the light of dawn and as they all had about the same degree of mechanical knowledge, there were as many opinions as individuals.

On the third day, as a last resort and without telling Benjamín what they thought was a brilliant idea, the soldiers decided to jettison the Time Ship's ballast. With no regard for type or condition, they began throwing boxes and crates out the hatch, starting with the ones closest to hand. They had just about finished their task when Benjamín, attracted by the thumps, entered the hold.

"Scoundrels! What are you doing? Stop!" he shouted, out of his mind.

"Our mount's too big in the belly!"

"But you're leaving us without foodstuff, and our situation is dreadful. We've been shipwrecked in the sky!"

That cry was the signal for panic. All hope, in effect, was lost, and through unwitting bad luck they had no provisions, for what remained would last barely forty-eight hours.

Such peril was surely the gravest they had yet faced.

"Who will be able to come to our aid?" asked the pupil, her own ones filling with tears.

"Don't you worry; maybe one of those tightrope walkers who go up in balloons will come by and throw us a line," said Juana, optimistic enough to give the famous Doctor Pangloss[74] a run for his money.

"Aeronauts, here?" wailed the dispirited archeologist, checking the coordinates. "Don't you realize it's the year 1645 BC and we are above the Wilderness of Sin?"

"If you'll give me a cable, I'll scoot down and check th' horizon," Pendencia offered.

But no rope of sufficient length was aboard, and even if such a descent were possible, the valiant Andalusian must not risk being left on the ground should the vehicle decide to set off again as inexplicably as it had stopped. So the shipwrecked travelers commended themselves to that faint but only chance of rescue and, as a precaution, cut back on rations.

Six days after coming to a halt they had nothing to put in their mouths. On the seventh, they had to mash substances that contained liquids and concoct a type of flour from the pulpy remains. By the eighth day, fever had overcome the ranks. By the ninth, all resources had been exhausted and the air that came in from the open windows was insufficient for those poor souls, choked by thirst and gaunt from hunger.

By dawn of the tenth day, the explorers lay strewn about the lab, whose appearance had much in common with a battlefield littered with corpses.

"We must decide. What shall we do?" gasped Benjamín with a breath wrested by sheer force of desperation.

"Draw lots to devour each other," yelled a soldier. This proposal was met with a chorus of approval by the sons of Mars, who closed their ears to the pleas of the distraught women.

"A moment of reflection," Luis said, thinking of Clara. "Perhaps someone can come up with a less bloodthirsty plan."

"No. Let's draw lots," the soldiers cried, adopting a threatening stance.

"They're right," Benjamín put in. "There's no salvation for us. The equipment hasn't moved in ten days."

"'Specially th' digestive equipment."

"Hunger besieges us and the instinct for self-preservation counsels a radical choice."

"What a pity the Jews killed Don Sindulfo," mumbled the loquacious Juanita. "If only he were here."

"What for? Another mouth to feed!"

"No, sir; to cook his goose."

Hearing the word "goose" made the travelers sit up; but convinced they had been the victims of an illusion, they swallowed a sigh and slumped down again.

"No more truces!" the petitioners insisted.

Shipwrecked in the Sky

"Mercy," murmured Clara, clinging to Luis's hands.

"For the last time," the enamored captain pleaded to his comrades, "I beseech you to spare the women."

"Yeah. Let's spear them now!"

"No!"

"Very well, but I give my life for hers."

"That's different. Approved, 'cause all of us will have t' kick th' bucket in turn. Now you'll be convinced of my love, Juanita."

"How so?"

"Cause I've told you a thousand times, 'I love you so much I could eat you.' And if you draw a low number, I'll prove my love."

All notions of humanity and respect lost in the face of hunger, the soldiers stood up and insisted so vigorously that their demands be met that it would have been rash for Benjamín to take the law into his own hands and risk letting chance decide what fate would otherwise settle.

"I'll have to resign myself," said Benjamín. "Let's get to work. We must write down the names. Paper!"

"Paper? We've eaten everything down to the banknotes."

"Very well, let us draw straws."

"No, we can suck their juices."

"I know," continued the polyglot. "Here's my collection of minerals and gemstones. Take the one whose color matches the first letter of your name. Luis, lazuli; Pendencia, pearl; Clara, coral."

"Benjamín, you should take the *burple* one."

"Purple is spelled with a *p*."

"This isn't some spelling *pea*."

Once these newly contrived lottery tickets were distributed, they placed them in a handkerchief and prepared to begin.

"Come now, an innocent hand."

"For that we'd have to use the mortar's handle . . ."

"You, Miss Clara."

"I don't want to be responsible for the death of a fellow man," the pupil said, declining the offer.

"You, Juana."

"No, because I'm sure to pick the J. Let the empress choose. It's only fair that she should be first. Aren't all Chinese people lucky?"

They were about to give Sun-che the handkerchief when a bulge that was detaching itself from one of the ventilators made all heads turn.

"Don Sindulfo!" yelled the archeologist, dropping the stones.

"The lunatic!" cried everyone else, not daring to believe their eyes.

It was indeed the beleaguered tutor who, aroused by madness though feeble from hunger, appeared before them looking like a talking skeleton.

How did he get there? Quite simple. When he was hurled into Vesuvius, his body, rather than plunging to the bottom, got caught on one of the rocks jutting out from the crater's interior. The immutability treatment he had undergone not only allowed him to survive the fall unscathed but protected him from the high temperatures in that fusion cave. When the volcano erupted, he was launched into space along with the crag that held him. And because at that very instant the Time Ship, fleeing Pompeii, intersected the parabola that Don Sindulfo was describing, one of the exhaust tubes swallowed him up like a mailbox does a letter, producing that strange sound which the travelers took to be a rock striking the vehicle.

"So, when the volcano bowled you skywards you squeezed into one of the Time Ship's air tubes?"

"Yes, so I could take my revenge."

"How?"

"When I heard my niece and Luis being carried away on the wings of joy and saw that the rival of whom I judged myself free was alive, jealousy exercised its fateful power over me and I conceived a plan by which we would all perish together."

"But, by what means?" asked his colleague.

"Using a secret device no one knows about, I anchored the Time Ship so that you would be condemned to immobility in endless space and I could enjoy your drawn out death throes."

"You fiend!" exclaimed the soldiers. "Kill him!"

"Yeah, kill him; let him be th' first bull we sacrifice in our hollowcost."

"Go ahead and kill me; I'll merely be preceding you. Your fate will not change."

"He's right," protested Benjamín, "we don't gain anything."

"Yes we do, we gain a meal," the Pinto lass countered.

"So, there's to be no mercy?"

"None. Let us all die."

"Agreed; let's all die. But you'll baptize th' slaughterhouse. Get him, men!"

The soldiers threw themselves upon Don Sindulfo in spite of Sunche's opposition; gesturing, she pleaded for forgiveness of the man for whom she felt such invincible affection. They were about to administer the fatal blow when a benevolent rain coming in through the skylight stayed the hand of the thirsty men.

"Water!" they said, opening their mouths to receive the heavenly dew.

"It's snow!" Juanita exclaimed, seeing that it looked more like snowflakes than droplets.

"Nope, it ain't snow, either!" Pendencia joyfully replied after tasting it. "There's somethin' like peas inside."

Benjamín, who up to now had remained silent, smacked his forehead and said, drunk with delight:

"We're saved!"

And he ran to find the Bible that was in the cupboard, while Don Sindulfo pulled his hair in desperation, seeing that defeat was upon him.

"Look, everyone," said the polyglot, reading from the book. "Exodus, chapter sixteen. 'The children of Israel came unto the wilderness of Sin, which is between Elim and Sinai.' That's where we are."

"So?" asked those gathered around him, noting with astonishment that the rain falling through the skylight contained hundreds of birds that enlivened the laboratory with their fluttering and song.

"'And it came to pass, that in the evening the quails came up and covered the camp: and in the morning the dew lay round about the host.... And when the children of Israel saw it, they said one to another, It is manna.'"

"Manna! Praise God!"

And they all knelt.

"And now will you persist with your criminal pursuits?" Luis asked his uncle.

"And their wandering lasted for forty years," interjected Juanita. "So between now and when supplies run out, you'll have plenty of time to see how they bill and coo."

"It's pointless to struggle," the vanquished and humiliated tutor cried. "Take me wherever you wish."

"To the land of Noah in Ararat," shouted Benjamín.

"So be it," stammered the sage, but in a low voice he added, "I can still be avenged."

And the voyagers, after gathering up a substantial quantity of that heavenly bread and restoring their lost strength, forced Don Sindulfo to unblock the Time Ship's movements. Afterwards, they took the precaution of locking him in the clock room so they would not be vulnerable to some new flight of madness.

"Make sure no one eats th' plum-ij, it'll make a nice feather duster fer th' sage."

"Didn't I tell you, mistress?" Juana said. "We're like a punching bag dummy; even when they knock us down, we land on our feet."

And the Time Ship resumed its majestic journey above God's chosen people, whom they had occasion to see crossing the Red Sea on dry feet while its waters, closing behind them, made a wide tomb for the armies of Amenophis IV.

CHAPTER 20

The Best One; Not Because It's Better but Because It's Last

THE shepherds were napping peacefully in the mid-afternoon, their flocks scattered either along the hillsides or on the banks of two crossing rivers that seemed to hug each other goodbye as if aware they would eventually separate along their course, never to be reunited.

In the valley the peasants and their families were hiding from the sun, dozing inside their tents, dreaming perchance about the pickings that could be gained later during the night raid on the neighboring tribe.

The women, whose status was at that time lower than man's least cherished pet, were tanning the hides for hefty Triptolemus and tireless Nemrod to wear, or preparing the dried meat over whose scraps they fought the dogs and that were their reward for being mothers.

Towering over the camp on a smallish hill stood the chief's tent, the place where he and the elders organized the skirmishes and settled the tribes' differences by issuing verdicts that had nothing in common with justice.

The Time Ship's landing in that pleasant valley caused the nomadic natives to have the same cowardly, superstitious misgivings the unknown always arouses in the uneducated. Rudely awoken by their sentries, they all picked up their slings, grabbed their shepherd's crooks, ran to the council meeting place and frantically asked if they were to prepare themselves for attack or defense.

Although the vehicle's descent had something of the supernatural

The Best, Because It's Last

about it in their eyes, and the travelers' attire added to the confusion, their low numbers, relative to their tribe's, restored their confidence, making them decide to let the newcomers proceed in order to strip them down at a later opportunity and share out their women-folk among those who would distinguish themselves the most in the raid on the enemy camp that night.

Just then, a blackish cloud that had been climbing over the horizon filled the valley with shadows and discharged a torrential rain.

"Anyone home?" shouted Benjamín when he and the others reached the elders' tent.

"I have a feeling they'll welcome us as happily as they would the landlord," whispered Juanita picking up on people's demeanor.

"Why do you come to trouble the peace of our land?"

"We are errant travelers and ask for your hospitality."

"Pay for it."

"Witness our state of exhaustion," pressed the polyglot. "Give us a bite to eat so we may restore our strength."

If truth be told, they were sick of eating quail and would pay any price for a humble bowl of garlic soup.

"Swap that bite for your clothes," answered the chieftain. "We don't give anything away here for free."

The deal struck, an order was given to serve them milk, fruit, and a couple of suckling calves.

Meanwhile, the thunderstorm kept howling and the echo of the electric discharges crashed stridently down the valley.

"Look, just look at that collection of venerable elders!" an obsessed Benjamín said again and again, ecstatically hoping those snow-covered heads would make his dreams come true. "Just tell me they don't possess the secret of immortality."

"How old're you, grandpa?"

"Five hundred and seventy-five," answered the old man once Benjamín made him understand Pendencia's question.

"Here's your twin," Juanita said to Don Sindulfo who, looking pensive and lost in thought, merely smiled in satisfaction every time a ray of reddish sunshine lit up the tent.

"You must've met Mohammed."

"I think it would be best, Don Benjamín," observed the Captain of Hussars, "that while they dish out the victuals, you solve your puzzle so that we may be on our way back to our land."

"Yes... I'm going to make my golden dream come true."

Trembling with emotion and surrounded by his companions who, after so many hazards, were hoping to taste the sweetness of victory, the paleographer produced the pieces of string found in Pompeii and greedily showed them to the tribe's chieftain.

"Let's see," Benjamín asked him, "if you are able to decipher this writing for me, since I've only been able to translate the first few characters."

All those present were holding their breath. The centenarian times five fondled the knots with his fingers and gave a huge belly laugh.

"Look!" he cried out as he circulated the *document* among his people, who joined in the elderly man's mirth with obvious signs of contempt.

"And, so?" inquired a bewildered Benjamín.

"This is that dreamer Noah's silly nonsense; it's some advice he's been circulating among all the tribes so we may cure ourselves of what he calls the corruption of man."

"What?" exclaimed all those around him, fearing disappointment.

"He knows we're only made happy by stealing, pillaging, and scandal and claims that God, whom we've never met, is going to punish us in his wrath."

"It doesn't look like the Flood has made you learn your lesson," objected Benjamín, faced with such a clear and shameless confession.

"The Flood? I don't know what you mean. We come from a far away land."

"And you haven't experienced a general inundation?"

"Not in my time."

"I was so right when at the Ateneo Club I declared that debacle not to have been universal. Oh well, getting back to our subject, it says here 'If you wish to become immortal, go to the land of Noah and...'"

The Best, Because It's Last

"And he," continued the old man interpreting the writing, "teaching you to know God, will give you eternal life."

The travelers could not repress a stir of indignation against Benjamín upon seeing what they took for a cherished empirical recipe be reduced to a moral precept. It all had a perfectly simple explanation. The pieces of string, handed down through generations, had been buried under Nero's statue by some Christian living in Campania eager to escape the first-century persecutions. The Westerner who took refuge in China, a descendant of his and possessor of the secret, had entered Henan to spread the Savior's doctrine, thus preceding the glorious conquests of the Catholic missions in the Far East.

"Th . . . therefore . . . ?" stammered the polyglot, blushing.

"Therefore you've made us go through hell," retorted Juanita, "just to find out what we already learned as kids from Father Ripalda's catechism."[75]

"You're really a coupla clever milords."

The ranting and cutting remarks would have gone on forever if a terrifying explosion that seemed to shake the world's foundation to its core had not triggered a deadly silence.

Rain suddenly burst down as if vomited by waterfalls and everyone instinctively tried to leave the tent, but a wild-eyed sentry came inside and said in terror:

"Save yourselves! The sky is splitting open; the rivers have broken their banks and the valley has disappeared under the waves of a massive surf. To the mountains!"

"To the mountains!" cried the whole tribe vanishing at the same time as the tent, the former set in motion by panic, the latter by the hurricane.

The women fainted, thus delaying the travelers who, to their horror, saw the dead floating on the waters, the living lifted up high, serpents of fire lighting the sky, and the roaring liquid mass rising up over the black horizon to reach the top of the hill on which they stood.

"This is some shower, ain't it! Could this be th' Flood?"

"Impossible," said Benjamín. "That disaster took place in the year

3308 BC and we have stopped in the year 2971; 337 years earlier, that is."

"What about my revenge?" cried Don Sindulfo with a cheery, devilish satisfaction.

"What?"

"You locked me up like an animal in the clock room and I set them all back so that, led astray by false calculations, you and I might become victims of this universal inferno."

A long, drawn-out roar followed the words of the cold-hearted madman. The situation was untenable; the waters made the rocks on the hill crumble away beneath the travelers' feet, and the darkness was so deep that one could not see anything two steps away. Luis's strength was waning under the weight of his precious cargo. He tried to make it to the top but a gust of wind knocked him down and Clara, falling from his arms, was engulfed by the abyss.

"Let me go. I swim like an anchovy!" said Pendencia, and he dove toward the water. But as he fell, unharmed due to the powers of immutability, instead of plunging into a liquid body he crashed into Clara's inanimate one that was laying on a hard, solid surface. A few rays of lightning brightened the sky, making it possible for the intrepid soldier to gauge the endless bounty of Providence as he dedicated a hymn of praise to it, delivered in the form of a sharp cry.

"The crab!" he exclaimed, recognizing the Time Ship and remembering its retrogressive abilities.

It was indeed the vehicle which, having been dragged by the current, was floating on the waves near the hill that had turned from harbor to tomb.

A bloodshot-eyed, furious Don Sindulfo was the first to go inside.

The boarding proceeded smoothly through the gallery that had received both Clara and the orderly and, a few seconds later, the voyagers tore through a curtain of water and fire and continued on their course through the most sheer and serene of primitive atmospheres.

Busy as they were, tending to the ailing ladies and worried about how long their fainting spell was lasting, everyone noticed they were moving, yet no one thought to ask who had switched on the great machine. Luis, fearing that his poor uncle would commit another

The Best, Because It's Last

reckless act in his present state, assigned four men to watch him and put four square feet between him and the machine's levers.

During the first few hours they feared for the lives of those unconscious souls who had been so resilient up until then. But, even when conquered, youth tends to remember the indisputable right it has to life by bringing on fits as swift and thorough as the one that gave our charming lady travelers their faculties back.

Having hugged each other as they would do after every great peril, which I think may be reason enough not to wish for danger but not to fear it either, nobody thought of anything else but the happiness awaiting them upon their return.

"Oh!" said Juanita. "When I think of the day I'll hear the Correspondencia[76] shouted out on the streets of Madrid...!"

"C'mon now, every Jack to his Jill. Cap'n, you with th' miss, Don Pichichi with th' empress, and me with th' maid (pardon my pointing)"—meaning the loving smack on the back he had given the Pinto girl—"let's get down to th' local church, have th' priest scrawl his signature, and we'll eat, drink and be merry."

"If we keep this pace up, we'll be there in no time," offered Luis. It was then the polyglot noticed the vertiginous speed they were making but, unsure whether recklessness was on their side, he said nothing and simply looked at the clocks. To his great surprise, he found they had been disassembled; their hands pointed to 3308, the year of the Flood, which they had left behind six hours ago.

"What's this?" he wondered, alarmed. And he tried to pinpoint their position by opening one of the laboratory's observations disks. What he saw was terrifying. Light and shadow alternated as fast as the vibrations from an electric buzzer whose transition from sound to silence leave no discernible space in between. Once in a while the Time Ship would come to a dead stop as if taking a break. After resting, the new Wandering Jew would set out once more as if a hidden voice had bellowed: "Go!" Benjamín, eyes glued to the telescope, witnessed Nature's disintegration parading before him through these, for him incomprehensible, phenomena. At one point, traversing Ancient Greece, he stole one of mythology's secrets when he realized the Cyclops were none other than the first men to go down below the surface of the Earth to explore its mines sporting a lantern on their forehead, which poets then turned into eyes. At another, reaching the limits of Asia and America, he found out that the Siberians had been the first to populate the lands discovered by Columbus, since he saw a group of them crossing over what at that time was an isthmus, later to be covered by water and form the Bering Strait. The Mediterranean did not exist; the Alps were a valley; the Libyan desert a sea. After the sons of Cain, up came Abel's dead body; after Paradise, Creation.

A guffaw shook Benjamín out of his stupor. It was Don Sindulfo who, taking pleasure in the archeologist's astonishment, was shouting in a frenzy of madness.

"You have forced my revenge and I'm not giving up on it."

"What?" screamed everyone, fearing some new misadventure.

"You thought you were advancing and, as you can see, you're still moving backwards."

"But will our troubles never end?" Juanita said.

"'We forgot t' tie him up."

"Let's change course."

"Yes, let's."

"It's no use," the madman continued, laughing spasmodically. "Don't you realize we're traveling at five times our regular speed? No one can stop us. I have destroyed the regulator and the Time Ship is headed straight for the primeval burning mass."

"Horrors!"

"Death awaits us in Chaos."

"Chaos!"

"Look!"

And, indeed, a soft light—the origin of natural order and the end of atomic dispersion—could be seen shining through the disk. But, the chaotic mass was gradually becoming denser as it drew back and the thick glass was not strong enough for the onslaught of water, earth, and fire flung about by the wind, which kept stopping the course of the vehicle with violent, irregular jolts as it floated along the burning mud. The immutability fluid had lost its properties. The walls radiated a great heat; asphyxia overpowered the travelers until, finally, the melting glass became a torrent of igneous substances as it exploded with the boom of a hundred volcanoes.

It turned out to be the audience at the Porte Saint Martin theater showing its appreciation for Jules Verne's inventiveness after a performance of one of his plays. Juanita, along with Pendencia and the military attachés sent by our government to the Paris Exposition, occupied gallery seats. Clara and Luis, married the day before and enjoying box seats, drew curious glances. Accompanying his niece were the tutor and his inseparable friend the archeologist, who had been an integral part of Don Sindulfo's existence since he lost his mute wife on the beaches of Biarritz. They both had been lured to the modern Babylon by the charms of the universal competition.

One may guess the rest. The tutor had fallen asleep and dreamed. While on their way back, he told his family his dream and they all laughed heartily, something I fear did not happen to the readers of my tale. And yet, one must admit that my work has at least one merit: that a son of Spain has dared try to unravel time, when it is a well-known fact that *whiling away the time* is the almost exclusive pursuit of all Spaniards.

Notes

Introduction: *The Time Ship*'s Place in the History of Science Fiction

1. Augusto Uribe mentions the possibility that Gaspar was inspired by Mouton's *L'historioscope* (1883), which features a device that can see into the past, but concludes that *The Time Ship* was conceived two years earlier. Writes Uribe, "I have compared it with . . . Gaspar's next manuscript, *La lengua* [The Tongue], a comedy first performed in 1882, and the paper and ink are the same, leading one to conclude that it was composed in Macau in 1881. Furthermore, he and other critics note that, when referring to the 1860 Battle of Tetouan, the narrator observes that he is writing twenty-one years after that historical event. Uribe, "The First Time Machine," 15.
2. See Tomás Albaladejo's "Imaginar la realidad, imaginar las palabras" for a comparative linguistic analysis of the words "anacronópete" and "time machine," understood as neologistic constructions that add their own creative dimension to their respective works of literature.
3. For example, Euhemerus' *Sacred History*, Iambulus' *Islands of the Sun*, and Lucian's *True History*.
4. Alkon, *Origins of Futuristic Fiction*, 3.
5. Poyán, *Enrique Gaspar: medio siglo*, 131–33.
6. Margot, "Jules Verne, Playwright," 4.
7. Evans, "Science Fiction vs. Scientific Fiction in France," 7.
8. Geraldine Lawless, "Unknown Futures: Nineteenth-Century Science Fiction in Spain," 253–69.
9. Verne, *From the Earth to the Moon*. Heritage Press ed., 87–88.
10. Díez, *Antología*, 13.
11. Dendle, "Spain's First Novel of Science Fiction," 47.
12. Wells, *The Time Machine,* ed. Leon Stover, 58.
13. We noted a few inconsistencies between Gaspar's description of the ship and Soler's illustrations of it. Although the author first says there is one large crystal disk in the observation room, later passages and

Notes

Soler's illustrations indicate more. And while the hull is described as swelling out like a belly between the upper decks and the hold, in Soler's drawings it is flat.

14 Quoted in Nahin, *Time Machines*, 55.
15 Wells, *The Time Machine*, ed. Leon Stover, 81.
16 Hammond, *H. G. Wells's The Time Machine*, 24.
17 Díez, *Antología*, 11.
18 Santiáñez-Tió, "Introducción," 23.
19 Kirschenbaum gives as his source for this recollection a profile of Gaspar published in the *Las Provincias* newspaper in 1898. Leo Kirschenbaum, *Enrique Gaspar and the Social Drama*, 318.
20 *Epistolari Llorente*, vol. 1, Biblioteca literaria de l'oficina Romanica, Biblioteca Balmes, Barcelona, 1928–29, Letter 302. In Poyán, *Enrique Gaspar: medio siglo de teatro español*, 39.
21 Kirschenbaum, *Enrique Gaspar*, 324.
22 In *Epistorali Llorente*, vol. 1, 58–59. In Poyán, *Enrique Gaspar: medio siglo*, 65.
23 Ibid., 64.
24 Kirschenbaum, *Enrique Gaspar*, 329–30.
25 Kirschenbaum, *Enrique Gaspar*, 331.
26 Gaspar was a devoted family man who once said of his children, "They're the two most perfect works I've ever produced without it costing me much effort; what's more, I made them with pleasure." Ibid., 332.
27 Kirschenbaum, *Enrique Gaspar*, 334.
28 See for example Canals, "Post Mortem: Enrique Gaspar," 163–66, http://hemerotecadigital.bne.es/cgi-bin/Pandora.exe
29 Poyán lists the following works as dealing with scientific ideas: *El anacronópete*; *La teoría de Darwin* [1893?; Darwin's Theory]; *La sordera política* [1900; Political Deafness]; *La cura prodigiosa* [1866?; The Prodigious Cure]; *La metempsicosis* [1887; Metempsychosis]; and *Pasiones políticas* [1895; Political Passions]. Poyán, *Enrique Gaspar: medio siglo*, vol. 1, 152–58; vol. 2, 17–19.
30 Introduced to Spain by Julián Sanz del Río (1814–69) and based largely on the ideas of the Austrian idealist philosopher Karl C. F. Krause (1781–1832), this philosophy embraced liberalism and progress. In

Notes

31 Spain, Krausism was associated with religious skepticism, tolerance, and a belief in a free-thinking education that included the students' physical and artistic development.

31 Both E. Pardo Bazán (in *Nuevo teatro crítico* 30) and H. Gregersen (in *Ibsen and Spain*, 130 and 133) have mentioned Gaspar's Ibsenism, citing as an example the character of Henny in *Huelga de hijos*. However, it can also be found before this, in the character of Lola or in Carmen in *La ola* [1888; The Wave].

32 Poyán vol. 2, 11–16.

33 See E. Pardo Bazán "Un ibseniano español," 240–55; J. Yxart, *El arte escénico en España*, 146–54, 166–81, and 304–9; and J. Cejador y Frauca, *Historia de la Lengua y Literatura castellana*, vol. 8, 292–95.

34 Adapting plays into novels was not unusual for Gaspar: both novels *Un problema* [A Problem] and *Las personas decentes* are adaptations. As mentioned earlier, *The Time Ship* first took shape as a zarzuela. Another of his novels of scientific ideas, *La teoría de Darwin* [Darwin's Theory], also started as a zarzuela with the title *La teoría de Darwin, humorada comico-lírica en un acto dividido en tres cuadros* [1893?; Darwin's Theory, a Comical-Lyrical Humorous Play in One Act Divided into Three Scenes]. The manuscripts for both of these zarzuelas may be found at the Spanish National Library in Madrid.

35 J. A. Hormigón recently edited his play *Las personas decentes: comedia en tres actos y en prosa*. Madrid: Asociación de Directores de Escena, 1990.

36 To learn about the friendship between the two playwrights, see Luis López Jiménez's article containing several letters from Gaspar to Galdós that show Gaspar's genuine affection and admiration for the better-known author.

37 The zarzuela's full title reads: *El Anacronópete. Viage hacia atrás verificado en el tiempo desde el último tercio del siglo XIX hasta el caos y dividido en tres jornadas y 13 cuadros*. [Backwards Travel Verified in Time from the Last Third of the Nineteenth Century until Chaos and Divided into Three Acts and Thirteen Scenes].

38 Santiáñez-Tió declares *The Time Ship* to be "of much lesser quality" than Wells's work and observes that it had no literary repercussion whatsoever ("Introducción," 16). Uribe laments that the ending of

Notes

Gaspar's novel is explained away in "twenty unfortunate lines that are unnecessary and incongruous" (10).

39 Ayala, "La obra narrativa de Enrique Gaspar: *El Anacronópete*."
40 Santiañez-Tió, "Introducción," 17.
41 Poyán, *Enrique Gaspar: medio siglo*, 26–27. The concept of metempsychosis also appears in Chapter 16 of *The Time Ship*, where it is treated in much the same comical, irreverent way.
42 Santiañez-Tió, "Introducción," 18.
43 To learn more about Gaspar's treatment of female characters and his modernizing intent, see Maryellen Bieder's "The Modern Woman on the Spanish Stage," 25–28.
44 An abridged list of the political events, minus their consequent social upheavals, would read as follows: the abdication of a king and declaration of the first Spanish republic, lasting only one year and governed by four presidents; three simultaneous civil wars; and the restoration of the monarchy after a coup d'état.
45 "Francesc Soler i Rovirosa," Generalitat de Catalunya, accessed 25 May 2011, www.gencat.cat.
46 "Set Design," Generalitat de Catalunya, accessed 1 June 2011, www.gencat.cat.
47 Francesc Miralles, "En recuerdo de Francesc Soler i Rovirosa," *La Vanguardia* (Barcelona), 25 November 1984, accessed 26 May 2011, http://hemeroteca.lavanguardia.com.
48 Ibid., accessed 26 May 2011.

Notes

The Time Ship: A Chrononautical Journey

1 Laurium was a mining town in Attica, Greece, famous for the silver mines which were one of the chief sources of revenue of the Athenian state. encyclopedia.jrank.org
2 During the 1794 battle in Fleurus, Belgium, against a Coalition Army and the Habsburg Monarchy, the French used a reconnaissance balloon that had a decisive influence on the outcome of the battle, which ended in French victory.
3 Narcís Monturiol Estarriol (1819–85) was a Catalan Spanish intellectual who, fascinated with the possibilities of underwater navigation, designed the first combustion-engine submarine. Between 1859 and 1862 Monturiol completed over fifty dives in his *Ictineo I* or fish-ship, a replica of which can be found at the Maritime Museum in Barcelona.
4 Salvador Sánchez Povedano, known as Frascuelo (1842–98), was a legendary Spanish bullfighter.
5 In English in the original.
6 Parfumerie Violet was one of the earliest French perfume houses, its perfumes appearing as early as 1810. At the 1900 Paris Exposition it was awarded the Grand Prix for its fragrance *Ambre Royale*. The celebrated French perfumer Edouard Pinaud (1810–68) was a favorite among the royals and aristocrats of the day, his brand Ed. Pinaud, being the equivalent of today's top luxury brands such as Guerlain, Dior, or Chanel. The Ed. Pinaud company famously introduced the hair grooming product "brilliantine" at the 1900 Paris Exposition.
7 A mezzo-soprano, although she commonly sang soprano parts, María Malibrán (1808–36) was one of the most famous opera singers of the nineteenth century. Malibrán was known for her stormy personality and dramatic intensity, becoming a legendary figure after her death at age twenty-eight. Contemporary accounts of her voice describe its range, power, and flexibility as extraordinary. María Bernaola was a woman who in 1677 was assaulted by a man named Domingo Gómez but managed to escape unharmed, only to have her life threatened by her assailant later on. See Renato Barahona, *Sex Crimes, Honour, and the Law in Modern Spain*, 62.

Notes

8   This refers to the mixture of reality and myth surrounding the disappearance of the nephew of Philip II of Spain, King Sebastian of Portugal, who presumably died in battle without an heir in 1578. The king's death gave rise to the legend that he would return someday to aid Portugal. The pastry maker from the town of Madrigal was Gabriel de Espinosa, a man who famously impersonated King Sebastian, adding to the confusion regarding Sebastian's disappearance.

9   An inn in Madrid's Alcalá Street. This inn is mentioned in the historical novel *Pedro Sánchez* by the regionalist writer José María de Pereda (1833–1906). Published in 1883, four years before Gaspar wrote his *Anacronópete*, Pereda's novel depicts the political disillusionment of a provincial newcomer to the capital.

10 This refers to the Spanish expression "to be like Ambrosio's rifle," meaning "to be as much good as a poultice on a wooden leg"; therefore, it is meant to have a comical effect.

11 The First Spanish Civil War (1820–23), fought between royalists and liberals, was brought about by King Ferdinand VII not accepting the liberal constitution of 1812. Here, the "loyalist army" must refer to those who did not join the liberal military coup led by Major Rafael Riego that started the war.

12 Bartolomé Espartero (1793–1879), prince of Vergara, was a liberal general who fought the Carlist factions and twice forced them to raise their siege of Bilbao. The Vergara reference is to the treaty that ended the Carlist wars, known as the "Embrace of Vergara."

13 This is a reference to the so-called "Progressive Biennial" of 1854–56, a two-year period of liberal political reform during the monarchy of Isabel II.

14 This is a reference to Empress Eugénie, wife of Napoleon III, who in 1854 built a palace on the beach of Biarritz, in the French Basque country.

15 Maritornes, a character from *Don Quixote,* is an ugly, but sprightly and kind-hearted servant at an inn in which Don Quixote and his squire Sancho spend a night.

16 Given as "miste" [*sic*] in the original.

17 A reference to the old, jealous character in Rossini's *The Barber of Se-*

Notes

  ville who, not unlike Don Sindulfo, is guardian of a beautiful young girl (Rosina) whom he hopes to marry.
18 A type of cigar.
19 In the late nineteenth century, a phylloxera parasite epidemic in Europe ravaged many French vineyards and extensively affected Spanish wine-growing regions as well.
20 Don Francisco Tadeo Calomarde y Arría (1775–1842) was a ruthless political leader who during the reign of the weak King Ferdinand VII used his power to prosecute the liberal forces in Spain.
21 The Paris Commune was a worker's revolt that lasted three months (March to May 1871) and was formed in the wake of France's defeat in the Franco-Prussian War (the Franco-German War).
22 In 1870, during the Franco-Prussian War, the French army's defeat at Sedan brought about the capitulation of Emperor Napoleon III and the collapse of his Second Empire, thus "leaving a crown orphaned." This caused the 1871 insurrection of Paris against the French government (the aforementioned Paris Commune).
23 The famed battle on the banks of the Guadalete river in 711 was decisive in the eighth-century Arab domination of the Spanish peninsula and the virtual destruction of the Spanish Gothic empire, its last monarch, Don Rodrigo (Roderic), probably dying during the battle.
24 Spain's "tragic" defeat to the Moors is explained in a romantic legend based on historical characters. According to the legend, King Don Rodrigo abducted and dishonored Cava, the beautiful young daughter of Count Don Julián who, in turn, treasonously delivered Spain into the hands of the Moors to get his revenge.
25 Cesare Cantù (1804–95) was an Italian historian of the Romantic school; Juan de Mariana (1536–1624) was known for his *Historiae de rebus Hispaniae*, a history of early Spain; Modesto Lafuente y Zamalloa (1806–66) wrote a monumental *Historia general de España*, a comprehensive history of Spain.
26 Musa Ibn Nusayr (640–716) was the Umayyad governor of the Muslim provinces of North Africa. He directed the 711 conquest of the Gothic kingdom of Spain and is popularly known as "Muza the Moor" in Spanish ballads.

Notes

27 This was a week-long battle fought near Tetouan, Morocco, in 1860 during the conflict known in Spain as the African War (1859–60). The Spanish victory over the Moroccan Army in this battle was considered a great triumph, since it brought about the cessation of hostilities towards the Spanish towns of Ceuta and Melilla, located in northern Morocco, and allowed the capture of the city of Tetouan for the Spanish crown.

28 Charles Castellani (1838–1913). The reference is most likely to *"La Bataille de Tétouan,"* one of his many panoramic depictions of famous battles.

29 Tetouan is a northern port city in Morocco situated very close to the Strait of Gibraltar, in the midst of the Martil valley, where the Martil river flows, although Gaspar calls this river the Martin river. The Spanish military headquarters was located in the Geleli Tower which was the site of a long battle. Gaspar's geography is a bit confusing here, since the city of Casablanca would be to the west of Tetouan, but much further south down the coast.

30 A Berber people (*kabilas* in Spanish) named after the mountainous region in the north of Algeria they traditionally inhabit. Gaspar also refers to them as "Rifeños." Most probably, the author simply uses both terms as synonyms for Berbers or Moors.

31 There are multiple conflicting accounts of the early history of Confucianism and Daoism and the lives of their founders. Except where noted, we have chosen to remain faithful to Gaspar's version of ancient Chinese history. We made every attempt to confirm the identities of the people, events, concepts, and objects he names in this and subsequent chapters, but were not always successful, in part because of the difficulty of following Gaspar's transcriptions from Chinese to nineteenth-century Spanish.

32 Although Gaspar uses the words *Dios* (God) and *ley* (law) in his discussion of Daoism, it is neither a theistic school of thought nor a legal system. The commonly accepted English translation of the Chinese character "dao" (道) is "the way." Our thanks to Scott Relyea for noting this.

33 There is no universally accepted English translation of the title; our rendering derives from what Gaspar wrote in Spanish.

Notes

34 It is possible that what Gaspar called "doctores celestes" are the Celestial Masters, proponents of the Tianshi Tao ("Way of the Celestial Masters"), a movement founded in China in AD 142. There are some significant parallels between this movement and the events described in Gaspar's novel.

35 Buddhist monks.

36 These two sects might be a reference to the commonly accepted distinction between religious and philosophical Daoism.

37 Tai-hio and Liun-in may be imprecise transliterations, Tai-hio of the Tai xuan, a Han text attributed to Yang Xiong, and Liun-in of Lunyu, the Analects of Confucius.

38 Mencius (fourth-century BCE) was an influential philosopher and one of ancient China's leading exponents of Confucianism.

39 Gaspar may be referring here to Yang Zhu and Mozi, Chinese philosophers during the Warring States Period (roughly 475–221 BCE) whose thinking ran counter to Confucianism.

40 Alopen was the first Christian missionary known to have reached China. He was a bishop, probably from eastern Persia, who arrived in the Chinese capital in AD 635, leading a group of two dozen monks and bringing 530 religious documents in the Syriac language.

41 The Nestorian Stele.

42 The Yellow Turban Rebellion (AD 184–204), also translated as the Yellow Scarves Rebellion, was a peasant uprising with ties to secret Daoist societies that contributed to the fall of the Han dynasty. Its name comes from the color of the scarves the rebels wore around their heads.

43 Gaspar is describing the collapse of the Han dynasty in Imperial China. Hsien-ti (181–234) was the last emperor of the Eastern Han dynasty; Tsao Tsao (155–220) was a celebrated statesman, poet, and warlord who was instrumental in putting down the Yellow Turban Rebellion; his son, Tsao Pi (187–226) forced Hsien-ti to abdicate and initiated the Three Kingdoms period and a new dynasty when he became Emperor Wen of Wei in AD 220.

44 Abu 'abd-Allah Muhammad XII (ca. 1460–1533), known as Boabdil (a Spanish version of the name *Abu Abdullah*), was the last of the Nasrid rulers of Granada in Iberia. In a bid for power and influence,

he led an invasion of Castile but was taken prisoner at Lucena in 1484, only obtaining his freedom three years later by agreeing to a series of concessions that favored King Ferdinand and Queen Isabella. King Boabdil holds a special place in the Spanish cultural imaginary both as a romantic, tragic figure and a cowardly, "unmanly" ruler.

45 Andreas Agnellus of Ravenna (ca. 805–46) was a historian from the city of Ravenna who served also as chronicler of the Tigurian gate event Gaspar alludes to here.

46 During the Middle Ages, every Sunday in the city of Ravenna people divided themselves into two parties, those from the Tigurian Gate and those from the Porterula Gate, and fought each other with slings outside the city limits. Gaspar is alluding here to a terrible revenge that happened at the close of the seventh century whose end result was the destruction of the Porterula neighborhood, the district being known thenceforth as "the brigand's quarter." See Ferdinand Gregorovius and Annie Hamilton, *History of Rome in the Middle Ages*, 205–6.

47 Much of the rest of this chapter borrows heavily from Cesare Cantù's prodigious *Storia universale* [1840–47; Universal History].

48 Your envoy behaved very boorishly.

49 Several Chinese terms from here to the end of the chapter were, as spelled in Gaspar's 1887 book, unfamiliar to our Chinese consultants, although they did recognize them to mean what Gaspar's Spanish (and our English) translations say they do. Because the exact spelling from 1887 might interest some of our readers, we were faithful to the originals in the narrative, but offer them in pinyin here: tie tsee (tie zi); fei sin (fei xin); sie putsin (gan xie bu jin); te-tsui (tai de zui); ki can (can kui); tai-man (daiman).

50 Huangdi, the Yellow Emperor, is the mythical progenitor of all Huaxia Chinese and figures prominently in Chinese legends.

51 A French sinologist (1797–1873) who was known for being controversial in his time. A prolific scholar with wide-ranging interests, Julien authored or translated numerous works on linguistics, vernacular literatures, Chinese porcelain, the production of silk, and other subjects.

52 As a subject of little value, not worth doing.

53 Although it is tempting to see the character Sun-che as a fictionalized Empress Fu Shou because of the latter's court intrigues and dramatic

Notes

death, the dates do not support this. Fu Shou, Hsien-ti's first wife, was executed in AD 214, six years before our time travelers reached China. In AD 220 the emperor would have been married to Tsao Tsao's daughter, Cao Jie (d. 237), who survived the fall of the Han dynasty and outlived her husband by three years.

54 Pendencia here means they will have to sacrifice something valuable in order to save something even more precious. His phrase refers to an episode of Spanish naval history that occurred on 2 May 1866, during the Battle of Callao (between Spain and an alliance of Peru, Chile, Bolivia, and Ecuador), in which the option to sink the frigate Santa Barbara was offered to the Spanish commander Victoriano Sánchez Barcáiztegui in order to avoid its destruction by fire. He refused to do so, saving the frigate in the end.

55 The line comes from the volume on Titus in Gaius Suetonius Tranquillus' *De vita Caesarum* (known as The Twelve Caesars), written in the second century AD.

56 There is a play on the word *levantisco* (levantine), an adjective which, in addition to referring to the Mediterranean coast of Spain, means "irascible."

57 The Great Fire of AD 80.

58 In Greek mythology, Ceryx (English translation: "herald") was a son of Hermes and, like his father, a messenger of the gods.

59 Gladiators who fought wild beasts.

60 The *postulatitii* gladiators were maintained by the Roman state treasury, whereas the *fiscales* were gladiators supported by the Emperor's private resources.

61 A standard bearer in the Roman cavalry whose *draco*, or standard, resembled a fierce dragon.

62 In *Don Quixote*, Sancho Panza is repeatedly implored by his master to work off some of the 3,300 lashes he must self-inflict in order to free Dulcinea from an enchantment.

63 Here Gaspar begins an extensive borrowing from Juan Bautista Carrasco's *Mitología universal* [Universal Mythology], which was published in Madrid in 1865 by the Imprenta y Librería Gaspar y Roig.

64 Jean-Baptiste Du Halde (1674–1743), a French Jesuit historian special-

izing in China, is just one of the many scholars and works Carrasco cites in his study.

65 Giovanni Francesco Gemelli Careri's famous multivolume travelogue, published in Naples between 1699 and 1700.

66 In Greek mythology, Iphito was an Amazon who served under Hippolyte.

67 Today called Bago, a city in Myanmar.

68 An old unit of linear measure, based on the length between elbow and fingertips.

69 *Frascuelo* (see note 3) and Rafael Molina Sánchez, *Lagartijo* (1841–1900) were two very famous, masterful bullfighters of the time.

70 *Gallus*, both the Latin word for an inhabitant of Gaul (France) and for cockerel or rooster.

71 Traditionally, the fifth bull to appear in the ring was the one considered the healthiest and the bravest.

72 José Delgado Guerra (1754–1801), alias Pepe-Hillo, was known for his stylized, artistic manner of bullfighting. He also wrote a treatise on tauromachy.

73 This is a miscalculation on Gaspar's part, as thirteen years before Noah's death would be the year 2971 BCE, as Benjamín states in the final chapter.

74 This character's excessively optimistic philosophy is caricatured in Voltaire's satirical novel *Candide* (1759).

75 This catechism by the Spanish theologian Juan Martínez de Ripalda (1594–1648), a personal friend and confessor of St. Teresa of Avila, was published in 1616. Its basic summary of Catholic doctrine is still widely used around the world today.

76 *La Correspondencia de España* (1859–1925) was a conservative-leaning newspaper that became quite popular as a news-driven journal, shouted out on the streets under the name "La Corres."

Bibliography

Albaladejo, Tomás. "Imaginar la realidad, imaginar las palabras: 'Anacronópete'/'Time Machine.'" In *Creación neológica y la sociedad de la imaginación.* Ed. Fernando Vilches. Madrid: Universidad Rey Juan Carlos, 2008. 17–36.

Alkon, Paul K. *Origins of Futuristic Fiction.* Athens: University of Georgia Press, 1987.

Ayala, M. de los Ángeles. "La obra narrativa de Enrique Gaspar: *El Anacronópete.*" In *Del Romanticismo al Realismo: Actas del I coloquio de la Sociedad de Literatura Española del Siglo XIX.* Ed. Luís F. Díaz Larios and Enrique Miralles. Barcelona: Universidad de Barcelona, 1998. 403–9.

Barahona, Renato. *Sex Crimes, Honour, and the Law in Early Modern Spain: Vizcaya, 1528–1735.* Toronto: University of Toronto Press, 2003.

Bieder, Maryellen. "The Modern Woman on the Spanish Stage: The Contributions of Gaspar and Dicenta." *Estreno: Cuadernos del Teatro Español Contemporáneo* 7.2 (Autumn 1981): 25–28.

Cabello de la Piedra, X. y F. "La escena española en el siglo XX: Enrique Gaspar." *Gente Conocida*, 31 July 1902.

Canals, Salvador. "Post Mortem: Enrique Gaspar." *La ilustración española y americana* 34 (15 September 1902): 163–66.

Cejador y Frauca, J. *Historia de la Lengua y Literatura castellana.* Madrid: Tipografía de la Revista de Archivos, Bibliotecas y Museos, 1918.

Dendle, Brian J. "Spain's First Novel of Science Fiction: A Nineteenth-century Voyage to Saturn." *Monographic Review/Revista monográfica* 3.1–2 (1987): 43–49.

Díez, Julián. Prologue. *Antología de la ciencia ficción española: 1982–2002.* Barcelona: Ediciones Minotauro, 2003.

"Enrique Gaspar." *Enciclopedia Universal Ilustrada Espasa Calpe.* 1924 ed.

Evans, Arthur B. "Science Fiction vs. Scientific Fiction in France: From Jules Verne to J.-H. Rosny Aîné." *Science Fiction Studies* 15.1 (1988): 1–11.

Bibliography

Fernández Bremón, José. "Crónica General." *La ilustración española y americana* 34 (15 September 1902): 154.

Gaspar, Enrique. *El anacronópete: Viage hacia atrás verificado en el tiempo desde el último tercio del siglo XIX hasta el caos.* Autographed manuscript, 20.707–19, donated to Madrid's Biblioteca Nacional by Doña Inés Gaspar.

Gregersen, Halfdan. *Ibsen and Spain. A Study in Comparative Drama.* Cambridge: Harvard University Press, 1936.

Gregorovius, Ferdinand and Annie Hamilton. *History of the City of Rome in the Middle Ages.* London: G. Bell & Sons, 1896–1905.

Hammond, John R. *H. G. Wells's The Time Machine: A Reference Guide.* Westport, CT: Praeger, 2004.

Kirschenbaum, Leo. *Enrique Gaspar and the Social Drama in Spain.* Berkeley: University of California Publications in Modern Philology, University of California Press, 1944.

Landers, Clifford E. *Literary Translation: A Practical Guide.* Clevedon: New Jersey City University, 2001.

Lawless, Geraldine. "Unknown Futures: Nineteenth-Century Science Fiction in Spain." *Science Fiction Studies* 38.2 (2011): 253–69.

López Jiménez, Luis. "Enrique Gaspar y Pérez Galdós: Una amistad inédita." In *Homenaje al Profesor Antonio Vilanova.* Ed. Adolfo Sotelo Vázquez and Marta Cristina Carbonell. Barcelona: Universidad de Barcelona, 1989. 327–33.

Margot, Jean-Michel. "Jules Verne, Playwright." *Science Fiction Studies* 32.1 (2005): 150–62.

Nahin, Paul J. *Time Machines: Time Travel in Physics, Metaphysics and Science Fiction.* 2nd ed. New York: Springer-Verlag, 1999.

Navajas, Gonzalo. "La modernidad como crisis: El modelo español del declive." *Anales de la literatura española contemporánea* 23.1 (1998): 277–94.

Pardo Bazán, Emilia. "Un ibseniano español." *Nuevo teatro crítico* 30 (November 1893): 240–55.

Polanco Masa, Alejandro. "Enrique Gaspar y la primera máquina del tiempo." *Historia de Iberia Vieja* 45 (February 2009).

Poyán Díaz, Daniel. *Enrique Gaspar: Medio siglo de teatro español.* 2 vols. Madrid: Gredos, 1957.

Bibliography

Ríos-Font, Wadda C. *The Canon and the Archive: Configuring Literature in Modern Spain*. Lewisburg, PA: Bucknell University Press, 2004.

Santiáñez-Tió, Nil. "Introducción." *De la luna a mecanópolis: Antología de la ciencia ficción española (1832–1913)*. Barcelona: Quaderns Crema, 1995. 7–35.

———. "Nuevos mapas del universo: Modernidad y ciencia ficción en la literatura española del siglo XIX (1804–1905)." *Revista Hispánica Moderna* 47.2 (1994): 269–88.

Stableford, Brian. Introduction. *Lumen*, by Camille Flammarion. Middletown, CT: Wesleyan University Press, 2002. ix–xxxv.

———. "Science Fiction before the Genre." In *The Cambridge Companion to Science Fiction*. Ed. Edward James and Farah Mendlesohn. Cambridge: Cambridge University Press, 2003.

Uribe, Augusto. "Las protomáquinas del tiempo de la literatura fantástica española: El Anacronópete de Gaspar fue antes que la Máquina de Wells." In *Apuntes para la historia de la ciencia ficción española*. [Madrid?] Privately printed, n.d. (3–23).

———. "The First Time Machine: Enrique Gaspar's *Anacronópete*." *New York Review of Science Fiction* 11.10 (June 1999): 12–15.

Verne, Jules. *From the Earth to the Moon*. Norwalk, CT: Heritage Press, 1970.

Wagar, W. Warren. *H. G. Wells: Traversing Time*. Middletown, CT: Wesleyan University Press, 2004.

Wells, H. G. *The Time Machine: An Invention. A Critical Text of the 1895 London First Edition, with an Introduction and Appendices*. Ed. Leon Stover. Jefferson, NC: McFarland & Company, 1996.

Yxart, J. *El arte escénico en España*. Barcelona: La Vanguardia, 1894–96.

The Wesleyan Early Classics of Science Fiction Series
GENERAL EDITOR
ARTHUR B. EVANS

The Centenarian
Honoré de Balzac

Cosmos Latinos: An Anthology of Science Fiction from Latin America and Spain
Andrea L. Bell and Yolanda Molina-Gavilán, eds.

Imagining Mars: A Literary History
Robert Crossley

Caesar's Column: A Story of the Twentieth Century
Ignatius Donnelly

Subterranean Worlds: A Critical Anthology
Peter Fitting, ed.

Lumen
Camille Flammarion

The Time Ship: A Chrononautical Journey
Enrique Gaspar

The Last Man
Jean-Baptiste Cousin de Grainville

The Battle of the Sexes in Science Fiction
Justine Larbalestier

The Yellow Wave: A Romance of the Asiatic Invasion of Australia
Kenneth Mackay

The Moon Pool
A. Merritt

The Black Mirror and Other Stories: An Anthology of Science Fiction from Germany and Austria
Mike Mitchell, tr., and Franz Rottensteiner, ed.

Colonialism and the Emergence of Science Fiction
John Rieder

The Twentieth Century
Albert Robida

Three Science Fiction Novellas: From Prehistory to the End of Mankind
J.-H. Rosny aîné

*The Fire in the Stone: Prehistoric Fiction from
Charles Darwin to Jean M. Auel*
Nicholas Ruddick

The World as It Shall Be
Emile Souvestre

Star Maker
Olaf Stapledon

The Begum's Millions
Jules Verne

Invasion of the Sea
Jules Verne

The Kip Brothers
Jules Verne

The Mighty Orinoco
Jules Verne

The Mysterious Island
Jules Verne

H. G. Wells: Traversing Time
W. Warren Wagar

Star Begotten
H. G. Wells

Deluge
Sydney Fowler Wright

About the Authors

Enrique Gaspar (1842–1902) was a diplomat and a dedicated playwright who strove to bring social realism to the Spanish stage. In spite of lengthy postings abroad, he published over seventy plays, *zarzuelas* (light operas), novels, and essays during a career that spanned half a century. In *The Time Ship* Gaspar employs humor, romance, and adventure to explore scientific and social ideas.

Andrea Bell is professor of Spanish and Latin American Studies in the Modern Languages and Literatures department at Hamline University in St. Paul, Minnesota. She is the coeditor/cotranslator with Yolanda Molina-Gavilán of *Cosmos Latinos: An Anthology of Science Fiction from Latin America and Spain.*

Yolanda Molina-Gavilán is professor of Spanish at Eckerd College in St. Petersburg, Florida. She is cotranslator of Rosa Montero's *The Delta Function* and author of *Ciencia ficción en español: Una mitología moderna ante el cambio.*